RIGHT O

Also by Pauline McLynn

Something for the Weekend
Better than a Rest

RIGHT ON TIME

Pauline McLynn

headline

First published in 2002
by HEADLINE BOOK PUBLISHING

10 9 8 7 6 5 4 3 2 1

Cataloguing in Publication Data is
available from the British Library

ISBN 0 7472 6997 1

Typeset in Meridien by
Letterpart Limited, Reigate, Surrey

Printed and bound in Great Britain by
Clays Ltd, St Ives plc

HEADLINE BOOK PUBLISHING
A division of Hodder Headline
338 Euston Road
LONDON NW1 3BH

www.headline.co.uk
www.hodderheadline.com

For
my agent, Faith O'Grady,
and
my editor, Clare Foss,
– guardian angels extraordinaires

PROLOGUE

The day they pulled Tiny Shortall's body from the river, I was hammering on the door of the Register Office in Molesworth Street trying to gain entry in order to record a man I'd never met marrying for the fifth time. His other four wives were alive and well and curious to see his latest choice. A bag lady pushing a shopping trolley full of her life pointed out that this was lunchtime and the office was closed. For all I knew she was the latest bride and therefore apprised of the opening hours of The House of Fun. If so, her dress was unconventional, but who am I to question another girl's sense of style? I checked my watch which adamantly stuck to its story that it was 2.15, and ten minutes later it was calling the same tune so I gave in to the idea that it had stopped. Whether that had been at the previous a.m. or p.m. only time could tell, and it was staying quiet on the matter.

I wasn't feeling good. I'd had a tummy bug forever and couldn't seem to shake it. Nausea had become the norm and I was dizzy and fed up. I decided to hit base, seven minutes away in Temple Bar. I would spend the lunch break there, perhaps asleep, and return to photograph the happy event later when, hopefully, I'd be a little more human. And less inclined to soil the bride's frock.

The sun beat mercilessly down from a cheerful blue sky, burning white light into my fried brain. Every step on the bone-dry pavement ricocheted through my body, jostling my stomach before heading to my pounding head to wreak havoc. I slowed my pace to ease the jerking nausea of movement. This will pass, this will pass, I chanted to myself. It had to. 'Pass, pass,' I urged. 'Pass, pass,' I begged. This really *had* to end. My hair was wet-plastered to my neck, stray wisps criss-crossing my face, my tee-shirt had moulded itself around my torso, thighs chafed against damp linen and my feet slid across the soles of strappy, flat sandals. Equilibrium was a memory and disaster a certainty.

I was stepping off the kerb outside a designer clothes shop full of couture without price tags when a van sporting a BBC logo rounded the corner at speed, presumably dashing a scoop to the company's studio in a nearby mews. I hopped back to avoid collision in the manner of comic-book heroines who often have the aid of supernatural powers – I wished. I had overestimated my agility and instead fell into the bag lady's trolley and from there on to the street. The jolt caused all the air in my body to evacuate with an impressive 'whoosh' and proved too much for my beleaguered system. I found myself gagging into a Dublin gutter, without the benefit of a punchline.

My name is Leonora Street and I am a Private Investigator. Welcome to my world.

ONE

Two blue lines. I looked again. Not one, but two. *Two* blue lines. I shook the stick and looked again. Still TWO, no change. I waited five minutes and had another peek, same result. Every fibre of my body began to hum with tension, tingling at the edges of my sanity. A weight on my chest refused me breath. My heart fizzed and ripped away from its moorings, plummeting below me, beyond me, beyond the ground beneath my feet, down, down, until it must have hit the office two floors away operated by a solicitor who chased ambulances for a living. He was welcome to it.

Suddenly, all my feelings centred on the ball of cells growing within me. I struggled to breathe, trying to restore normality in this vast cavern of amorphous despair. Independent of my will, my mind decided that if I didn't get off the toilet, soon, I would deserve the brand of the seat across my flabby bottom. I was oddly grateful that something useful was still functioning automatically, however basic and unheroic. I stood and fixed my clothing into its requisite place with a measured speed: it suggested calm.

I was anything but.

What I was, was pregnant. And single. And self-employed. The folks at home were gonna love this one. While I was adjacent I turned and had a last gawk into the porcelain telephone. I trust the message got to whichever god is in charge of unwed mothers.

The parallel blue lines were still shimmering against their white background. Abstract and beautiful, they might signify infinity in a modern painting, I thought. Here they marked my humanity at its most elemental level: the high art of creation. I was mesmerised, and blinked to clear my vision, hoping to clear one of the lines too, to erase it. The blinking didn't blinking work. I forced my eyes away again. The grit between the tiles above the hand basin was like so much dirt under a fingernail; expected yet distasteful, almost beyond control.

I was not particularly in the habit of examining the workings of this bare, and relatively unpleasant, room but on that particular day I was content to stare at the imprint of decades of life's other travellers, while trying both to ignore and digest the news I had just received: duffed, preggers, up the pole, bun in the oven, going halvers on a baby. But how had I got myself into this fine mess? I looked into the mirror at a vaguely familiar, ghostly face, flattened by life and the day's humidity.

'You tell me,' I said. 'You're the detective.'

My reverie was interrupted, I am glad to report, by vigorous banging on the door. A pair of disembodied voices discussed the matter.

'There's obviously more than one person in there. Unless it's some class of lunatic talking to themselves.' (Female, reedy, worryingly familiar.)

'Now don't get overexcited. Sure, who'd climb up all this way for that?' (Male, reasonable.)

'A lunatic would.' (Her again.)

The hammering began afresh. Come out, come out, who-ever you are.

'Come out of there, whoever you are,' said Mrs Mack, erstwhile cleaner and self-appointed patrol woman for my office building.

I had learned much from this woman over the years we had shared here, and was therefore wise to her habit of checking bins for interesting rubbish. I carefully wrapped the parapher-nalia of pregnancy testing and secreted it in the massive bag I carry with me. I'll freely admit that I have adopted some of Mrs Mack's tactics in my work; she has a lot to offer to the professional snoop. I rinsed my mouth with water and splashed my face. It didn't make a helluva lot of difference, but that's what happens in the movies so it was worth a shot. Then, with stinking breath held tight, I opened the door.

'Well, I was nearly right,' she smugly told her husband, Kevin, who was diligently stationed by her side. 'I might have known it was you,' she directed at me.

'I didn't realise I was making such a racket,' I said, with plenty of fake innocence.

'You look terrible,' she went on. 'Are you sick or on drugs or something?'

'Actually, never better. I'm a bit stressed is all.'

Mrs Mack pushed by me to check that I hadn't damaged any of the precious fittings; some of them were so old as to be antiques, so maybe she was being prudent. It was also a blatant sweep for other interlopers: it's a terrible thing when trust is on an indefinite vacation.

'I see you've decided to stay with us,' I said to Mr Mack,

5

who had been deputy sheriff while Mrs M was on a pilgrimage six weeks back, and now seemed unable to leave again.

'Oh, you know yourself,' he said sheepishly.

To be honest, everyone in the building was thrilled with the arrangement, because Kevin Mack applied himself to the tasks in hand, whereas his wife, first name unknown, had the loosest of grasps on her job description: CLEANER. With Kevin effectively carrying out the contract the building was just that.

'You do look a bit pale,' he said.

'I know. I have a stomach bug and I'm off my food. But I've got to the root of the problem now, so I'll be able to deal with it from here.' (Oh, how smoothly the truth dripped from my lips, sounding like a lie and feeling like betrayal.)

'Be sure you do. Your health is your wealth, you know.'

'I do,' I said. 'And I will.'

We both heard the sound of machinery ferrying between floors. I was shocked.

'Did you leave the lift working?' I gasped.

'She wasn't looking,' Kevin whispered.

Mrs Mack was not keen on the elevator being available to anyone but herself and her enormous vacuum. Neither of them had done a tap in decades and exercise would probably finish them off altogether. A point worth noting, I thought. It's always handy to know your enemy's Achilles heel.

The metal doors of the lift accordioned open and Ciara Gillespie emerged, jingling and clanking with belts and body piercings. She took one look at me and announced that I was death warmed up, or that's what it translated as in more genteel parlance. To put it plainly, my assistant is as blunt as a first-degree trauma. On cue, the loveliness that is Mrs Mack re-entered our orbit. She eyed Ciara up and down. The neo-goth attire, so beloved of my staff, cut no mustard.

'Back to the dustbin look, I see.'

Ciara grinned impishly and said, 'Yeah. I know it really annoys you.'

The older woman's mouth almost curled before she snorted and declared grandly, 'On your own head be it.'

The banter had begun, but it was an agony to behold. Although the two enjoyed themselves greatly during these impromptu sessions, everyone else lived in fear of a real battle some day, wusses that we were. Kevin Mack and I stood back in neutral territory allowing the combatants to spar without hindrance. I was grateful of a cold wall to lean on. Damp clothes chilled my feverish back and the resultant shivers were delicious and distracting as my life continued to reel and spin. The bout was short, as luck would have it.

Ciara added, 'That shade of beige you're wearing is just so you. I'd never be able to carry it.'

'True,' said the older maestro. 'But your time will come.'

She gave a beatific smile, wide enough to scare the entire Foreign Legion and a few regiments of Gurkhas into the bargain. Ciara shivered at the thought and took off. I nodded respectfully at the Macks and followed the teenager through a door, which declared the legend 'Leo Street and Co.' on frosted glass. My legs were weighted jelly and the buzzing in my head was still making a racket. I was amazed no one seemed to hear this aura of nervous fright crackling around me.

Ciara's hands were shaking as she busied herself preparing the coffee percolator. The smell did nothing for my condition.

'Peppermint tea,' I muttered, as I lowered myself wearily into the ancient leather armchair usually reserved for clients. I couldn't look across the desk because the semi-circular window behind it beamed cruelly with summer sunshine. It was bright enough to create the illusion of a halo around Ciara Gillespie, which ranks it as something of a miracle. On any other day it would have warmed my bemused cockles, now it just plain hurt.

I closed my eyes but the light rendered my lids' frail membranes, ineffectual against nature's joy. On a rose-pink background small dots of orange and yellow exploded on cosmic impact; ideas and dreams vaporising before my very eyes. I tried looking at the floor, but the black and white squares of linoleum insisted on moving. Were my feet beginning to swell? Was I getting paranoid? Does the bear steal food from the campsite? With my head between my legs, I closed my eyes again and burbled some more. And, yes, I considered kissing my ass goodbye.

'Oh, I get it,' Ciara said. 'This is where you murmur something that sounds like "peppermint tea" and expire, and I'm left to figure out what you meant, but it turns out that peppermint tea's *not* what you said at all, but *again* being the clever and quick-witted individual that I am, not to mention top Private Investo, I solve the mystery with great aplomb.'

'Sorry to rain on your mackintosh and trilby but I really do want a cup of mint tea. It's good for the digestive system,' I explained, wondering if it was too early to have a craving, other than wanting this all to end, that is.

'Well then, you're going to have to go and buy some. And while you're on the town, why don't you go see a doctor and get yourself fixed up?'

'You may have a point there,' I conceded, wallowing momentarily in my knowledge of the situation and Ciara's lack of it. 'I can't do all that till later, because I messed up on the Mulholland wedding.'

Ciara consulted her watch. 'How can you have messed up

on something that hasn't happened yet?' She frowned across at me, then quickly added, 'Don't answer that, I don't think I'm ready for it. I'll deal with the wedding, you rest up. I want you in tiptop shape for our date this evening.'

My stomach pirouetted and I groaned. I have nothing against a good time, but this night out of ours was not a traditional one. In fact we were both working undercover in a club called Moonlites trying to find out how the regular staff were fiddling the system. It was smelly, horrible and bleak, which was apt for my situation at that moment. I tried lifting my head up, but decided against it very early on in the move.

Ciara's voice was far off as she asked, 'Where's the mutt?'

No. 4 was the third member of our team and, as a dog, headed up the canine division of the firm. He was paid in love and food and, so far, hadn't proved a huge help with case-solving, but life would have been duller without him. We'd decided to hook up as a team after a case in Kildare, and my three house cats were still coming to terms with this moment of madness on my part. Ciara had been peripherally involved in the Kildare events, but had only recently become a salaried member of the company, so seniority was with the dog. I did not pry into the internal arrangement between the workers. I suspected they took me to be the dead wood now, but foolish questions on my part, or trying to be boss, might spur a schism or a coup and one or other would be costly and unwelcome. My charm would stretch only so far. I did harbour dreams of No. 4's animal wisdom rubbing off on me and perhaps a smidgen of Ciara's teenage pain-in-the-ass sass. Either would have been handy then. Instead, I answered the question.

'He's with Molly, minding the parking lot. They enjoy each other's company.'

Molly was the alias of an ancient codger who had laid claim

to a derelict patch of gravel and muck a few streets away. He operated it as a haven for those of us who couldn't afford the spiralling rates in the concrete multi-level car parks dotting the ever-yuppifying inner city area. His real name was Malachy, and he had galloping rheumatics, imagination and the type of hacking cough that would make a tabloid journalist proud.

'If the dog is with Molly, he can't be eating the files or the furniture here,' I added.

'Boredom is a fearsome thing,' my assistant said. 'Though I'd still love to know how he got the filing cabinet unlocked and the drawers open that time.'

'He has skills,' I acknowledged.

I chanced raising my head and it went moderately well. My watch was still in its warp, but I thought it was probably time Ciara got to the Register Office and told her as much.

'You'll spot Mulholland, no problem. He's small, roundy and bald. Brimful of energy too, if he can sell books all round the country by day and keep going to at least four partners in rotation at night.'

'He'll also be the one in the suit with a grin a mile wide. Dead give away.'

'Happiest day of his life,' I pointed out.

'Again,' Ciara added.

I watched in awe as she stripped her nose and ears of a half ton of jewellery, took off her black, sleeveless PVC jacket and replaced it with a perfectly ordinary blouse.

'Mmn, beige,' I observed.

'I know. That old bag will be the death of me yet.'

She wiped a moist cloth over her face, removing all traces of punk, and dragged a comb through her spikes, rendering her hair a respectable short back and sides, softly waved by nature. She checked her new look out in a compact mirror, but drew

10

the line at powdering her nose. Ciara was not that kind of gal.

'Oh, yes,' she said, remembering a detail. 'I have a little surprise for you. It'll arrive later.'

Normally the threat of a Ciara 'surprise' would have scared the living daylights out of me, but I felt that nothing could top my earlier display of shock or even come close to matching it.

'I'm sure it will brighten up my day,' I retorted, trying to inject an element of spirit into my voice.

She gave me an unconvinced look, loaded up her gear and was gone in the sort of whirl my body cried out to be able to achieve without hurling.

Alone, now, in the office I had too much space to myself, and time to put far too much perspective on my situation. I missed No. 4. I missed Ciara. Even the sight of Mrs Mack's tiny, permed head and brown checked workcoat (a mockery of contradiction in itself) would have provided some welcome distraction. Most of all I missed my old life, which I'd had until only a half hour ago; it might as well have been half a century. And still the damned buzzing sawed away in my skull, reverberating through my traitorous loins and shaking me like an eight on the Richter Scale. This was not the best of days.

And of course it got worse.

TWO

As self-employed proprietor of a company of three, you might reasonably assume that I would welcome a new customer. Snoop women and hounds need to be fed, clothed and so much more. For this, money is important currency, if not the best. And with each new job comes a potential source of said currency. So what bothered me about the case that landed in on top of me? Well, for starters, it was a 'missing person'. And I hate those. But how do you sit opposite a distraught mother and tell her you can't take her on because you don't need the aggro or the sorrow that comes with her circumstances?

People disappear for all sorts of reasons. Sometimes they want to escape the consequences of their lives, or to change the course that life is on. But a smaller percentage than one in several thousand ends up on a paradise beach with a piña colada and only the weather to worry about. I have been in too many mortuaries and I've delivered too much bad news, even about the still-living. So why did I agree to help this mother? Did her anguish touch me at the right time for her and a disastrous time for me, as I struggled to come to terms with my unwanted problem? Well, I listened to her story and I offered her a cut-price rate. I can't call it her lucky day, but then again it wasn't mine either. And it was very poor business practice.

I looked to Mick Nolan for advice or, rather, I consulted his portrait photograph sitting on top of the filing cabinet. He was doing the inscrutable thing, which was worse than when he felt he had to share all of his opinions with me, all the time. Mick was an ex-cop and family friend who had trained me, when it turned out I was too short to be a policewoman (I blamed my parents, and with some justification, given the double helix of DNA they'd supplied me with). He'd died on a golf course a few years back, but only properly left the firm with the arrival of Ciara. Funny, though, I still felt him agitate every so often when I did something really reprehensible (in his eyes). Now he was giving grief to the players on That Great Links in the Hereafter and bemoaning his handicap of nine. He kept schtum on the missing person case. And that was no surprise.

Mick was a good policeman, one of the best. But he hated politics. And as any Garda worth their blue uniform will tell you, politics plays an increasing role in police work. Mick had hated to think that he was toeing any sort of line, and some would say he went out of his way to annoy various heads of the Force. He got results, though, and results mattered. Then came the case of Anthony Butler, an eleven-year-old runaway who no one cared a jot about except Mick. He defied authority and flouted the rules until he found Anthony. It was too late for both of them by then. I remember the only time I ever saw Mick cry was when we buried that little boy, and the only people at the funeral were the two of us, a priest, and Anthony's mother, who was drunk enough not to remember it later. Mick paid the expenses and he paid the price too. He left the Force just before he was pushed.

I tuned back in to Mrs Mary Clancy, my latest client. Her grey head was bent over her task, as she rummaged with red-knuckled hands for photographs and other snippets on her daughter Nina. Her face was lined with fine purple veins, which told of a life of outdoor work, digging fields and tending cattle. I was willing to bet that she wrestled with her dirty clothes in a twin tub and washed her own dishes: murder on her arthritic joints. But she was made of the stern country stock that never gives in. She was mid-sixties, which meant having had Nina at fifty, late enough in the day to tackle raising an infant. But that was probably as nothing compared with what she was going through now.

I looked at the meagre pile Mrs Clancy had placed on the desk. It's amazing how little information we have to hand about loved ones, simply, I suppose, because we never think they'll come to harm and we will have to describe them to strangers. Perhaps it's human trust in a kinder nature than is in charge. All I know is that the world does not protect the vulnerable; if they're out there they'll be preyed upon. I did not share this thought with my client. Instead, I took her details and a deposit, and promised to do my best. Had I offered her too much, particularly in the hope department? Mick seemed to join his bushy eyebrows, but for once he was not judgmental. This made me very uneasy.

Nina was sixteen and had left school early with no interest in continuing her formal studies. She was wilful and wayward, and when she announced that she was off to the Big Smoke to get a job and a life less ordinary, no one could make her change her mind. She waved a letter at her mother, offering her a position as a chambermaid, and took off.

'To tell you the truth, Miss Street, I thought she'd be back within the fortnight.'

Nina hated her new boss on sight and left as quickly. She didn't give anyone a forwarding address and soon the phone calls dried up too. A few motley postcards brought up the rear; with messages like, 'Am fine. Will call soon, Nina x.'

'She was never much for letter writing,' Mary told me.

After waiting a reasonable, though not excessive, time, her mother had contacted the police. All the relevant bulletins were put out and followed up, but to no avail. In time the police turned their attentions to other pressing cases, some with a better chance of resolution. They released a skeleton file to Mrs Clancy when she suggested getting outside help.

On the face of it the cops had done as much as they possibly could. I have a lot of time for the job they do. As a one-time wannabe, I often envy them their power and camaraderie (though not that uniform, needless to say). They do their level best, for the most part, in an ugly and difficult world. And on this occasion they had helpfully released their information to a frantic mother. Now it was up to me to use the only real advantage I had over the police: a lesser workload. I had the time, patience and energy to expend on this one. Or at least I normally did when I wasn't pregnant and out of my mind with worry about it.

Sweet Holy Mother of the Divine, what are you going to *do*? asked an inner voice, which I later recognised as my own.

In the Street book of rules and logic, a decision deferred is a boon. This rationale doesn't work for everyone, and a lot of people would probably shun it. But I was not exactly on an even keel, so it seemed perfectly workable to me. I got busy

with distracting myself and established a few more facts from
Mary Clancy; she had been a widow some six years and Nina
had two siblings, both older, a brother and a sister. Nina had
not been troubled, barring the usual fuss, with the flying
hormones, tempers and earth-stopping crises of identity of
adolescence. In fact these never go away, I observed, and Mary
Clancy looked at me as if I'd announced I was off to join the
circus. (For all too brief a moment the idea held appeal.)
However later, when she was leaving, she seemed a little
happier, so that made one of us at least.

'Mrs Clancy, there is a question I have to ask, no matter
what you may think of it.'

'Away you go,' she instructed.

'Why was Nina so keen to leave home altogether?'

Mary thought a moment.

'I think I know what you're getting at, but if there was any
trouble I never knew of it.'

She paused again.

'Clunesboro is a very small place. Everyone knows your
seed and breed. And there's always someone who'll blame
your family for their prize bull dying that time, or think your
lot brought the blight on the town the time of the Famine.
Nina couldn't stand how . . . oh, what's this the word she
always used? . . . how . . . parochial it was. Yes, that's it.'

I studied the last photograph that had been taken of Nina
outside the family home in Clunesboro, Co. Meath. She was
wearing a sleeveless navy dress with big, white buttons down
the front and matching piping on the pockets; scowling at the
camera, a pixie face with dark features and unruly curls.
Behind her stood her brother Aidan, looking equally cross,
and peeping out from a doorway was her sister Deborah. It
had been taken by a neighbour on Nina's sixteenth birthday,

17

shortly before she took off. For some reason, it made me shiver.

'She loves that frock,' Mrs Clancy told me, proudly. 'I made it for her from a picture in a magazine. I'm fierce handy that way. It's a shann-elle, Nina said. Oh, she'd take the eye out of your head with the glamour, wouldn't she?'

Nina Clancy was clearly the apple of her mother's eye. I hoped I wasn't going to end up being the pip.

'It's an absolutely gorgeous dress,' I said, and I meant it. 'Did she bring it with her to Dublin?'

'Yes, she did. And a pink bouclé skirt and jacket suit I made her. As well as scruffy jeans and the other stuff the youngsters love these days.'

'Would you say yours is a close family, Mary?'

She looked perplexed.

'What I'm getting at is, I don't understand why Nina wasn't in contact more, even when she was keeping in touch. Wouldn't she have known you'd be beside yourself with worry?'

Mary let the question settle.

'Nina lives in her head a lot. And she hates not doing well, except for school of course. I don't think she could see the point of that at all. So, maybe she wants to have good news when she calls again.'

All present tense, then 'or maybe . . .'

We both let that last pause linger, unable to take the curse off it quickly. Neither of us wanted to voice the possibility that Nina hadn't been in contact because she was no longer able to. Neither of us wanted to use the word 'dead' or any of its unalterable relatives.

I broke eye contact and scribbled notes as Mary Clancy checked me over.

'Do you mind me asking, Miss Street, but are you all right?
You're very pale.'

'It's Leo, and I'm fine,' I assured her. 'I missed lunch.'

'Ah, well, now, if that's all it is, then I have the cure right
here.'

Mary Clancy was back in her magic bag of tricks, this time
pulling out a foil-wrapped mountain of sandwiches. She
peeled back the aluminium to reveal a classic of the softest,
meltingest, white bread encasing thick slices of home-cured
ham with a tincture of butter. Strangely, my stomach rumbled
in delighted anticipation. I realised that my nausea had passed,
gradually but definitely, from the time I had read the legend of
the blue lines. It was as if my body felt vindicated once I knew
my state, and it had no more to broadcast, for the moment.
Thankful for this small mercy, I dug into the heap of food with
relish.

'I can't stand them auld plastic things they sell in the bus
station. And they're not afraid to charge for them neither.
Fools and their money's the only ninnies buying that stuff.
Sure, it'd stick yer guts together, so it would.'

I nodded and smiled and scoffed some more. Before she left,
we filled Mary's thermos with proper tea and real milk to save
her from the 'pettril' they serve up for the poor unsuspecting
travellers wandering the roads bewildered.

A thought hatched in my head. 'Did Nina and Deborah
share a bedroom?' I asked.

'Yes, they did. They do,' she corrected herself.

So, then, Deborah might be privy to secrets: a salient point.

As Mary reached the door I had to check a last detail, 'Do
you own a washing machine?'

She smiled. 'Indeed I do. A lovely front-loader, with a
separate dryer.'

I practically smacked my forehead for foolishness: I had made an assumption and that was an A-range sin in my books. Work to the facts, Street, forget whimsy; savour the concrete, not the imagined. As I silently berated myself, Mary put her head back around the door. I swear her eyes glittered with recognition as she let me off the hook.

'I only got them a couple of years ago. Before that I had a hoor of a twin tub and the sink.'

It seemed I was taking on the charge of the atmosphere surrounding me. While Mrs Clancy was in the office, I felt as if I too had quiet strength and maybe even the chance of a little dignity in the face of adversity. Now, the void left by her absence returned me to emotional chaos and a physical reality I didn't feel able to deal with yet. I was in need of a mammy, but preferably someone else's till I figured out how to handle mine and my latest piece of hot gossip. Oops, nearly got to thinking things through there, I realised, so I quickly organised a courier to come collect Nina's photograph and bring it to my favourite laboratory to be copied, ready to be distributed wherever and whenever.

A gentle tap on the door saved me from more decision-making hell. It opened on command to reveal a young man in combats and a long, light, anorak with a snorkel hood. I couldn't quite pinpoint why he was familiar to me.

'Where do I know you from?' I asked, shaking my head at this early onslaught of senile forgetfulness.

He stood in a knot of embarrassment, then suddenly bolted forward with great and unexpected speed. Turns out he'd been thumped from behind by a returned Ciara. She's a boisterous girl at the best of times, but this was behaviour unbecoming even for her.

'Ciara,' I exclaimed. 'Please do not attack members of the

public like that. We've talked about this before.'

She laughed into my face. 'That's not the public, that's Ronan, the feckin' eejit.'

He nodded in agreement.

'He's the little surprise I was telling you about.'

Believe it or not, Ronan completed Ciara, if such a thing were desirable or necessary. They were the twins born to the Gillespie parents as proof that chalk and cheese can mix and match. It was a stroke of luck for the family that the two were not identical, so there was only one of Ciara rather than double trouble; she was that all by herself.

'Ronan's a geek, but he's a useful geek,' she was explaining. 'And frankly, that computer system of yours is not worth a bucket of shite. It's as slow as my mother's sense of humour and it's driving me nearly as mad. So the boy is going to soup it up for us.'

'For you, you mean,' I pointed out.

'Whatever,' she replied loftily.

My technophobia was well known on several continents. I just don't 'get' it. And I don't want to have to. On the information cyber highway I was road kill. I favoured the traditional approach of searching for information through paper trails and person-to-person information. A look on a face can be worth a lot more than the proverbial thousand words. And though I sincerely believe in asking many, many questions, my experience with technological data is if you don't word something precisely to the last letter, you can spend hours shooting moose. I'm too old to learn a big new trick.

Ronan was listing strangely and stepping from foot to foot.

'Are you in, eh, difficulties?' I asked.

He nodded vigorously, and forced out the words 'Bio break'

before disappearing into his anorak collar in a red cloud of blush.

'Out the door and up the stairs on the left,' I instructed.

'Sheesh!' Ciara shrugged. 'Feckin' Alpha geek! And who would wear that get-up in this weather?'

'I've ordered a courier to collect a photo for copying, so you can send in the film from the wedding with that,' I told her.

'Yep, grand.'

'How did the bride look?'

'She wouldn't get a kick in a stampede, so she must have money.'

'That should please Cheryl.'

Cheryl was the ringleader of the wives. At five foot two and as wide as she was long, she figured herself to be the wisest of the women, if not the longest married to Mulholland. That honour fell to Madge, a nervous wreck who didn't care if she never saw him again as long as the mortgage was paid and the gin plentiful. Cheryl's plan was to gather the wives, confront Mulholland, stop any further marriages and draw up a rota whereby they could all enjoy the man (barring Madge who'd opted out of that part), and live happily ever after. They liked the little guy. Apparently, he was kind, funny and a marvel in the sack. Bigamy is against the law, certainly, but it wasn't my place to foul up a happy circle of spouses who had gone to such efforts to ensure their collective happiness.

Ronan returned, looking slightly less uncomfortable. He even chanced taking off his huge anorak, revealing a slim, well-built body and fantastic buttocks, I was shocked to notice. For goodness' sake, I had enough trouble with the present and not-so-present men in my life without lusting after a mere child. Between Ciara and Ronan and Ronan's pants and me and My Problem, the office was now officially packed and I was feeling a mite claustrophobic. This was not helped when Ciara launched into techno gobbledegook, telling Ronan that they'd start with the corrupted index on the database. The look she gave me indicated that I was responsible for this sin; a mortal one in every sense. I packed the Clancy file into my bag, catching the briefest fright-sight of the used pregnancy test, and told Ciara that I'd brief her about the new case when I'd made sense of the information available. Then, in a spirit of furthering science and perhaps the capabilities of our little company, I made way for progress. In other words, I left.

But outside on the stairs I found that I could not leave. Not yet. In spite of myself I sat and began to face up to my uncertain future. Nausea returned. And the main question to be asked was a tough one: who had fathered this child?

THREE

I could have called this dilemma an inconceivable one, but it would have been an appallingly poor choice of words. I could not believe that I found myself even having to ask such a question as, 'Who might have fathered this bundle within me?' I tried to detach myself from the notion that I was carrying a baby in there. At a mere six weeks, surely it didn't merit that? Or perhaps I did not want it to. And why opt for that particular time frame? One that might not necessarily include my live-in partner, Barry Agnew. Another name stirred on the sidelines waiting for a call-up; a name from my past and my present, whether I liked it or not. But was it a name for my future? In truth, probably not. My heart began to hurt. I turned to the facts, breathing steadily, maintaining just enough calm to stay conscious. Stick to the facts, Leo, do what you do best.

I hovered above the body of a lonely thirty-year-old female, private investigator, sitting in a stairwell, panicking. She had a steady boyfriend whose stock in trade was acting; like her, he told lies for a living. They didn't have much money and they didn't have much of a sex life, but there was a little of both and perhaps enough to get them by if neither was fussy; neither appeared to be. Barry Agnew was a one-night stand which had stretched into years without retaining the passion of the original outing. He was a story that seldom changed: a handsome, self-centred, party animal bent on a well-paid career in show business, and as few ties as possible to bog him down in what the plain people of Ireland might call real life.

The actor had just landed a part in the main urban soap on Irish television and was now garnering a regular wage, which ran to supporting his wholehearted interests in beer and clubbing and therefore eased the pressure on the household's finances. He had yet to stump up money towards the mortgage, which was in the woman's name, as the house was hers. The television series was called *Tiger City*, in keeping with the current late-twentieth-century economic boom in the country, and Barry Agnew played Fintan McCaul, a handsome public relations cad who shagged anything that moved and made loadsamoney. The fan mail had already started to fall on to the couple's Welcome mat, although he had only appeared in five episodes so far.

They shared a house on Dublin's northside with three cats of dubious parentage and a mongrel dog of dodgy pedigree. The animals displayed robust moral fibre, which was more than could reasonably be said of the woman of the house. She was recently pregnant. She had recently been unfaithful. She was in a bind. And alone.

There, in black and white, was the ugly truth. In all honesty, it wouldn't have looked any better in colour. I had been unfaithful to Barry, several times in one night, I'll admit. It was a case of doing the right thing with the wrong person. And I had loved it, at the time. To complicate an already complex matter, I had also slept with Barry since the fateful night. And so I had no way of knowing whose genes were whose. Lovely. I don't think I could have made it worse if I'd tried, and it was just as well that I hadn't. I had merely given in to carnal desires with no thought as to where they might lead and was now left on my own to deal with the consequences.

The name I could not let myself utter was Andy Raynor. And in a way this was no surprise.

Andy Raynor and I grew up in each other's pockets. He'd been around since before my memories began, and I knew him well enough to fight with him as if he was family. He was a handsome devil type who'd played puck with hormones north and south of any border you could care to mention for his thirty-something years on this earth. I was never immune to his considerable charms, but it had been clear for many years that he and I could never be an item. Oh, sure, there were dalliances, maybe even teenage love of a sort once, and there was no doubt that he was still a considerable presence in my life, but there was no question of commitment. Fortunately, for him, unfortunately for susceptible women, he had the wit, physique and charm of Robert Mitchum at any age, and that did it for me without even listing his other charismatic traits. He was probably an all right bloke too, if you could overlook the legions of women who followed him around. I was told he had the same effect on men, though whether he toyed with their hormones as much was beyond my ken to know. Andy Raynor was free-range, walking erotica. If he had anything to do with this pregnancy, I was in deep emotional trouble.

I found myself clutching the banisters of the ancient refuge for down-and-out chimney sweeps our office block had once been and staring at the ground far below. When had I stood up? Why? I dragged my eyes away from the vertiginous drop, got myself wall-side and started slowly down the stairs. I had not exactly calmed my anxieties but I had acknowledged them, and like the stairs I would take them one step at a time. I needed to employ my favourite form of self-defence again, that old friend displacement of emphasis. I would get out of the building, buy the emergency supply of mint tea, collect the mutt and go home to the one place I felt loved and cherished: under my duvet.

I was on the first-floor landing when I heard Mrs Mack laugh. The terrible peal of delight echoed through the corridors and stairwell, building up a head of maniacal steam. It really threw me, and I felt sure I didn't want to know what the cause of her mirth was; the Satanic is only ever a breath away from that woman. My body broke into jitters, pulsing in time with the laughter's reverberations. I began to run, taking *two* steps at a time, lodging the action in my brain for further analysis and comparison with life, i.e. could I apply this tack elsewhere? My own hurried footsteps resounded in the hall, mocking my cowardice. 'You can run, but . . .' they seemed to taunt. Despair was giving in to sheer 15-denier panic and I was hyperventilating as I burst through the open front door from quiet shade into another bloody beautiful day. The outside world blazed, full of happy people blistering and burning with scant regard for proper sun factor; we Irish like to worship that which we seldom see. I felt my arms and face immediately begin to freckle. The sense of optimism buoyed by the sunshine was palpable. Honestly, there are times when good weather can really get a girl down.

The health food shop seemed as good a place as any to start my rehabilitation. I headed for 'The Hippy Seed' deep in Dublin's trendy Temple Bar. The least hip, or even hippy, bit of the area was my office building and a handful of others that didn't have a U2 name on the owner's list or a solar panel to save their battered reputations. Oh, and no über-pub lodged in the renovated basement catering to stag and hen parties each and every weekend, as well as any day with a 'y' in it. I tottered across cobbled streets, stopping occasionally to admire all manner of outrageous cushion in the bric-a-brac emporiums along the way. Economic growth should probably be measured by how much frivolity a nation will buy. One shop had a display of toilet seats. The most unsettling was made of clear perspex with barbed wire embedded in it – hopefully very well embedded. Was nothing safe anymore?

I was crossing a shining, grey piazza, headed stolidly for my goal, when a woman with a squeaking buggy ran over the back of my ankle, slicing it evenly and painfully across its width. I screeched in a very unmusical way and grabbed the injured area.

'You should look where you're going,' she told me.

It was the last straw across my humpy back. I practically exploded with fury. I hated her. I hated her kid. I hated my predicament. I kicked the buggy and suggested that she fuck right off.

'Ooh,' she chimed. 'Someone should be taking their HRT more often.'

'Take yourself and your rat out of my sight,' I warned.

It was an appalling display. And I wasn't proud of myself either. Clearly motherhood was somewhat beyond my grasp at that moment. I hobbled away muttering petty vulgarities – who says a convent education is a waste?

In the incense-fogged sanctuary of 'The Seed' I got bogged down in the first macrobiotic, vitamin-enriched, organic, diuretic, bulk-building, high-protein, isotonic, low-fat, carbohydrate-enhanced, energy-laden, microlite, anti-fatigue, de-tox, pro-aerobic aisle and limped to the counter to request my mint tea. I began to have fellow feeling for the seekers of the Holy Grail. A goatee-ed cliché in a colourful waistcoat offered me mint, organic mint, hill mint, valley mint, mint with ginseng or mint with caffeine before I stopped him with a firm palms-up gesture and the word, 'STOP.' He got the message and parted with a basic brew, muttering that I needed a little more vitamin D in my life. No, I felt like explaining, I need a fat bank balance and very possibly a husband, for propriety's sake, by sundown. And I used to think it was bogus to say we get more right-wing as we get older. *Pullease.*

Next I stopped off at a twenty-four-hour huckster chain to be overcharged for cat food. This is a filthy habit of mine: I cannot go into a shop to get anything without thinking of the pussycats at home and buying emergency stock just in case. It's clearly a guilt thing: if you've ever had a hungry cat look THE LOOK at you, you'll know where I'm coming from on this. All I wanted was an evening paper, needless to say, but the Hairies rule and who was I to argue the toss?

The headlines told me the body of an unidentified man had been fished out of the Liffey earlier and the paper would keep all us folks informed. It was nice of them to think of Joe and Josephine Public in the midst of so much death and disorder. Time to collect the superpup and head for the hills.

True to form, Molly and No. 4 were in high good humour. They both dozed side by side on matching striped deckchairs in the makeshift lot, surrounded by tightly packed cars and duly protected. Not that they offered much of the same as a return favour. I watched them for a while, envying their abandon. Unconsciously my hand drifted to my stomach. I shook myself roughly and called to the dog. He didn't exactly kill himself rushing over. Instead he gave several yawns before stretching his muscles and daintily hopping to the ground for a leisurely canter over. He gave two little 'rups' and by then Molly had rejoined human consciousness. The carkeep followed up with some barking of his own. It began with low growls, then a few dry rasps, a rumble from deep down and finally a hoick of something green flew out to points unknown, behind a red Mazda. It was enough to turn me a pale frog colour.

'Better out than in,' Molly commented. 'Isn't the weather grand altogether? Meself and Lucky here are enjoying it no end.'

'Lucky?' I was puzzled. The dog answered to nothing but No. 4 from me.

The two passed a conspiratorial look between them and left me to wonder.

'Lucky,' I repeated, savouring the name. 'I like it.'

'Now, I could be wrong but I think he likes it too. He can have his moments, though, so I wouldn't go putting my savings on it.'

No. 4 yipped in agreement with Molly.

'Point taken,' I assured them.

I was turning to go when a dazzling black Porsche took my fancy.

'Wow, Molly, you're going upmarket with the old clientele,' I observed.

'Mmn,' he said. 'I'm not sure about the lad drives that yoke. Bit of a wide boy, I'd say.'

Must work in finance so, I thought. I have a poor opinion of anyone who takes wadges of my hard-earned moola every day, while pushing pens and inventing new and previously unthought of numbers at a comfy desk in a posh office. Really, they should get out more.

'Honest to God, you wouldn't be able to turn a sweet in your mouth without him knowing,' Molly offered. 'And we're not keen on his associate either, sure we're not?' he said to the dog.

No. 4 agreed by jumping clear into the air, all paws flying, then chasing around the car, growling and barking.

'He's a bull terrier,' Molly revealed.

I was lost and sought to clarify the information. 'The associate?' I ventured.

No. 4 barked, Molly nodded. 'Name of Rocky,' the human told me. 'Looks nasty.'

No. 4 cast his vote by cocking a leg against the back bumper of the Porsche and wazzing lightly on its brilliant German engineering. Thankfully, the car did not have a vanity registration plate or I would have had to join in the protest. Goodness only knows what action would have been necessary if I'd met the awful Rocky and his chauffeur.

'Off we go then,' I said to the furred one, slipping his leash on to his collar. He did a farewell dance then took off with my arm halfway out of its socket. Just as well we were only travelling on foot to the other side of the yard. My car had recently morphed colour from green to blue in circumstances far short of divine intervention and I was finding the change hard to adjust to. No. 4 had no problem with it and between us we were managing. He hopped on to the passenger seat and looked envious as I put on my battered sunglasses.

'Believe me, I need them far more than you do today.'

I swear he snorted in derision; the cur had no respect.

I got to wondering if I could tell anyone of my change of circumstance. Did I have someone to talk to? Everyone and no one, was the answer, it seemed. I was close to my family, but they were *too* close for this. I didn't have a regular gal pal, by dint of bizarre work hours and a consequent inability to keep in regular touch. I didn't regard any of this as a shortcoming. I liked my independence. And besides, I had three cats and one dog who were very good listeners. As we crossed the bridge on to O'Connell Street I finally told No. 4 what was on my mind, and indeed in my nothing-to-write-home-about body. Afterwards, I was left with the unhelpful feeling that the truth really could be improved upon. The dog was wise enough not to express an opinion. I pushed the point.

'Lucky,' I asked. 'What do you think I should do?'

No. 4 insisted on yapping at a traffic warden. Normally, I would applaud all forms of abuse extended in that direction. Today I was a dog with a different bone.

I was still in prime position for a rousing festival of self-pity, but even I knew that was a waste of time. Now was the hour for defiance, for swimming not sinking, or at least for staying afloat.

'Black dog be gone,' I said. 'Let's be having the white and black and pale brown terrier of happiness.'

Its representative woofed beside me.

All along the sea front people took advantage of the glorious weather. Pets were walked, bodies exercised in a run or a stroll or simply a laugh. There was a lot to be glad about, if you just looked around. The sea sparkled gaily, sails raced through the surf, the cotton was high. And still, a shapeless misery persisted deep down inside me.

As I saw the borough of Clontarf hove into view, I had what alcoholics often refer to as a moment of clarity. I didn't like what I saw, but I gave voice to it.

I said: 'There's no rule says I have to have this baby.'

I found no comfort in the statement, whatsoever.

FOUR

Christmas had come early to number 11, The Villas, Dublin 3. Blood and feathers adorned the small narrow living room leading to an equally festive kitchen. I suspected some poor birdy had breathed its last earlier in the day. Snubby, Bridie and Noel were rank and file along the couch, natural habitat of the actor Barry Agnew. Detective that I am, I deduced by his absence from this locale that the young man was not in residence. I was relieved. One less chance for confession, one less discussion slated for debate for the human element of the household.

I had gleaned from previous returns that it was best to keep No. 4 on his leash, that way no Formula One chasing could ensue. Call me a spoilsport but they had a lot more legs than I did and, thus, a lot more speed. A few ugly ornaments had met their ends on the initial learning curve, for which I was grateful, but a halt is always a good thing to call.

'So, my wild and crazies, who's the hunter today?' I asked.

The poor creatures were trapped in a beam of light streaming through the voile curtains sapping what energy they had left over from their derring-do. It pinned them to the seat and forced their eyes shut with heavy, relentless torpor. Noel stretched an elegant limb and went back to sleep, very much his version of cat-anetics. The ladies of the troupe eventually managed to struggle off the sofa and complain about life, which was gratifying, in an inexplicable way. I was reminded of a death notice I'd seen in the local rag the previous week telling of the death of Harold O'Connor 'to the inexplicable grief of his family'. I could not help thinking that language hadn't quite served the family's needs there.

Looking back, it's odd that I wasn't plunged into stomach-churning nausea at the state of the rooms, given my fragility, but I was not. I cleared away the remains, wishing that cats wouldn't do what nature designed them for, and all the while careful not to scold. I'd made that mistake with a dead rat they'd offered once, and they brought one twice the size the following day. Later, it was explained to me that it had been their contribution to the pantry and when I wasn't pleased they thought it too small and made efforts to rectify the error.

I was washing my hands at the end of the exercise when I noticed a fat envelope on the draining board. It was addressed to me so I opened it, although as any sea worth its salt knows I would have even if it hadn't been. (I am a very nosy person, and have learned to reason my way expertly around manys the moral dilemma this has produced over time.) The envelope contained one thousand pounds in fresh, clean and, as far as I could tell, un-forged notes along with a note from Barry.

Dearest Leo,

I know I haven't exactly pulled my weight financially up till now, but the times are a-changing. Here's the start of the good times, babe.

I love you.

Barry, xxx

I sat at the table with my head in my hands. SHITE! Barry had turned good guy. Was nothing sacred? I had a weird mental flash of that barbed wire toilet seat.

In the years we'd been together, Barry had never stooped to such an act of selflessness. Any money garnered from his spells on the dole or sporadic bouts of stage-acting had been channelled to pay for his wardrobe and social habits. I lie, he once paid an electricity bill which had been written in red ink. Then he nobbled me for fifty quid a week later and we were more than even.

This was a crisis and no mistake about it, so I reached for the potatoes and a peeler and went to work. The cats saw what was happening and had the good sense to abandon ship. No. 4 was a rookie and knew no better than to sit at my feet waiting for wayward morsels of any food group at all to fall his way.

When Leo starts to make mashed potato and lots of it, something big is up and something bigger going down, particularly as I am possibly the worst cook this side of 1900. Except for baking bread, that is, a talent with which I was blessed late in life. So much so, I have a thriving sideline in supplying the Ladies Who Have Other Ladies To Lunch circuit on a regular basis. My cheese and cardamom loaf is the talk of the Howth peninsula.

The mashed potato lark was an achievement, considering that I once couldn't boil water with much success, let alone put an egg in for good measure. It had been a struggle but I had prevailed, and learned in the process that butter (lashings of) will render any charcoal-based feast edible. Mmn-*hmn*. I sure was lucky to hit on that one.

I never move far from the stove when a culinary adventure is unfolding; cruel lessons have been learned is all I'm prepared to divulge on that. It made for a sweltering on such a fine day, but I could not risk the consequences. I took out the Clancy folder to make initial notes and draw up a resumé for Ciara. Normally this would be done at the office but I had adapted the formula for changed circumstances. Clever and expedient right down to my toenails, that's me, workwise. Shame it doesn't stretch further in my life. I got as far as finding a pen and a scrap of paper from the end of an outstanding Amex bill when Maeve Kelly rang me on my mobile. This was very considerate, I thought, otherwise I'd've had to go all the way to the land line in the other room, and that was a full eight feet away. There are days when you're as weary as Moses listening to the settlers' complaints – 'I got caught in the splashback of that sea closing up again and my good jacket is ruined' . . . 'Where is *this* place?!' . . . etc, etc – and this was one of them.

'Your mother has invited me to a barbecue tomorrow.'

'Sorry about that.''

'Don't be. I'm filming with some *very* eccentric Americans who have *far* too much money and a flimsy grasp of Irish history, so I welcome real company.'

'My mother is about as real as it gets.'

'*True.*'

'How did she corner you?'

'Made me give her my number when you brought her to that hosiery launch a few weeks back.'

'The bum uplift tights?'

Maeve laughed. 'As opposed to which *other* hosiery launch?' Duh!

'She said it would be good to be able to contact me directly *just in case*. I didn't delve.'

'Recruiting a mole for stealth spying on her only daughter,' I confirmed, grimly. My mother was good, very good, but I was learning.

'I take it you'll be there?'

'Royal Command Performance, what do you think?'

'*Nice* one. *That* means you'll have to wear a dress and all.'

'And all, yes.'

'A *last* point in what seems a succinct call so far. Your *emails* are coming up in strange parts of my inbox.'

'Ooh, Matron!'

'*Quite*. They're all dated 1904, interestingly. Which makes *you* the inventor of that black art.'

'And still my mother thinks I've done nothing with my life.'

'I know, I know, they just *cannot* be talked to. I'll see you tomorrow then.'

'More than likely, unless I get so drunk first that I can't see you.'

'I'll understand, *fear not*.'

I just love Maeve, and so does every male in Ireland and lots of females too. She's our leading thirty-something actress and a contemporary of Barry, through whom I met her. We forged an unlikely friendship, as the actress said to the detective. She's kind, good-looking, talented, sexy, wicked, and damned good fun to be with. It was very acceptable to me that I would have such a decorous and able bolster the following day if things got sticky: mothers *know* stuff and mine was no slouch in the guessing arena. Now that I had a secret, that thought frightened me so much I had to go pee.

The water and potatoes were still in harmony when I returned to my post at the kitchen table. They would be swapping ions for another ten minutes so I took the time to phone the Garda in charge of the Clancy case. According to the file he was a Hugo Nelson, posted to the sprawling Garvel Place station, Dublin 1, at the heart of the inner city; a lawless place with too few crime fighters. I doubted he'd want much to do with me, but I dialled the number and was surprised by a soft Cork accent which purred at me to meet him Monday lunchtime.

'If there are no major incidents to deal with here I might have time for a sandwich,' he said. 'Maybe even a cup of tea.' Then he gave a hollow chuckle.

Something attractive in his voice made me want to offer to ride shotgun if he was called out, but it wasn't appropriate behaviour on a first date so I filed it under 'later'.

I scanned the cards Nina had posted home. They were ordinary tourist fare, including the 'Dublin at Night' which is entirely black and adapts to anywhere in the world. What caught my eye was the extra message on each: 'boo to Debs,' sometimes a 'p.s.', sometimes written on top. This seemed tantamount to a code. I reached for the phone and dialled Clunesboro. I hit paydirt when Deborah answered. I explained that I had been hired by her mother and had been given free rein in the case.

'What does "boo" signify?'

I expected a silence and I got one. I asked the question again. 'I have all day,' I told her.

'It's . . . nothing, really,' she stammered. 'It just means she's okay.'

'Do you think she is?'

'I . . . yeah. Well, I don't know now, 'cos it's a while since she's been in touch.'

'Was there a particular reason why she left, Deborah? I have to know.'

'No, no, no reason. She just wanted to get away from Clunesboro and see the world.'

I only half believed her.

'Did she have a boyfriend?'

She took time for a few breaths, then, 'No. No one serious. The usual school discos and hanging around the chip shop. No one special.'

'Did anyone else leave town with her?'

No hesitation this time. 'No, definitely not. I have to go now, someone's at the door. Goodbye.'

Deborah knew more than she was prepared to admit. She would be hearing from me again.

It was nearly Treat Time so I made one last quick call. It was to the Clunesboro Garda station. They had no report of any other missing person besides Nina. Perhaps she had left town alone.

The mash tasted like nectared manna. As I licked the last spoonful (it was not a fork moment) and held the fluffy carbohydrates in my mouth to savour, my eyes drooped with happy weariness. With superhuman strength, I swallowed the mouthful and dragged my sated body upstairs to duck under the haven of feather and down. (Actually, the duvet is polyester because I'm a bit allergic to the good stuff. Also cat hair and dander while I'm at it, and dog's too. Still, that's what scientists invented antihistamines for, whether they knew it or not at the time.) Sleep enveloped me and my cares pissed off for an hour and a half.

I woke with a big, fat head full of marshmallowed thoughts

and forgotten dreams. It was a lovely way to be and I luxuriated, until I remembered that I had to go to work in Dublin's version of Hades, a.k.a. Moonlites, disco bar and late-night vomitorium. My heel ached from its run-in with the buggy earlier. I hauled my carcass to the shower and let it give me a no-mercies workout and hose down. It stung the heel a little, a small price to pay for rectitude. I was pink with cleanliness when I emerged. And still raw around the edges after all these years.

The cat colony was back on the sofa sans human company, which was a relief as I was still spooked by Barry's largesse. No. 4 had opted for an armchair. It was seven o'clock and all was well. Except that I was pregnant. I guess you can't have everything all at once.

I got into a black skirt and white blouse, the uniform of the nightclub staff. It could have been worse. I'd seen employees in animal costumes in one of the other hot spots in town. With all due respect to the creatures of the earth, no grown man or woman should have to impersonate, say, a rabbit or a lemur, unless it's for charity, although when you think about it most night-spot work counts as that, given the wages involved. I dabbed make-up on my various facial blemishes, added some mascara (waterproof, in case I burst into tears at any point, you never know) and lipstick, which always encourages me to smile. Hey, I'm not averse to accepting tips, of the cash variety, even if I am undercover. I ruffled my mouse-brown hair and to my chagrin a clumpful came away in my hand. I may have overreacted, perhaps it was just a strand or two. Whether or which, instead of windswept danger, I plumped for a neat librarian bun as there was no point in moulting into a customer's drink and sharing my DNA needlessly. There was enough of that going on already, I felt. A quick check in the mirror revealed that I was no oil painting, but I wasn't the back end of a bus either. This would do.

I filled the menagerie's food bowls and hid the envelope of money, just in case Barry changed his mind about generosity as a way of life. It's not so much that I'm suspicious, just realistic about people and their foibles. I see a lot of the grim and the grubby, even if they start out well-intentioned. I felt a niggle of guilt at my own mean-spiritedness so I rearranged the magnets on the fridge door to spell out 'Thank you, Baz'. The niggle retreated.

A questionnaire from a local politician adorned my letter box asking a) did I want to join his party? and b) did I feel safe in my own home? I was feeling civic-minded so I ticked 'no' for a) and 'yes' for b), it's the outside world I have more of a problem with. Then noticed that I was to return the survey to him at government buildings. But no stamped addressed envelope? Right, like that's really going to happen. I chucked the thing. And politicians wonder why the public think they're out of touch.

The season had gone to The Villas' head. The cul-de-sac was, frankly, mad with house 'n' garden activity. I sneezed my way to the gate in air thick with the aroma of fresh paint, grass cuttings and petrol mowers. Who needs cocaine to mess up the sinuses when pollen and neighbours can do the job for free? The good weather had given scope to rivalries none of us had known existed, and fierce competition had exploded in the herbaceous borders of the estate. My street was a riot of clashing pinks, reds, yellows and oranges, with the odd cool blue and purple vying for attention, and a bit of white to calm the contrasts. All number 11 boasted was some overgrown weed-infested grass in all shades of green, a single theme which looked tasteful under the circumstances. Restful, even.

All right, I'll admit, there was a certain amount of interest added by the colourful sweet wrappers and cider cans which had blown in, so I removed them, then turned my back on the emerald aisle.

I could see Marion Maloney, Official Borough Gossip, waiting to pounce for those intimate details of my life that she couldn't garner through voodoo and the imaginative use of lace curtains, so I made a run for the car at the kerb. Miraculously, the keys slid in without protest and I was behind the wheel and firing up the engine before she got within two houses of me. I pulled away as she reached ground zero, a little too close for comfort and something to watch out for later. I waved cheerily as I sailed by. Marion was fit to be tied. I knew she would strike another day, but for now I was safe. Barry would probably be cornered instead, and now that he was a star of a TV show, it was bound to be a gruelling gruelling. I smiled as I pictured it.

Our shift didn't start till nine o'clock, but Ciara and I were in the habit of meeting for a cup of coffee beforehand to discuss any tactics we might have for the evening. We sat in the long pews of a recently converted basement, now renamed The Vaults, furnished with recycled convents and monasteries.

'That reminds me,' Ciara said. 'Con called to arrange a meet up. He's settled into his new parish and wants to fly the nest a bit.'

Father Con Considine was a friend we'd made on a cookery course in Kildare. He had since been transferred to Dublin, which was great news for urban sinners, especially myself and my quirky assistant. I was lulled into a false security by this and the fact that I was enjoying my *latte grande*, so I didn't see Ciara's broadside Internet attack coming. After fourteen light years of scorn about my ignorance of computers and technology I got us back to the job in hand.

'Let's go over what we know for sure here.'

Ciara gave an exaggerated sigh and prepared to knuckle down.

'We know the staff have glued coins in the bottom of the spirit measures,' I began, 'so they're clawing back bottles that way.'

'Very, very slowly. It takes ages, so you'd wonder why they even bother.'

I shrugged. 'Just for the sake of it, I suppose. Everyone wants something for nothing. But that's humdrum stuff and putting in computerised optics will deal with it. Still doesn't explain the amount of money being salted off the top.'

'The waiting staff is making a mint from not giving people their correct change. You know the way no one ever knows how much a pint costs these days?'

I nodded. Truth was, I didn't know how much it was in Moonlites myself, just rang the code in and waited for the machine to do the hard sums. I had enough trouble remembering the order, never mind the prices. I was a bad barmaid.

'And if they're drunk enough,' Ciara continued, 'they can't remember if they gave you a ten or a twenty. No one ever asks for a receipt. But I don't get the feeling that it's organised, I think it's opportunism on various individuals' parts. There's no central kitty that I've heard about or seen. So I'd regard that as petty.'

'Agreed.'

'Well, that didn't take long,' she commented.

'No,' I acknowledged, reluctantly. 'We've got to follow the money here – back to basics.'

Ciara cocked her head at an angle. 'And that's the plan?' she asked, a little incredulously.

'Yes,' I said firmly. 'It's a basic rule: follow the money trail.'

'You're pointing again,' she told me. 'It's very common.'

The offending digit was poised mid-air.

'Back in the holster, Leo,' she ordered.

I blew the gunpowder off and tucked the finger back at my side.

'You could have someone's eye out with that.'

'True. It's a very bad habit.'

We finished our coffees in silence, lacking a brilliant plan to discuss and put in motion which would ultimately ensure our release from Moonlites and its many horrors.

As we started to leave, a posse of guffawing men flooded The Vaults. I wondered idly if the original Order in these pews had been a silent one. In their midst and fuelling the fun was none other than the actor Barry Agnew. This sight was as welcome to me as a night of Belgian Symbolist Theatre (which, incidentally, he'd made me endure a few weeks earlier). I hid behind a pillar as the group passed, and was instantly ashamed of myself. I didn't do anything to rectify matters, though, and carefully snuck out the door without attracting attention. I needn't have been so concerned, Barry was revelling in his extended collection of sycophants, and only had eyes for himself.

Outside, Ciara was pensive.

'I know that guy from somewhere,' she said, frowning.

They had not yet met through me, I knew. Ciara had only worked for Leo Street and Co. for a couple of months and the opportunity to introduce them had not yet arisen.

'Probably off the telly,' I suggested. 'He's an actor.'

She spoke again before I had to explain any further.

'No, it's not that. I know him from somewhere else too.'

Wherever that was didn't sound like a good place to be and I didn't follow the matter up. Perhaps what I didn't know wouldn't hurt me, this time. It was handy to believe that, so I did. Denial is so much more than a river in Egypt to a Dubliner like myself.

A beggar stood by an upturned hat collecting change. He was too busy talking on his mobile phone to pay us any heed so we passed without making a contribution. He'd be sorry when he couldn't afford his next top up.

'A snoopçon of poking about where we're not wanted?' I asked my Sancho Panza.

'I think that just might pay the bills,' she replied. 'Let's go get some bad guys.'

And off we went to search out our windmills.

FIVE

Rope lighting surrounded the legend 'Moonlites' and blinked spasmodically as we approached. Epileptics beware.

'It's like a circus,' I said to Ciara, injecting an element of adventure into proceedings, I thought.

'Freak show, more like,' she replied.

At the door a bulky, male figure bulged from a dark, shining blouson jacket with 'Security' emblazoned in luminous yellow across the back. Meanwhile, his corpulent belly poured out over tight black trousers, pockets gaping open to reveal cream linings with the strain; if they could, they would have screamed, I was sure. He was poking an ear-piece into place with one hand and picking his nose with the other, unperturbed by his audience. Eamonn Davey was an off-duty policeman who did nixers as a bouncer at weekends under the official title of 'Security Consultant'. I was willing to bet that the Tax Man was not aware of this lucrative sideline.

His comrades this evening were a lanky git who had a black

belt in karate, and whose name I had never bothered to memorise, and a bodybuilder called Sam, who was rumoured to be a woman. These latter two were playing with a water cannon installed for emergency crowd control. They were itching to use it on real punters, but the opportunity hadn't yet presented itself.

The head barwoman at Moonlites, Val Tobin, had taken a scunner against me from my first night. It wasn't personal, to begin with at least, but part of a power struggle between her and the General Manager, Simon Cadogan. She also preceded Simon in her job by six months and never missed an opportunity to remind him of this. My information was that she had applied for the post of General Manager, and it must have rankled to be passed over for a man. I liked neither of them. If they hadn't hated one another they would have been a perfect couple; both ruthless, grasping power-junkies.

At the end of the spangled diamante chain we were all answerable to Pleasure Holdings Inc., run by entertainment mogul Declan Barrett, who hired and fired. His only concern was making money, and it was he who had spotted the Moonlites scam from the fall in revenue. Simon, apparently, was too new in the job to know what to look out for; that in itself would have ruled him out as a candidate for manager in my eyes, but people willing to take on this crap job were thin on the disco-lit ground. Except for Val Tobin. Word was that she was too good a bartender to lose to a 'desk' position. According to Declan Barrett, profits had been hit for approximately six weeks, so everyone working at Moonlites within that time was under suspicion. In spite of their animosity towards each other, Val and Simon were tied at the top of my list. He banked the money into the various safes every night and had to be involved somewhere in the crookedness;

Val took the money in via her staff, and supervised the handing over of the cash at the end of trading. Follow the money.

Moonlites had the capacity for a thousand people, and achieved that figure most Saturdays. The entrance fee was £6 on the busiest nights, a fiver or less at any other time, although not everyone paid to get in. The door money was counted by Simon and locked in an internal safe by 1.30 a.m. Bar takings were in the club safe by 2.15 a.m. and everything was tallied and ready for the night safe by 3 a.m. Then Simon, accompanied by the door security personnel, lodged it in the fortified wall of the nearby bank. The main common denominator in all of this was the General Manager.

Cadogan was clucking around Tanya in the entrance booth. It could be argued that Tanya was the missing link between conversation and noise, but she was easy on the eye and forgiven much as a result. Her boss dragged himself away to mark his territory.

'Barrett wants you at the company office three o'clock Monday afternoon,' he barked, spraying us with spit for good measure. 'Looks like your marching orders to me.'

'Full charm by-pass in operation,' Ciara mumbled.

'My pleasure,' I told Simon, smiling; the lipstick had been a good move.

Tonight he looked like a badly suited Mormon. Whatever cologne he'd selected smelled of carbolic soap and gave him a taint of fifties industrial school and lice. I shivered to remember my own recent attack of hair dwellers, courtesy of my niece and nephew. Simon didn't need to worry overly about that kind of activity as his head was swathed in the finest tonsorial elegance money could buy. Gossip had it that he owned a range of rugs, each a little longer than the other,

51

which he phased in and out to suggest haircuts and so on. It didn't always go to plan: he'd stinted on glue a few nights earlier, using it only at his sideburns, and an unexpected wind lifted the toupee from his pate like a parachute all evening. It was truly mesmerising, and even Val was moved to let me off for five minutes to go have a look.

In the hour before opening, the club was a strange twilight zone. The purple carpets and velvet upholstery fringed with silver braid looked tacky and sad. A vast mirror ball looked bemused on high, wondering how it could have ended up there, without the adoration it deserved. Ceiling lights in the shapes of the moon and stars dangled aimlessly, travelling through a non-time without proper purpose, poor relations of the cosmos, a plastic universe. The smell of spilled booze and stale romance perfumed the dark cavern and its satellite booths. My feet slurped across the sticky floor.

This silence was the freakiest part. Later the air would thrum with persistent bass, now it was hushed. Barry was the club connoisseur of the household and he declared he wouldn't touch Moonlites with, what he liked to call, his ten-foot pole. My queasiness returned, happily without a vengeance on board.

Ciara worked the floor with an army of other lovelies. They were encouraged to wear short skirts and tight tops. Most did because the tips were easier earned that way. Even Ciara showed a section of thigh and, minx that she was, often wore patent boots which stretched above her remarkably elegant knees. This was because I was paying her too little and forcing her to exploit her body, she assured me. The boots were stored at the office for fear Mrs Gillespie might do away with them if she knew they existed. Ciara didn't mind encouraging heart attacks in her parents at all, but she couldn't afford to replace the thigh-highs, hence the untypical caution on her part.

My post was station three in the main bar. This was midway along the counter and always very busy. There were two stations to my right, two to my left, and two more at a small back bar in the dim recesses of the club. There was also a scabby VIP area, which was no fun whatsoever, had bad table service, no dance floor and seldom held anyone, let alone a celebrity. It was designed to look like a space capsule, but had the effect of making revellers feel they were trapped in a tin can. The runt of the security team worked its periphery: a dim theology student from Trinity College, accepted by Academia because he was good at rugby, had played for St Mary's and now bolstered the college ranks against the dreaded UCD who always won the annual Colours Match. (The other university had also got James Joyce, because he was a Catholic and therefore precluded from attending Trinners in his day, although somehow the college could take that easier than the sporting defeats.)

I counted out my float and signed for it, as did the others on each of the stations. My fingers began to feel greasy in anticipation of the coin and paper exchanges ahead of me. Money is dirty business, a truly filthy commodity. All along the production line glum faces got ready for a night of rictus smiles at drunken assholes; showbiz right down to our fallen arches. Val Tobin stood close by, nursing a glass full of cola; I knew from experience that it was also well topped up with vodka. Whatever gets you there. When she realised that she was staring at me she looked away. Okay, I'll admit that I stuck my tongue out at her, thinking it might break some ice and let us share a laugh. A misjudgement, as I was soon to discover.

Val was short and mean with it. Her height, or lack of it, had kept her from many of the jobs she coveted, including that of

General Manager at Moonlites. It's always better for a trouble-maker to have to look into the eyes of, or preferably up at, authority. She was skeletal enough to fax from place to place and was in the habit of dying her hair outrageous colours; last week had been fuchsia, this was magenta time. Perhaps she had 'issues' that she was working through. As long as they didn't always involve me, I was happy.

It was unusual for anyone to stumble into our hovel before pub closing time, but tonight was to be an exception. Shortly after ten o'clock, a dozen men in dark suits arrived and set up a kitty. They picked a quiet spot in Ciara's jurisdiction and proceeded to drink pints and shorts without conversation for at least half an hour. If this was a stag party it needed serious livening up. It wasn't. In fact, it was a wake.

'Did you see the story in tonight's paper about a lad who drowned in the river?'

I nodded as I filled Ciara's drinks order.

'It was Tiny Shortall.'

'And that would mean what to me?'

'He's a regular in here. That's his identical twin over there.' She pointed a lacquered nail at the table of sombre-suited men.

'Oh, him. I thought that *was* him, if you know what I mean.'

Ciara flashed me a C-Special Scather.

'I mean, I didn't know there were two of them.'

'People think us twins are freaks,' she said, shaking her head at humanity's ignorance.

I remained silent.

Nicknames tend to reflect the essence of a person or the complete opposite, I have found. In the case of 'Tiny' Shortall, it was the latter. If he'd been identical to the man Ciara indicated, he was tall, broad-shouldered, with a tendency to a few extra pounds around the midriff, wavy auburn hair and blue eyes. In short, not bad for a minor thug-type.

'What's this one called?' I asked the font of knowledge.

'Shorty, would you believe?'

'I would.'

'They're not a bit happy about Tiny's death,' she continued.

'That can happen.'

'Bet you a fiver there'll be singing before the night is over.'

'No way am I betting on a certainty, witch. It's like saying that they'll raise a glass to a fallen comrade.'

With that the table stood and muttered, 'To Tiny.'

Ciara returned to hustle more orders, shimmying a flash of upper leg and a lot of boot. She was *so* going to make the readies tonight.

Val Tobin chose that moment to step on my sore heel and spill some ice down my back. Oopsadaisy. 'Wet', 'hen' and 'mad as' were all words which sprang to mind, but I wiped myself down, saying, 'You shouldn't drink so much sherry with your breakfast, Val. It will always find you out,' in my most pleasant tones. And they can be pretty annoying, if I say so myself. I know I should have left it but, dammit all, I still had a little spirit left.

Simon Cadogan arrived to pay his respects to the mourners, and to order them a drink on the house. Least he could do, really, as they were about to blow a lot of money in our humble hole that evening. He joined their company and spent a long time wringing Shorty Shortall's hand. I wondered if they were on more than speaking terms. Whether they were or not might not be pertinent to the job in hand but, bowing to force of habit, I noted it nonetheless. He also took the opportunity to feel up Ciara's bottom and was rewarded with a cold drink in the crotch and profuse apologies. Don't mess with what you can't afford, swamp boy.

My eyes roved the faces around me, unconsciously searching for Nina Clancy. Well, that sort of coincidence is the vital twist in lots of Hollywood movies, so it can't be completely impossible, can it? The Moonlites clubbers were a fairly young crowd and I was certain a goodly number had fake ID to prove they were legally allowed entry and alcohol. After an hour, they all began to look the same to me, and if Nina came within my orbit, I missed her.

By midnight the joint was heaving. The dance floor was stuffed with humanoid marionettes pulsing to the beat. The youngsters on Ecstasy charted the evening's progress most vividly: starting with a broad smile and lots of energy, they danced confidently and invaded others' personal space without noticing. As the night wore on, the muscles keeping the grin in place tired and faces began to droop, while still retaining an element of the original happiness, not unlike a face after a stroke. They drank water by the bucket, and rarely touched alcohol, which was the only usual difference between them and the regular punters. By two a.m. the batteries were running low and most were uncoordinated and had to be helped out the door. A great time had by all.

We ran the full gamut of petty thefts that evening, from short measures to unreturned change to stolen brollies and a very nice leather jacket that Tanya just had to have. Same old same old, really. At the end of proceedings the table of gents was very drunk indeed and collected on cue by a fleet of taxis ordered in advance by the party itself, a professional operation to the last detail. They vowed to return the following night and I had no doubt but that they would, and that Ciara hoped they'd sit with her again. We stacked the dishwashers, wiped down the bar surfaces, bagged the money and put things to rights. There didn't appear to be anything moody about the transfer of the cash from the ten tills to the bank bags, but that was the point of a good scam: there shouldn't be. We were still no closer to knowing how it worked.

I was feeling very, very ropey by then so Val, the twisted little bonsai, put me on puke patrol. She would have made a wonderfully cruel mediaeval ruler. I should have refused but I didn't want to give her reason to sack me. It wasn't a large vomit but it was enough to turn my innards. Ciara, bless her (and I don't often go in for that), came to my rescue and helped swill out the affected booth.

'Admit it,' she said. 'You were annoying Val. Again.'

'I couldn't help myself. She was getting my goat. Again.'

'You and your livestock, Boss.' She shook her head, mystified.

It was traditional for the staff to have 'one for the road' in the back bar. Buying and selling alcohol after hours was illegal, but drinking wasn't, so we all put our money in a kitty to go into the till the following night. I chose a white wine, which was as wet and nasty as you'd expect in a dive like Moonlites. I wanted a 7-Up but it would have attracted too much attention, especially from Ciara. I wasn't up to telling the world my good news just yet. If I waited long enough the world and its mother (mine too) would be able to see for itself, as my body expanded to behemoth proportions. I groaned to picture it.

'It's your own fault,' Ciara said.

I started with fright. How could she know?

'Pardon?' I gasped.

'You brought it on yourself,' she continued in a self-satisfied tone, which I did not like one little bit.

I was sweating in a most unladylike way and fighting to

contain the contents of my stomach.

'You know well that the wine here is rot gut.'

Ah. I let out a long sigh. Safe, as yet.

Tanya did a tour of the floor in her ill-gotten gain. The jacket certainly suited her, but I couldn't resist pointing out that she could never wear it to the club, in case the real owner returned and claimed it. She was not the greatest at thinking a situation through. Then again, neither was I or I would have employed safer methods of contraception – like never having sexual intercourse. Which I would not, ever again. As if to bolster my feelings towards the opposite sex, Eamonn Davey, in the off-duty cops' corner, belched like a fart bag and dug into his pint, swallowing it whole. No wonder he was big enough to see from the moon.

'Tonight was a strange one,' Simon commented.

Everyone nodded.

'You did well,' he said to Ciara.

'Thanks.'

'No. I mean you did well on tips,' he clarified.

She didn't bat an eyelid. 'That's 'cos I'm the best,' she offered.

He didn't like the cheek but let it go, lacking a suitable put down. With Ciara there was no point in going off half-cocked, which was what Cadogan was if Ladies' room graffiti was to be believed.

The Trinity rugger throwback slid on to the banquette beside Ciara, clearly bent on engaging her in conversation with a view to fun times. He'd been pursuing her for as long as she'd worked here and had got precisely nowhere. Tonight she was mellow and allowed him to breathe in her general vicinity. He took this to be a good omen and even had the temerity to ask a question.

58

'What were they like?'

'The Shortall Gang?'

He nodded, beaming like a vampire at sunset.

'Them,' he verified, dipping his head up and down some more, like a toy dog on the back seat of a car. 'Them.'

I did say he wasn't the brightest bulb on the Christmas tree.

'Fine, really, for villains. And there was great storytelling and theorising about Tiny. They say someone took him out.'

Now, we were all listening intently. My big nose itched with curiosity, professional parker that I am.

'Really?' I said, by way of encouragement.

'Yeah,' Ciara continued, delighted with the spotlight. 'They say he was murdered and that when they find out who did it they'll wreak a terrible revenge. All very *Pulp Fiction*, I have to say.'

And how was your day at work, dear?

Nothing could match that for exotica, so I took my leave. As I reached the door I heard a low, dangerous growl. A little of the Trinity boy went a long way and Ciara had had enough.

'Warren, if you do that again,' she promised, 'I'll snap it right off.'

I prolonged my journey for all it was worth because the sooner I got home, the sooner I would get to bed, and the sooner I would fall asleep, and the sooner tomorrow would come, and the sooner I would see my family and sundry neighbours. It was the opposite of Christmas, really, when you couldn't wait for your presents and rushed things along by going to bed early. Tomorrow was Barbecue Day and I could look forward to the fate of a grilled martyr if my mother found out the state I was in.

Summer nights have always seemed brighter to me than

their winter cousins. This was a beauty, balmy air ruffling the leafy trees and toying playfully with my smoke-scented hair. I always smelled like a full ashtray after a Moonlites session, one of the many drawbacks to working in a service industry. Suddenly, passive smoking was a newer, greater threat, harmful to both me and the baby. This brought me neatly, and uncomfortably, back to the question of whether or not to continue with this pregnancy. I didn't have an answer, yet, and I didn't like that the terminology already included 'baby', not 'foetus'. Was my body acting the traitor on all levels? Around me the city was going about the business of living and dying; I felt myself do a little of both.

SIX

I lay splayed across my double bed the following morning, blissfully unaccompanied and for once free from nausea. I found the remains of another human being downstairs on the couch: unconscious, snoring merrily and upsetting the wild-life. Come to think of it, Barry was an awful lot wilder than any of the sundry animals casting disgusted looks his way. He had not brought any offerings home and neither had the cats or dog; I gave myself a quiet high five.

Today was Family Day at the Street residence further into the wilds of Dublin's northside. Now *that* made me feel ill, but I resolved not to dwell on my problems and to enjoy the morning instead. Well, what was left of it, which was twelve minutes until noon. The sun was wantonly streaking across a clear June sky and the very ground hummed with energy. I chanced a weak cup of caffeined tea and was well pleased. My toothpaste would fulfil the mint remit for the time being. I decanted smelly tinned fodder for the quadrupeds and they seemed pleased too.

'See, almost lunchtime and still no trouble. How sweet it is.'

After a bracing shower I went in search of clean, girl-type clothes, as favoured by mothers the world over, settling on a blue linen pinafore dress over a crisp white blouse and white plimsolls. I was the picture of unblemished innocence after scraping my hair into a ponytail, and applying some rather clever under-eye concealer and blusher to rosify the image. It would keep my mum at bay for all of six minutes but that would serve as a useful lead in to the afternoon. While I was about it I even applied a little perfume. Reckless me. I was distrustful, though, of feeling so normal, wondering when an attack of the gastrics might strike. Short-term crisis intervention came in the form of chicken soup from a can I unearthed in the kitchen. A bowl of universal elixir later, I was ready to tackle the world, so I started with Barry.

It was not easy. I tried waving coffee under his nose. I tugged and pushed. I whispered sour nothings in his ear. I shouted worse. Eventually, I set No. 4 on him in a devilish attack-by-licking initiative. The manoeuvre was a total success and soon we were trading insults like any other couple who'd been together too long. I enjoyed it greatly, until things got accurate with Barry accusing me of blatant, cynical dressing up.

'And what's that I smell?' he asked, sniffing the air. 'Eau de Suckuptothemammy, unless I'm tragically mistaken?'

'Better than spilled pints and whacked out anecdotes,' I responded, aware that my riposte was nowhere near championship form.

'Feeling the pain of that pathetic remark yet?' the big Feck asked.

I resorted to violence; most satisfying. But I had kept my best ammo for my finale.

'Are you ready for this barbecue then?'

He gave a strangled cry. He'd forgotten. I glowed in a short-lived triumph.

Barry dashed to the bathroom, showered and changed in a matter of nanoseconds. He had gone from hobo to *homo superbens* in a thrice. A fashionable day-old stubble graced his manly features, complementing his smoky, decadent eyes. He'd opted for a James Dean look: tight tee-shirt and jeans. The question 'Would you . . .?' was emblazoned across his muscular chest. This ensemble would send my teenage niece Lucy over the edge of her massive crush on him. We were in matching colour schemes, I noted, his 'n' hers, how cute: if that didn't make me vomit perhaps I was fit for the afternoon ahead.

'What's all this in aid of again?' my paramour asked.

'Primeval urges,' I explained. 'The boys want to make fire.'

'Mmn, evil urges, my favourite.'

Barry wrapped his arms around me and kissed me full and long on the mouth. I responded in kind, tasting the mint of his toothpaste, feeling the pleasant rasp of his chin against mine, breathing in his scent. It was most acceptable, all in all.

'Will I phone a cab?' he asked, his voice loaded with the suggestion of bed and sex first.

I was tempted, but the little knot within me had changed the rules of engagement in a way I had not worked out yet. Best not complicate an already messy mess.

'No need, I'll drive. I won't be drinking much. I have to work at the club later, and my stomach is still a bit ropey.'

'I hope it's confined to just the one end,' Barry remarked.

If we could go there, we were obviously sharing way too

much, so I refrained from issuing a detailed description of my health status. That could wait till later, when I might even be able to deal with it myself. There was a grim satisfaction to the fact that it would frighten the pants off Barry, neat-fitting though they were. I allowed myself the tiniest of smirks. Well, I had to keep my spirits up somehow while headed for Geraldine Street's auto-da-fé.

'I'd better saddle up the dog creature,' Barry said.

'I wasn't going to bring him, actually.'

'Oh, no, no way is he staying here without supervision. Last time he ate my entire collection of Leonard Cohen bootlegs.'

'Yeah? Well, he suffered for it, he was depressed for two days.'

No. 4 was idly chewing yesterday's *Irish Times* and looking as if that old news was leaving him unfulfilled.

'Fair point, however. Leash the hound. Let's go chew some ribs.'

Marion Maloney was not to be thwarted two days in a row; she came at us with stealth, speed and accuracy. It was poetry, in a way.

'Look and learn,' I whispered to Barry.

'Awesome, isn't she?' he gushed, with genuine admiration.

Marion opened with, 'Oh, but ye're the elusive pair,' before a segue into an impressively knowledgeable set of televisual queries. Barry was put to the pin of his collar to answer one or two of the more obscure.

Marion finally got around to me and mine. 'Does that dog eat things?' she wanted to know.

I didn't like the direction we'd taken. I looked at No. 4, searching for a clue. He was unhelpful.

'Yes,' I replied. 'But nothing unusual, I don't think. Why?'

'There's a wheel missing off my new bin,' she informed me.

'I've seen him in action, it looks like something he'd do.'

Marion was so right and I couldn't tell her that. The little wretch even had the cheek to meet her beady eye then. It was a stand-off worthy of a Western with really tough guys in it. My nerve didn't hold, theirs did. I tugged on his leash and made for the safety of my car. Barry laughed for two blocks.

'That woman can hear the grass grow,' I pointed out.

'And that dog is outrageous.'

No. 4 was thrilled with his plaudit.

The first inkling I had that the goal posts had shifted on the family day was when I spotted balloons attached to the Raynors' gate rather than our own. Second was the happy chatter from their garden, as opposed to the silence of the Street house. It had all the hallmarks of a Mammy plot to join two dynasties. And I was the only available single member of mine, tarnished as I was. I linked Barry's arm proprietorially and boldly entered the fray wearing a smile that would stop an armoured car in its tracks.

Maeve was engaged with my mum, which was noble of her and would provide me with excellent back up. My two brothers and their wives were chasing various Street children; No. 4 quickly joined them. My father was scorching flesh with Frank Raynor at a built-in barbie, both of them clad in alarming golf trousers and novelty aprons. Neighbours lounged with exotic coloured drinks, trying not to poke their eyes out with the paper umbrellas stuck into the cocktails; they were lethal in every aspect, no doubt.

Breda Raynor came through the French doors leading from the house to the garden carrying an enormous bowl of salad. Following her, bearing platters of bread, was her son, Andy. Pain jolted my chest and I halted abruptly.

'What's up?' Barry asked.

'Nothing. Heartburn, that's all.'

Andy Raynor met my eyes and smiled, then casually left me hanging there, gasping for breath. Two could play at that game. I made my way to the opposite end of the garden and joined Maeve and my mother who were neatly framed by a honeysuckled arch. Barry scavenged for beer and my teenage niece Lucy.

Baby Rose Street was hanging over Maeve's well-toned shoulder and dribbling gently down her back in a picture postcard of contentment. She also smelt distinctly high. All very reminiscent of an early-morning Barry Agnew, actually. I exchanged the requisite kisses and stood back for my mother's examination. She nodded happily and said, 'See where a little effort will get you?' I returned a benign smile, because it's nice to be nice, you know? The back of my neck was still hot from the full body flush supplied by Andy, and my ego was smarting in a less than pleasant way.

'Why the change of venue?' I asked my mother, trying to keep any hint of an agenda out of my voice.

'Your father and brother had a practice run on the new gas thing they bought and nearly took out half the neighbourhood with their antics.'

'They're *not* allowed to play with matches anymore,' Maeve added, laughing.

'It's great to have handy men around, isn't it?' I commented, smiling.

My antennae were more finely tuned for foreign bodies than I realised. The hairs on the back of my neck twitched and I turned just as a mellifluous voice asked, 'Are any of you ladies in need of a drink?' My mother Geraldine simpered and extended her glass for 'just a half of that pink fizzy stuff'.

Maeve put in a request for champagne also, and I was despatched with Andy to help with the order.

I had ample time to study his back view as we made our way to the drinks table. He was looking fit and well in white linen which set off his perfect tan. His walk was an easy stroll, with a slight swing of the shoulders and just enough swagger in the hip department. He played many sports, all of them well, which led to his healthy colour and good condition. He told me once the exercise kept him calm; all aggression was gone after a good, hard game. I knew sex was another sport to him and here he was peerless.

'A tray would do just as well,' I muttered.

'But it wouldn't be half as much fun,' my host retorted.

I couldn't see his face and therefore couldn't tell whether he was teasing or taunting. His tone was perfectly measured. Damn, he was good. As we busied ourselves with the drinks he met my eyes again in that way I wished he wouldn't and asked, 'Why have you been avoiding me?' Nothing like getting down to brass tacks straight away.

'I would have thought that was obvious,' I answered, with closure clearly signposted.

'Not to me, it isn't.'

He was either maddeningly cool or maddeningly stupid. Either way it was maddening.

'Don't play me for one of your regular female twits,' I hissed. 'You used me, dumped me, then rubbed my face in your other affairs. Don't you dare come over all moral high ground with me.'

'I wouldn't dream of it,' he said. 'But if I were you, I'd check all my facts while preparing the apology you owe me for jumping to conclusions. And I think it might also be pertinent to remember that I don't live with anyone, whereas you do.'

Then he off and left me with my mouth hanging open. It had been a short spat but a bitter one, and I felt that he was as furious as I was about the situation. If he only knew the half of it, I thought, fuming.

'Jeez, Leo, who pissed on your pansy?' the unfortunate Barry asked.

'Fuck off,' I exclaimed, storming out the gate to cool off.

When in doubt, head for home, especially if you know it's empty. I sat in the back garden of my childhood beside the charred crater surrounding the doomed barbecue. The blast had been enough to singe an area four feet square, and the blackened grass and bricks seemed a metaphor for my life. I felt the scald of tears behind my eyes but stemmed the urge to let them flow. There would be time enough for those. In the sky, two cotton ball clouds gave chase to one another. That same sun up there was shining down on Mary Clancy and her family in Clunesboro, on Barry and Andy a few doors away, on me in my own private hell and on Nina Clancy in hers, if she was still alive and on this earth. I felt as low as I wanted to go that day. Those tears could definitely wait.

Only one person had noticed my departure and subsequent re-entry to the Raynor demesne. Andy did not bat a handsome eyelid, but swiftly looked away as I trudged back to my mother and her now extended company.

'Maeve has been telling us all about this power yoga she's up to.'

'Sounds painful,' I said.

'Oh, it *is*. And very, *very* boring,' Maeve assured me.

'You're doing it three times a week then?' I guessed.

'*Bang* on the money,' she revealed.

I shrugged at my mum. 'I know my gals,' I told her.

'You forgot this,' a man's voice informed me.

68

I turned to find Andy, bearing a glass of orange juice. A peace offering?

'That blue is a nice colour,' he continued, a little awkwardly, referring to my dress.

Same as the blue in a pregnancy test, I mentally observed. This thought remained unspoken as I was wisely supping the drink he had proffered instead. It's not good to share too much, too often, which is normally the way with me at family gatherings. Maybe I could learn new tricks after all.

Before we got into a full-blown discussion on the merits of the colour blue, Angela began to change her reeking baby girl. This occurred in full view on the grass and Rose enjoyed having an audience. When the used nappy was trapped in more plastic I took the moment to point out that not polluting the planet with disposables was one of the reasons I did not have kids.

'I'm doing my bit for the environment,' I explained.

'You could always use terry towelling nappies,' my mother countered.

That woman had an answer for everything.

The Street children, Dominick and Mary, dashed over to revel in the adoration of 'their' new sister.

'Do you know how we got her?' Dom asked Maeve.

'No. Would you like to tell me?'

'Yes, I would,' he nodded. 'Daddy sexed Mummy. He put his penis in her bagina and unleashed the power of the seed.'

'As good an explanation as any I've heard,' Andy commented.

'Before that, Rose was nothing,' Mary added. 'But I never was.'

'Yes, you were,' Dom taunted. 'Before you were born you were nothing too, but I was here.'

'I was not nothing,' his sister shouted. 'I was never nothing. Was I Leo?'

'No,' I reassured her. 'You were never nothing.'

And there was another truth for me to pick over.

The kids legged it. I guess you could say their work here was done. I tried to ignore the episode.

Angela hoisted a giggling Rose into the air and handed her to Andy.

'Have a go,' she offered.

Cue the coo-fest over the good-looking guy with the beautiful baby, and kiddiespeak of 'Rosie posie pooh' and 'Rosie posie puddin' and pie'. It was ridiculous behaviour from grown women. I was caught in mid-sneer and suddenly found myself in charge of the tot thanks to the manipulative Raynor. Then the fawning took place over me. I was back to a simmering rage with him. Andy had no idea what he was messing with here, but he would pay for it, I vowed. My tension was transmitting itself to Rose who tried to escape, so I calmed down and allowed myself to enjoy this quality time with my niece who, it must be pointed out, was the best baby in the world. I even decided to postpone the torture of Andy until another more appropriate time.

The wily fox saw his chance and wangled me into light conversation. He was a past master at charm and I was only human, so I found myself laughing at his jokes and bloody basking in his attention. How that man could scramble me, despite my firm resolves, was a bafflement. My mother was in one of the seven heavens. She even subtly engineered to cut the two of us off together at the edge of the group, rendering us an independent satellite. I really hadn't the strength to protest, and anyway it wasn't all that bad having the undivided attention of a man so easy on the eye. I had a shocking and very pleasant vision of me jumping his bones, and allowed myself to wallow in the memory for a good forty-five seconds.

Then things began to go pear-shaped for Andy – or should that be model-shaped? A slender twig, who looked like she should be draped across the bonnet of a sports car, wafted into the garden, obviously in search of him. He had the luck of charms though when she spotted a television star and made a beeline for him instead. She and Barry made a very plausible couple. We watched them flirt awhile, silent and unlikely conspirators. Then Andy muttered, 'Wouldn't that solve a lot?' under his breath and left to attend to the new arrival. I bet myself an ice cream that her name was Willow, or at the very least something plant-based. Last time I'd encountered Andy with a woman had been the unfortunate early-morning call I'd made to his house to declare my undying devotion. I'd interrupted him cosily ensconced with a Heather and given myself way too much heartache for a weekday. Or any day.

Later as I chewed on a Cornetto, waif-like Daisy asked me how long I'd known Andy.

'Forever,' I explained. 'Which is about a century too long for both of us.'

To admit this was a weight off my freckled shoulders, so I ran with the theme. I pointed at Barry, with the butt of the wafer.

'That's my fella there. Again, it may have gone on too long.'

Although Daisy didn't comment, I knew she was busy figuring out how a plain lass like myself could possibly carp about knowing two such gorgeous men and living with one of them. I guess I was just a tad fed up by then, and could see the end of my tether in the near-distance.

In a way, the afternoon was a breakthrough for me. It calmed me, oddly enough. I began to plan how to deal with my life without relying on the crutch of an Andy or a Barry; they could not be depended on, even if they seemed to be around from time to time. I had reached a decision. I would manage for myself, and now for a baby too. I thought of the Chinese proverb: 'You cannot see it, but through'. I was not sure it was entirely apposite, but it would do as a working model. There was no need to rush into telling anyone what was going to happen; the right time would present itself later. And in the meantime I had to get my body into top working order. Oh, and I probably needed to see a doctor. Already a list was forming and I felt excited. I also really, really wanted a choc ice, but settled for a green salad, pilau rice and two lamb kebabs: no point in encouraging bad eating habits in this kid from the outset. I felt wise and practical. Leo Street, mum-to-be, fecund and relaxed. I made the most of the fleeting moment, because it was obvious it would never last.

My dad and Frank Raynor were keepers of the flame. It took me a while to figure out what was different about my father, aside from the fact that his apron was decorated with the torso of a naked woman. (Oh those men, what japes!) His face was slightly 'off'. He didn't wear a beard ever, so that wasn't missing. Same deal with a moustache. And then it came to me. He had no eyebrows.

'But you should have seen them fireworks, Leo. Mighty altogether.'

'Unintentional,' I pointed out.

'Ah, yeah, but you can plan too much in life.'

Wisdom indeed.

The barbecue wound on its pleasant and charming way. I renewed friendships and heard the local gossip. The lady from the sweetshop was having a love affair with the lollipop man at the primary school. And why not? They were both widowed and their work was compatible. Fair play to them.

The residents were mounting a campaign to halt the development of a green belt into expensive apartments. Miles French, a notorious, ninety-year-old eccentric who still cycled his bike around the area, was trying to introduce a rare plant on to the land in question, pretending it had lived there forever. It was an audacious and imaginative plan and I wished him luck. He tapped me for twenty quid for the cause: small change in the march for the environment and I gave it willingly.

Breda Raynor ordered five loaves of bread to be delivered the following Tuesday. This covered my protest donation and the price of the ingredients, so the afternoon broke even. There aren't many days can say that for themselves.

No. 4 had to be carried to the car, his porky tum distended with stolen food and his short legs run off him from chasing humans. He'd had a wonderful party. Dominick and Mary were worried that he'd pushed himself too far. I told them it was hard to get rid of a bad thing. They seemed to know what I was getting at.

'He ate my lucky bag,' Dominick told me. 'There was a balloon in it and maybe he farted and the air went in the balloon in his stomach and that's why he's so fat now.'

All in all, a brilliantly thought through theory.

'Maybe Rose's nappy will explode with one of her farts,' Mary extrapolated.

This notion met with great approval from Dominick, for its scientific basis and incendiary possibilities.

I waved goodbye to neighbours headed to their own homes and gardens. Andy appeared at the gate with his dad, Frank, and Barry.

'I like the waves,' I told the elder Raynor, referring to his latest hedge design. Frank practised the gentle art of topiary.

'They're easy on the eye,' he said, proudly.

Barry shook hands all round and I pecked Frank's cheek.

'Thank Breda again for us,' I said.

There was no avoiding his son. Andy's eyes bored holes into mine, piercing my mind, unsettling me.

'You dropped this,' he said, handing me a note.

I had not.

'Give me a ring sometime,' he continued and I could have sworn I heard a whispered 'soon'.

'Sure,' I told him.

We both knew I didn't mean it. I tucked the note into my pocket. Might be good for a laugh later, to lighten the Moonlites load.

He leaned down for a kiss and I made sure I was turned slightly away. He almost missed me altogether and I have to admit that I sniggered. Well, well, well, was this the confident Andy Raynor, conqueror of all he surveyed? I wasn't stupid enough to think I'd done anything but dented his pride. He'd no doubt be wondering why I wasn't slobbering all over him; I'd done that enough over the years.

No. 4 gave an ominously loud belch. 'Time to go,' I announced.

I had kissed Dominick and Mary goodbye when the problem bothering them finally surfaced.

'Leo, which came first?' Dominick asked. 'Jesus or the Dinosaurs?'

Their dad, Stephen, arrived in the nick of time to save me from a lenghty discussion, which is what usually follows a question of this sort.

'They're big into religion at the moment,' he explained.

'And dinosaurs,' Mary added.

Stephen was in for rigorous intellectual argument later. I winked at Andy and Frank, who now each had a child swinging off them, then beat a hasty retreat with the male members of The Villas household. As we got into the car I heard Dominick proudly say, 'We gave Aunty Leo headlights.' That child was such a gossip. My scalp tingled to remember them and I felt a session with a nit comb coming on, just in case.

'That Daisy is some stunner,' Barry commented as we drove away.

'But deeply dull,' I said.

'Yes.' Barry gave me a sideways glance. 'What are you up to?' he asked.

I laughed. 'I have no idea what you mean.'

'You seem a bit, I dunno, happy.'

'It's a beautiful day, I have a night of drudgery ahead, why wouldn't I be happy?'

'You are a strange woman, Leo Street.'

'But not dull.'

'No, not at all dull, my love.'

Love, eh? Didn't some poet call it 'the crooked thing'? We sang along to the radio all the way home. It felt like one of the better days for a while.

SEVEN

Ciara was taking the surprise business seriously. When I got to The Vaults she was chatting happily with our corpulent friend Father Con Considine. We were all dressed in black and white, I noted. I told Con he could get a job at Moonlites without having to shed the uniform.

'It couldn't be any tougher there than where they've put me now,' he said.

Con was a recently appointed parish priest in an inner-city area close to Connolly Station. It was famous for high unemployment, drug abuse and prostitution, with dependencies on the black market and moneylending, each problem feeding the next in a vicious circle of despair. In spite of this, he was upbeat.

'I think I'm finally doing something worthwhile,' he said. 'I'd like to make a difference.'

His previous parish had been in the Midlands, where he'd shared duties with a rich aesthete who considered him shoe muck. I got the feeling he'd tired of sherry mornings with the local ladies and confessions from forty-year-olds who'd neglected their morning and evening prayers and cheeked their parents.

A detail from Nina Clancy's file came back to me. 'Con, Mayville Street is part of your new stomping ground, isn't it?'

'Yes, Why?'

'We're starting on a missing person case, a sixteen-year-old country girl who took off to Dublin and disappeared. The cops traced a phone call she made to a public phone on Mayville.'

'What's her name and I'll keep an eye out?' he said.

'She's called Nina Clancy. I'll get a photo to you on Monday.'

'Great. I've always liked detective stories on the telly, so it'll be a bit of a thrill to be involved in a real-life one.'

Ciara snorted. 'A very, very small thrill,' she promised.

I couldn't disagree. The glamour of the job had never presented itself to me, and I missed it. I enjoyed the TV sleuths, perhaps more than most, because I knew how far removed they were from the boredom of a real private investigator's days, spent sitting around waiting for someone else to make a move. Still, escapism is a wonderful modern aid.

We waved Con off when the time came to report at Moonlites. He headed home for some beauty sleep. The next day was Sunday and a big one for clergy. Ciara and I faced into another night of possibilities. I really wanted a break in this case and with it an end to the filth of bar work and the annoyance of people. Ciara agreed.

'I never thought I'd envy a priest,' she said. 'But, you know?'

'Oh, yes, I do,' I assured her, watching our friend's back

disappear into the shimmer of another warm evening. 'And he gets eternal happiness in heaven at the end of it all. Or the beginning, whichever way you look at it.'

'Yeah, we're not even getting a Social Welfare stamp from this one.'

'Let's stick it to the feckers, shall we?'

'Let's.'

Simon Cadogan was all over Tanya like a saprogenic rash. He hardly had time to growl at us as we checked in, so busy was he pawing the young woman. Tanya was thick enough not to notice the harassment, which was a mercy to her really. I wasn't sure she understood even the simplest concepts, like why the wheel was a good idea. I could picture her saying, 'The wheel? No, sorry, I don't get it.' Security continued to stare longingly at the water hose and Val still hated me. We were like a television sit-com starting out from the same place every episode, except for the paucity of humorous incidents.

The DJ was warming up a new set so we had sounds to accompany the ringing in of cash floats and the arrangement of stock. The practice run was a bit more tuneful than usual and I congratulated him on it. I was accused of being an old hippy.

'Less of the old and don't ever mention my hips again,' I warned, laughing.

Val barked me back to my station. I looked at my tatty little kingdom and wondered what the hell I was doing here. 'Earning a living to support you and your family,' I heard a distant inner voice mutter. If I have a soul, it's a narky one.

I enjoyed a brief, minty tea and the evening paper while Val was hiding with her first vodka and Coke of the evening session. The body in the river was the lead story. He was formally identified as Thomas Shortall, a native of Dublin's inner city, 'Tiny' to his friends. A post-mortem was being carried out even as we read. Police would only reveal that the circumstances of his death were suspicious.

A short paragraph on page five caught my eye: an unidentified body found near a dump in Castleknock, over to the west of town. What bothered me was that these were the remains of a young woman. I had been tardy in starting the Clancy case, reluctant to delve into the upset. I would ring the hospitals the following day. And the mortuaries. Maybe I would even take in Con at work, for luck or whatever.

I'm as superstitious as the next ninny, so I checked my horoscope. It said, 'Family matters loom large. An old flame returns. Money is tight. Be strong.' It was never any different, really. I read a few other signs and saw that they were all of a muchness; universal problems and solutions, one equation and one panacea working the whole of the cosmos. It made me feel less alone in life's struggle. For a glimmer.

Ciara's men were back with women in tow. Everyone was splendidly turned out, with black the main theme of the mourning partywear. It was business as usual, in one way, as Ciara had been offered dope, E and coke by one of the guys.

'All the way up to heroin,' she told me. 'It'll take ten minutes to collect and all I have to do is step outside then with my money.'

'At least they're not actually dealing on the premises,' I said, trying to ignore another unsavoury problem.

Ciara gave one of her trademark snorts. 'Small mercies.'

I took in the Moonlites demi-monde of crooks, shop assistants and students mingling before my eyes, hankering desperately after a good time, or perhaps to forget their lives for a few precious hours.

'The good news is that they're determined to give Tiny a great send off,' Ciara continued. 'The bad news is that they're starting on tequila. I'm almost tempted to give them all over to Warren in the VIP area and forego the tips. This could be one messy evening.'

Tiny Shortall's brother seemed diminished. He wore his suit carelessly and didn't seem to fit anywhere, not even at the table. I had not yet lost a human close to me, but if it was to be in any way like the deaths of my animal friends over the years I was not looking forward to it. This man was on a plane of grief unreachable to the rest of his company. He sat still as the grave itself and proceeded to drink himself comatose. Before he passed out, he gave a short pep talk to the troops.

'Two wrongs might not make a right,' he wailed, 'but they come close enough for me.'

Loud applause followed his cry to arms, and then more tequila. This time it was ordered from me personally by one of the types, as Ciara was otherwise distracted. He was of average height, stocky but well built, with a body honed by a gym. His black hair was slicked back off a smooth-skinned face. His eyes were extraordinary, almonds of pale grey ready to swallow a girl like a pool. They were framed by elegantly curved brows, the kind that cost women a fortune to buy in a salon. His lips were thin and pale above a dimpled chin and saved him from effeminacy on the one hand and downright good looks on the other. It was a face that would have looked at home in a sepia photograph. He was sober. He spotted that I had noticed and said, 'I don't drink. I'm an alcoholic. Not that it's any of your business.'

The menace might have been step nine and a half on his program. Whatever, it was effortless and fitted him as neatly as the Armani hanging off his body. I filled the drinks in silence, took his money and thanked him. Then I hoped never to encounter him again in my life. He refused the change due from the order.

'I don't do coins,' he sniffed. 'Ruins the line of my suit.'

I decided to regard it as a deserved tip, niggardly though it was; a girl's gotta make a buck.

Good old Moonlites remained seedy as a garden centre. The punters came and went, dancing, drinking, puking. The staff pilfered change from receipts and drinks from the measures. Ciara smacked a few wandering hands. Val spilled slops on my apron and jostled me whenever she could. Really, she was such a notice box, fighting so hard for my attention when all she had to do was talk to me. She was so under my feet at one stage that I unfortunately spilled a pint of stout down her legs and into her plimsolls. Simon Cadogan got tipsy or high, don't know which. We stultified in boredom and we sweated in the muggy heat exacerbated by too many people and too little air. We were regular as a high-fibre diet. And when commerce and the night and the music ended we counted out the money from the tills and bagged it and handed it over to Val and Simon, ready for the night bank. So where was the fiddle? Damned if I knew. I dreaded the meeting on Monday afternoon when I would be grilled on a subject I was no expert on, not even close. On my way out the door, Sam, the security person rumoured to be a woman, made a pass at me. I didn't know whether to be flattered or afraid. I settled on a slice of both.

Barry was stretched across the sofa in a state of mellow high at number 11 The Villas. I waved the smoke away and told him he was a sad bastard to be home so early on a Saturday, it being a mere 3.30 in the morning. His eyes were wide and doped. This was not his first joint of the evening, I felt. In fact, he was stoned up to his retinas.

'I was bored and I missed you,' he told me, slowly.

Maybe he even believed that. I pulled myself up short before giving voice to the thought. There's a thin line between scepticism and cynicism, I told myself, and neither state is attractive.

The thing I found worst in my rude health and sobriety was that drunks and grass fiends were so boring and repetitive. And I had thirty-four or more weeks of this tedium with family, friends and colleagues to go. No wonder the reformed alcoholic at the club had looked so cheesed off with his company.

The television was spewing out synchronised aerobics for mixed pairs on one of the many sports channels Barry had bought in on a satellite package. I know, because I remember writing the cheque. Noel lay on top of the set, watching the action upside down, and occasionally reaching a paw down to swipe at a waving, Lycra-clad leg. He was having great fun and saving me from dusting, the clever boy, as well as taking Noël Coward's theory that television was for appearing on, not watching, to a logical extreme. Barry was unable to focus on something so intricate as the couple's contortions and hummed along with the elevator music they were dancing to. Moonlites seemed almost plausible by comparison. Snubby and Bridie were AWOL, doubtless on stealth patrol through the mean gardens of Dublin 3. No. 4 was snoring loudly in a large paper bag from a shop called Surprise! It felt good to be home.

Barry staggered into the kitchen as I boiled the kettle for tea. He was clutching a letter and laughing.

'This one was hand delivered today. I must have a devoted fan in the area.'

I scanned the words, which were of the 'you're so great and handsome' category. Harmless stuff in itself.

'Wonder if it's from a man or a woman,' I mused.

Barry seemed taken aback, then thrilled. 'You mean, I might have cracked the gay market? Excellent. Double the viewing figures. Copperfasten my job.'

At least his ego was nurtured and that made for a happy actor. It's better to be talked about than not talked about, as the man said – Oscar Wilde, was it?

I didn't like that the letter had been delivered to the door, no matter how full of adoration it was. Normally fan mail was forwarded by the television company, and I had no doubt they filtered out the nasties. This one had been put through the post box by someone who knew where Barry lived, and this fact was not in the public arena. He wasn't even in the phone book. Maeve had been the target of unwanted attention some weeks before and I didn't want to face a similar situation in my own home. I held schtum but determined to keep a beady eye on our front door for strange visitors or deliveries.

I looked into Barry's happy, dopey face and felt nothing. No loin-stirring, no nerve-leaping, nothing. Not even curiosity anymore. Just a flatlining familiarity and the lethargy it brought with it. That said, the early hours of any morning after a shift in Moonlites were not the optimum time to go looking for romance or excitement in a life. But I wasn't even reminded of those, just aware of their absence. Not good.

I polished off the leftover heel of a honeyed brioche I had been experimenting with. Then I tried some toasted pumpkin soda. Suddenly I was inspired and up to my elbows in flours and nuts, creating new breads; some good, some bad, and some downright ugly. I avoided yeast recipes as it can be a cranky lad to work with in the wee smalls, and found that limitation an inspiration. Barry abandoned ship somewhere around a batch of wholemeal oat scones with a buttermilk and feta crust.

In those backshift hours of the day, the house was quiet and cosy, with snoozing animals looking adorable, a man upstairs, a pregnant woman glowing below and the smell of baking bread lingering wholesomely in the air. We could have sold the lot at a premium there and then – this picture-perfect domestic bliss and promise of content forever and ever.

It was 5.45 a.m. before I found myself washing my face and preparing for bed. My body clock had been put right out of kilter by this nightclub job and, at the rate I was travelling on the road to nowhere with the case, I was due an insomniac child with a serious aversion to daylight. Vampires and creatures of the night were all very well, but generally the devil to live with. The sooner I put the Moonlites gig to bed the better. I would pray with Con tomorrow for deliverance from the hours of darkness. That task actually sounded right up his street, and entirely desirable in mine.

Every step of the stairs took an age as I dragged one heavy leg after another. My eyes had closed by the time I reached the bedroom door and I felt my way blind to the bed. I was out and on my way to the dream world before my head was hot on the pillow.

EIGHT

I was bone weary as I clawed my way out of sleep later that morning. It took me a further fifteen minutes of contemplation and mental persuasion to get myself physically out of the bed, and I was a study in slow motion as I made my way downstairs to whatever life had to chuck at me. Thankfully, this involved only a little actual throwing up on my part, amateur stuff compared with the previous week. Conspicuously missing was the fuzzy edge of too much alcohol, and that cheered me no end. I was tired, yes, but up for action. And too late to have Father Con Considine save me through the Catholic celebration of the Mass. Ah, well, sometimes it's best to make do with what you've got. Which was bread, and plenty of it.

By the miracle of cloths and cupboards, I had thwarted No. 4's natural instinct to eat everything remotely edible in sight or within a range of five miles of his portly body. The cats were less of a threat when it came to bread, though Bridie was partial to a fruit slice. I buttered a selection of goodies and shared them with the dog, telling him how good he was not to have thieved in his leisure hours. I tried to get information out of him on the Marion/bin wheel situation, but to no avail. Well, it was worth a go. I showered and dressed in loose and unflattering sweat pants and a very worn top covered with cartoon cats smiling out from my chest. Then I set to on the job I had been postponing.

Death and misfortune did not take a day off just because it was Sunday. I opened Nina's file at 'physical description' and began to dial the hospitals and mortuaries, breakfast agitating my stomach with apprehension. No one wanted to deal with a 'lay' enquiry on a Sunday, but after some international-level cajoling, I got answers. It was a pleasure to put a line through the venues without her, and a harsh reminder of how many unclaimed dead and injured people were out there in the system. I had not forgotten the newspaper report of the young woman's body found the previous day in Castleknock, and left the City Morgue until last, when I might feel braver. I needn't have worried, they wouldn't deal with me no matter how hard I whined and I was told to try again on Monday when administration just might respond to my query. The pall of unpleasant expectation now hung over proceedings. Could it be Nina Clancy lying on that slab, alone and cold, far from home?

The telephone brought me back from the Arctic regions of one dread and put me in line for another.

'You should come over and see us,' my mother told me. 'I hardly got to talk to you at all yesterday.'

'Well . . .' I hedged.

No cigar.

'Your grandmother said she'd call too and you haven't seen her in an age.'

The phrase 'What's seldom is wonderful' ricocheted mischievously in my head, but stayed unspoken. Good, uncontroversial.

And then the sucker punch.

'She won't always be with us, you know.'

Certainly an unfair, and possibly illegal, fight manoeuvre, that, but The Mammy was The Mammy and I had no recourse to official complaint. I threw in the towel.

'I'll see you in twenty minutes,' I said, with a strong hint of annoyance in my capitulation which either sailed right over my mother's head or, and this got my vote, was completely ignored.

In order to convince myself that I was a far nicer and more humane person than my mum, I brought Barry a cup of tea and some of my delicious scones. I held my breath while in the bedroom, which was a mini-Moonlites in my own home, fugged up with body odour and the massive whiff of stale smoke and alcohol. My sense of smell was heightened beyond a joke now and I didn't want to encourage random queasiness on top of the regular stuff of morning sickness. He wasn't much into conversation, which was no great surprise, and a series of grunts did us for the time being.

I did have a fleeting wonder about modern romance and if this was all it had to offer me. But, on the understanding that it was probably still better than a poke in the eye with a pointy stick, I let my sunny disposition *du jour* push any further dark thoughts away. They went to fester at the back of my mind, with a feast of other juicy issues.

Noel was killing a sock around the lower half of the house. The shredded wool would never again cover a foot. I left him to his task. One sock was a small price to pay in the nurturing of such a talent.

I wrapped two loaves as a gift for the clan and shouted the news that I was off to my parents' from the bottom step of the stairs, just as I exited with No. 4. A muffled throat-clearing in return indicated that Barry had taken my afternoon itinerary on board. With nothing more to add, I skedaddled with the hound.

As we were passing The Sheds pub, on the Clontarf Road, I reached the end of my current list of options (it had not been a long one). 'I've got a home, a job, a regular-ish income. I could manage on my own.'

It felt good to have shared. Briefly, good. No. 4 looked entirely fed up.

'So you see,' I concluded. 'We don't need anyone but ourselves.' I liked the empowered sound of this when uttered aloud.

The dog gave me the eye and I went for broke, adding 'Lucky' and waiting for a response to the name. All right, more in hope than whatever. Didn't work.

'Okay,' I admitted. 'I need a husband.'

Again with the glare.

'*Really* need a husband,' I amended.

He continued to be rude on the staring front, so I retorted with, 'No need to be so traditional, mutt.'

That got a sulky response. Life is just a case of staggering from one insult to the next, for any of us, no matter who we think we are.

I jerked the car into a space opposite the ancestral bricks and mortar and made my way round to the back door. I would never dream of entering by the front, unless I had news of an undeathdefying cancer or something unbuyable to sell. This year's floral display was Victorian cottage garden, a pretty mix of real geraniums (blue) and their upstart non-cousins the pelargonium (slut-multicoloured), along with Black-eyed Susan, hollyhocks, larkspur, nasturtiums and some rather cheery poppies. I somehow think that the Poppy family cannot help itself in the cheek department. They should have Gillespie as part of their taxonomy.

No. 4 gave chase to that hairy, white monster Smokey Joe Street. He returned all yeowling, nose-scraped and indignant. The cat never broke stride. Smokey was the Christian Brother of the feline race, the armed wing of the mog militia.

'That dog has no manners,' my mother shared with me.

'That cat should have cloven hooves instead of claws,' I countered.

I held my offering out.

'Are they safe to eat?' my mother asked, regarding the loaves with all the enthusiasm of a Buddhist at a bullfight.

The question was understandable, as the family had endured much in the way of poisons at my incompetent culinary hands.

'Perfectly,' I assured her.

'We'll have to see, so,' my mother sighed, ever the Suffering Irish Mammy.

I was draping my cardi on the back of a distant chair when a neighbour arrived to return some borrowed cutlery and plates. I hung back to observe. A little of me died when I saw who had come-a-callin'.

'Andy,' my mum trilled, thrilled. 'What a lovely surprise.'

'Oh, now, I thought you'd be sick of the sight of me two days in a row.'

'Don't be mad! Isn't it just great to have a fine man dancing attendance?' Geraldine Street followed this up with a hearty laugh, laced, I might add, with considerable smut. 'Will you have a beer while you're here?'

'I'd love one,' he assured her. 'Mum is driving me up the walls, so I could do with a break.'

'That's what mothers are for,' my own said, touching her finger to her nose conspiratorially. 'So hush and don't tell anyone.'

They both grinned at that.

'Sure, isn't mine supposed to be on the way over too?' Geraldine said, raising her eyes to the roof. 'Leo, get Andy a beer, would you?'

Suddenly, six eyes were upon me, No. 4's included.

My mother was far closer to the fridge than I was, but this was no time to be picky. It was horrendous enough to be faced with this scenario without making it worse for myself with an argument. These are the times when you realise you are never going to be a grown-up until your parents are dead and buried very deep in the ground, or scattered far and wide enough to delay their resurrection on Judgement Day, should that be their bag. I handed Andy the can and asked him if he'd like a glass to go with it.

'Please,' he said.

My mother beamed at how well brought up he was. I knew he enjoyed making me work.

'You're so right,' my mother was wittering. 'I believe there're all kinds of diseases you can get drinking things straight from the bottle or the tin. Rats and all that.' She shook her head and put her hand to her chest to ward off the plagues that might settle upon her if she so much as said the word 'urine' or one of its many derivatives.

'Are you not having one yourselves?' Andy asked.

'I'm working later,' I told him, smugly.

'I'll join you in a sherry,' Geraldine said, her ladylike arm twisted high up her back. 'Let's all go through to the lounge, and have a nice sit down for ourselves.'

This last 'suggestion' was an order, so we all trooped into the front room of the Street residence where Smokey Joe was receiving.

That cat was the most outrageous pervert. Whereas he didn't particularly like being picked up, especially by me it seemed, he allowed strangers to do with him what they would. Andy scooped him on to his lap, where the white blob of malice purred and stretched as if all his wishes had been granted at once.

'So, Andy, what's the news?' my mum asked, in a pitch slightly too high for credibility.

'Oh, this and that,' he hedged.

'You're a terrible man altogether. Isn't he, Leo?'

'Yes, he is,' I agreed, in a monotone.

We had the makings of an awkward silence here, but there was also a Mammy on board determined not to have that.

'Breda tells me you're moping over some woman. Is that true?'

Andy choked on a mouthful and gasped, 'Mum told you *what*?'

His gobsmacked eyes darted from mine to my mother's and back again. Smokey Joe abandoned his perch with an indignant howl and outstretched claws, leaving poor Andy in disarray and pain of various kinds. I could not resist a laugh.

'Oh, come on, Andy,' I teased. 'Tell all. You're amongst friends here.'

He was saved by the telephone and Geraldine's retreat to answer it.

'You're enjoying this, aren't you?' he said, as he wiped spilled beer from his Lacoste polo shirt and gently rubbed the cat scrawb.

'Of course. It's not often I get to be on this side of the torture. In fact, I'd go so far as to say that I'm loving it.'

Then I left him to stew, by exiting for a juice. Of course, I offered to get him another beer while I was at it, so as not to appear too victorious. And I took my own sweet time getting the refreshments. When I returned with my spoils my mother was explaining that Gran couldn't make it till later that evening, which let me off as I had to be at Moonlites. It was moot as to which was a worse prospect to face, but the decision had been made for me and that was that. I was pleased to go with the flow.

'Where's Dad?' I asked.

'Oh, now, that's a story and a half,' my mother said with a shake of her head. 'He's finally got his old age pension and he's busy crowing about it as if there's no tomorrow.' She looked at her watch. 'He'll be in Kilbride's boring anyone who'll listen and showing off his Post Office book full of his ill-gotten gains. I wouldn't mind but the man has been paying taxes since he was seventeen years old and never took sick leave in his life, and still he's grateful to the buggers for giving him a pittance in the autumn of his years. Ah, this country gets up my nose sometimes, I can tell you.'

I caught Andy's eye. 'The new politicised Geraldine Street,' I confirmed.

'Sneer all you like, miss. When you're my age you'll know all about it,' she warned.

'I might take a stroll down to the pub to see him,' I said. 'The walk would do me good.'

'Why don't I get my dad?' Andy suggested. 'Then we can all go together.'

Before I could protest, my mother had declared this the best idea since the smallpox vaccine and decided to accompany us.

We were only a hamper short of the picnic now.

'I can't stay long,' I warned them, to a chorus of, 'Yeah, yeah, sure.'

An excitement became a fuss and soon I was driving an inadequate blue car jammed full of grown people and a dog to the pub; no healthy walk for Leo or No. 4. He looked happy enough on Geraldine Street's knee as she queened it all the way in the front passenger seat. She had advice about my gear changing, and my acceleration. Oh, and my signalling. All fell short of her stringent expectations, and this from a woman who could not steer a lawnmower. The lads in the back guffawed along and I threatened to throw the lot of them out more than once, although the fact that I was smiling may have undermined each deadly warning.

By the time we hit Kilbride's my brain was full to the brim with details of local shenanigans, including juicy stories of corruption, swinging and wife-swapping amongst the Tidy Towns Committee. My head was dizzy from this and the vast hunger that had overtaken me. I ordered two packets of peanuts for immediate consumption, and a ham and cheese toastie at the landlord's later but earliest convenience.

'Sure, it's more like a restaurant than a pub these days,' my father lamented.

'Get over it,' I told him, and was rewarded with a toothy grin.

'Well, Princess, did you hear the news about yer auld fella?' he asked.

'I heard a scurrilous rumour involving a pension, but as far as I know, my father's too young for that.'

He chortled and plopped his pension book on to the counter. 'There it is, in black and white and covered in stamps. And I'll be getting the free travel and all. Now! Hah?'

'Congratulations, Mr S,' Andy said. 'There's many said you wouldn't make it, I'm sure.'

'True, true. The bagses. Still, I beat the lot of them off. The good don't always die young, you know.'

My mother busied herself scoffing at the last statement.

There was a small war when I succeeded in paying for the round of drinks, men raising their voices to complain at the sexism of it all and pointing out their turn in the scheme of spending and the traditions defiled by my Jenny-come-lately gesture. It was a fascinating look at the Middle-aged Irish Male in his lair. And, of course, none of them was a bit bothered to have a drink bought for him, and it was of no matter who did the buying.

I was comfortable being back amongst my own, and that included Andy, I realised. But I didn't feel any need to engage his interest. I was self-contained, removed within my own secret world, gathering strength for the months ahead. Trying desperately not to sit with a protective hand on my belly. Wanting to share my treasure. Urgently keeping my secret from the world. Hardly daring to breathe it, even in private.

As the happy time continued, I underwent a delusionally relaxed period during which I decided to leave No. 4 with the others while I visited the Ladies. When I returned, an argy-bargy was in full swing at our table and the dog was looking guilty.

'Ah, now, be reasonable,' my dad was pleading with the barman. 'No one saw what happened and you can't throw the chap out for hearsay.'

'Is this something to do with him?' I asked Andy, pointing at No. 4.

'Yeah. Though no one actually saw him do anything.'

'What's the anything?' I wanted to know.

'Best forgotten about,' Andy assured me.

'If it happens again, he'll be barred and no maybes,' the barman announced as he stormed off.

'He's been barred out of pubs before,' I told our intimate assembly in hushed tones. 'And I didn't know what for then either.' I slipped the leash on to the dog's collar and began my round of goodbyes. 'Seems as good a time as any to leave,' I said. 'No need to overstay our welcome, particularly if His Lordship here is in a mood.'

'He's a feisty wee thing, isn't he?' my father declared, with a trace of envy in his voice. He loved a bit of villainy. 'It takes the shape off the day,' he would say.

Andy insisted on seeing me to the car.

'Did you get a chance to read my note?' he asked.

'No,' I admitted. 'I forgot all about it, actually.'

'Right. Well, never mind then.' He turned to go, changed his mind and said, 'I would like to see you sometime, you know? Like, on a date, eh, sort of.' He began to correct himself and stammer. 'I mean, I know you have a boyfriend and so it wouldn't, couldn't, be a, well, date, but to go out, you know? But not out. Em, yeah.'

'I do know,' I laughed. 'And I'll think about it. Okay?'

'Okay. That'll do for the moment, I guess.'

I would love to report that I felt completely calm and in control, but the truth is that I found it difficult to breathe without gasping out loud. And my jellied knees were threatening to prove that they were hinges and not rigid brackets.

I carried it off better than Andy, though, which must have been a first. This man had been messing with my hormones since I was a teenager, but now I felt in control rather than being controlled. It made for a pleasant, if unfamiliar, change. Of course, I really wanted to know why the beautiful Heather had looked most at home at his place very early one morning six weeks before, when I had called with the express intention of declaring an interest in seeing him formally for purposes of courtship and mutual fun. The question would have to brew a while longer, as I was desperately busy appearing dignified and aloof.

When he leaned in to kiss me, I allowed myself to face him and accept a hug and some lip-touching. And almost fainted in his arms. He felt good. I felt good. The dog didn't like being ignored. He piddled noisily on the tarmac of the pub car park, dangerously close to our two pairs of adjacent shoes. Andy bent down to pat him.

'Okay, pal, you can have her back. I can't say that I blame you.'

How easy it would have been to confess my pregnancy then. But that was the crux of the matter: it was *my* pregnancy. I didn't know if Andy was the father of the child, and if he were not, it would be unforgivable to involve him. I couldn't involve Barry for the same reason. It was looking starkly as if I would have to clear the boards of all men and venture forth alone. Big life and plenty of it, it's what makes a Sunday memorable.

NINE

Nina Clancy and her mother were preying on my mind. I decided to take a detour through Con's new parish and possibly drive by the public phone Nina had used to call Clunesboro, if I could locate it; telephones came and went at an alarming rate on the Skid Row of Dublin. It had more chance of survival if it accepted call cards only: cash in a metal box was a crime waiting to happen.

This part of town was close enough to the railway track to be on the wrong side of it. The skyscape was dominated by towers of flats built badly and wearing worse. Graffiti howled at the injustice of the world and fought with stripes of pigeon shit for space. There were houses too, some boarded up and empty, some with metal grilles protecting their lower windows; row after row in ordered grids attempting to tame the savagery of the surroundings.

Navigation of Mayville with a view to locating an address required local knowledge because everywhere had Mayville in its title. Accordingly, we had Mayville Street, Avenue, Court, Close, Lane, Mansions, Towers and so on to the power of 'n'. It was a grim example of disastrous municipal planning from the early-seventies, with no sign of hope apparent to the casual glance. Even on this fine summer evening the streets seemed deserted.

I stopped the car on Mayville Street by the remains of the public telephone and looked around. Nina Clancy would not have had much to phone home about if this was where she was shacked up. I decided to get out and walk around with No. 4. He didn't look like much of a threat, but he was a dog and that might put brigands and ne'er-do-wells off their stride. A smell of forgotten rubbish fragranced the air, and my tummy threatened to kick up again. The squalor underscored the depression and hopelessness of the area, making me sorry for coming here at all.

I was standing by the ruined booth when a young voice said, 'That's not workin' anymore,' in a heavy Dublin accent.

I turned to a boy, maybe ten or eleven years old, wiry and agitated, small for his age. His ginger hair was buzz-cut and he had attitude.

'So I see.'

'D'yeh not have a mobile?' he asked, incredulous. 'Every-one has one o' those these days.'

'I'm looking for someone, not trying to make a call,' I said.

He was quick to spot a market opportunity.

'I can get yeh a mobile if yeh want?'

'No, thanks. I'm trying to find a girl called Nina. I don't suppose you know her?'

'Nah,' he said, shaking his head. 'Women are nuthin' but trouble anyway.'

'Oh, right,' I said.

'Is he any good at fightin'?' the little guy wanted to know of the dog.

'He has his moments,' I told him.

'Do yeh want drugs? I can get yeh them, no problem.'

'No, thanks.'

He took various clear plastic bags from his pockets.

'Honest, look. I have charlie, blow or smack. I'm out of E at the moment, there's always a run on it at the weekends. The clubbers are mad for it, yeh know?'

Ms Middle Class was horrified and I stood with my mouth gawping open. 'Does your mother know what you're up to?' I asked in my best Clontarf twang.

'Who do yeh think sent me out to shift this shit?' he asked, letting me know what an idiot he thought I was.

I was rooted to the spot. When he saw that I was useless to him he ran off, shouting back, 'Fuck off so, yeh useless bitch,' as he went.

I was shaking when Father Con Considine came upon me a few moments later. When I told him what had happened he said, 'Ah, yes, that'll have been Billy. This is his patch. At least he's not on the drugs too, unlike his mother.'

'What kind of bubble have I been living in all these years?' I asked, not expecting an answer.

I didn't get one either.

Con fortified me with strong tea at his cottage, a few streets away on Mayville Lane, just across from his church, Saint Patrick's. There are probably as many churches named after that saint in Ireland as there were different Saint Patricks in the first instance. The cottage was what an estate agent would call 'bijou', without bothering to tell the 'surprisingly spacious' lie. It was basically a small reception room, a little kitchen, a tiny shower room and minute bedroom, all practically in the space of a postage stamp. But where lateral movement was in short supply, vertical distance was plentiful and this wrongfooted me. I was totally astonished by how far I sank into the chintz covers of an antique two-seater, and scalded myself on my tea in the process. The brew went down surprisingly well with my stomach, even if my thigh stung angrily for a time.

The room was sparsely furnished, yet packed to the gills. My eyes lit on a painting on the wall over the fireplace.

'Now that's an ugly thing,' I stated.

The picture was of a cartoon fox in a landscape, standing upright dressed in hunting gear. He had a smile playing across his knowing face.

'Mine, I'm afraid,' Con 'fessed up.

'Oh, sorry,' I apologised. 'It's probably a priceless heirloom.'

'You're half-right.'

'Story of my life,' I joked.

'It used to be on the wall of my bedroom when I was growing up. Always scared the heebies out of me, but I never told anyone. When I left for the seminary I thought I'd be rid of it, but my mother, God rest her soul, wrapped it up and gave it to me to take along. She thought it would help if I became homesick. I've never had the guts to throw it away. That fox knows where to find me.'

I asked about the youngster who was, even now, spreading dark tales of invading do-gooders from Clontarf.

'Believe it or not, Billy could be one of the success stories around here,' Con told me. 'He's a leading light in the local boxing club, says it helps keep "the kids" off the streets. He should be forty, the head he has on his shoulders. If you can ignore the drug-dealing, he's a good lad. I know that sounds a bit crazy, but everything in Mayville is relative. Billy has to look after three younger children. His father is long gone and his mother is out of it most days. Heroin.'

'He'll never have a childhood,' I sighed.

'No, that would be a luxury for someone like Billy.'

'I feel like a spoiled brat now, with my car and my house and my boyfriend and my pets.'

'You forgot your business,' Con teased.

'Sorry,' I said, and we both squeezed out a laugh. 'I just can't believe I thought I had problems, in the face of this.'

'And do you – have problems? Something you want to talk about?'

'Con, you're a brilliant man and thank you for caring, as our American brethren might say, but no, I'm fine. Nothing I can't deal with.'

'As long as you know that I'm here if you need me?'

'I do. But it seems to me that you have your hands full at the minute.'

'It's busy, I'll grant you. But we do have the odd success and that makes it all worthwhile. And it's important to help people with the ordinary, day-to-day problems, even if they're not very newsworthy, to bring a little comfort.'

He patted No. 4 and spoiled him with custard cream biscuits. I didn't object. The custard cream is one of the gackiest biccies ever invented. (*Street Biscuit Guide*, Chapter 1, Verse 1.)

'It may be time to get a guard dog too. Life is cheap and rough round these parts, no matter who you are.'

I was suddenly afraid for my friend and told him so.

'Leo, I prefer this to any of the sheltered carry on I had before. I have never felt so alive, and I'm determined to make a difference. I really feel it's what God put me on this earth for.' Con paused a moment. 'That sounded evangelical, didn't it?' He reddened and looked at his shoes.

'Well, that is your neck of the spiritual woods, really,' I told him.

We didn't get long to play catch-up: I left him dealing with a woman who called to the door crying, sporting a black eye and, I suspected, a broken arm. I felt like a low crawling thing as I skulked off. Con caught my eye and said, 'It's all relative, Leo, don't lose your perspective.'

Billy was back at his watch as I passed, deep in a transaction with a child of twelve. He cheerfully gave me the bird as I pulled away.

'All this and Moonlites to look forward to,' I said to No. 4. 'My cup runneth over.'

I was tired of ironing white shirts to wear to that blasted club. Instead I stole a Barry Agnew number, all ready and starched on a hanger in the bedroom. Obviously, there would be hell to pay but, man alive, I was tired of being a barwoman with its attendant annoyances. I would brave the wrath of man instead. A whiff of aftershave in the air suggested my roomy had gone out carousing. Barry's capacity for fun was endless and, now that he had the aid of money to bolster him, he was unstoppable.

He had left me his latest fan letter to giggle over. These were arriving at a rate of one a day now, and I didn't like it one bit. I wasn't in the least jealous of the attention lavished on my boyfriend, I was unsettled by the hand delivery of the praise. At least it wasn't lewd. 'Yet,' I muttered, to no one but myself.

I had time to kill after I'd fed me and my shadows, so I wrote an agenda for the following day which was busy enough for something important to get left by the wayside. Lists appeal to me, beguiling in their vistas of possibility and promise of fulfilment at their completion. I paper-clipped the legend 'Monday' to the front of the Clancy file and reluctantly left for town. A whole week of backbreaking, pint-pulling, barrel-changing tedium was nearly done, and good riddance to it. Of course, it had heralded a more permanent change to my life, so it would go down in the annals as memorable for all its tedium and lack of closure.

'This job is as fulfilling as watching cow dung go cold,' Ciara was complaining.

'Do you mean the club or the job in general?' I asked warily.

'The club. I mean, I'll be glad when we get to the root of the thing and all, and it'll seem worth it then, I suppose. But, Jayz, in the meantime I could chew nettles I'm so maddened by it.'

'Hopefully it won't be long now,' I said, with more optimism than I felt. 'At least the club is closed on Mondays so we'll have tomorrow night off,' I added to cheer us up.

'Yeah, but Tuesday is Mickey Money Day, and you know what that means.'

'Mickey Money' was the staff lingo for Children's Allowance. On the Tuesday it was paid out, Moonlites came down with women done up to their nines and casting their six sheets to the wind. It was the wildest night of the month and inevitably led to several bitch fights, which were frightening and fascinating in equal parts, but like a car crash, you wouldn't want to be in one.

'Still,' Ciara grinned, 'I have a booty call in for tomorrow and that should cheer me up. Believe me, I need it right now.'

She noticed my puzzlement and laughed. 'Get with it, Grandma! I've arranged a shag with no strings attached.'

'Er . . . brilliant idea?' I chanced.

'You are a lot squarer than you think,' she declared.

We finished our drinks in silence as I pondered my

105

squareness and wondered how it had got me into my present pickle. Then Ciara asked the question every detective dreads.

'Have you ever had to give up on something?' she wanted to know.

'Yep.'

I let that answer suffice because neither of us wanted to go through a litany of failures, not before a Sunday night at Moonlites. We left it hanging there, ready and waiting for another day.

'To be continued,' I acknowledged, sadly.

As we left The Vaults, Ciara began to chuckle. 'Maybe I'll break Warren's wandering hand, that'd liven things up. He is such a gob-shite.'

'Rugby?' I suggested.

'Rugby,' she nodded.

The excitement of the evening was that Val's hair was now purple, as was most of her scalp, so she looked like she was wearing a very unflattering cloche hat. That raised spirits. So did the punters, including the mourning party. Never die in Ireland at a weekend, because the despatch takes ages. The punters drank, danced, laughed, cried, sang and threw up; all six stages covered in depth. A woman hissed a fit as dark as Val's quiff at the cloakroom, demanding the return of her leather jacket or payment for the same. Eventually, Simon Cadogan persuaded Tanya to give it up, and a little bit of justice was served. By the end of our shift, my calves ached, my feet were downright sore and my head continued to pound consistently, though the music had long since stopped. I was glad to see the back of Moonlites and everyone associated with it. My heart sank to realise that I would return on Tuesday and forever until the scam was unearthed. I was really beginning to feel that there was a fine line between undercover work and a hostage situation on this one.

I was unable to resist the lure of Mayville on my drive home. Against all odds, I suppose I hoped to catch a glimpse of Nina, or a hint as to where to look for her. Billy's corner was occupied by an exhausted prostitute plying her wares. An abandoned car burned merrily opposite the woman, attracting no more attention than the moonlight itself. A gang of drunks sat on a rickety bench drinking sherry and cider and shouting gibberish from time to time to remind the world that they were still alive. Further along the thoroughfare, the business of selling flesh was conducted as desultorily as on Billy's erstwhile patch. Apparently Sunday nights were always slow because the johns brought their wives to the pub, instead of indulging their carnals for money. The things you learn.

The scene was what I imagined the days leading up to Armageddon would be like. I was profoundly depressed by the experience, and very worried about Nina Clancy. If she was out in that, she didn't stand a chance. I turned dispiritedly for home and my familiar comforts, ashamed of what I saw as my own cowardice in the face of 'real life'. All of the same questions were there for the asking, all of the same problems needed to be solved. 'Erase' and 'rewind' would be handy buttons in a life.

TEN

I was vaguely aware of Barry leaving shortly after I fell asleep in the first light of Monday morning. It was enormously satisfying that his filming hours were from hideously early till hideously late on a shooting day. Perhaps it would give him an understanding of my life and working regime while on a case. Then again, knowing Barry, it would not. The car had arrived to take him on to location ten minutes early, which caught him out. It felt good to stay in my semi-conscious cocoon as he moaned his way through dressing, thundered down the stairs and banged the front door shut. Oh, no, Mr Selfish Git, I thought, that won't work at all; I am not waking up. And I did stick to that promise. I finally surfaced at 8.30 feeling surprisingly refreshed, if a little down in the tummy, eager to tackle a brand new set of challenges. And a few old ones, I reminded myself.

The first phone call of the day should have been to the morgue to enquire after their young woman's body, but the awful fact was that she was dead and I was very much alive. Overly so. I acted in suit. Today was the day I would begin to look after myself in an adult and womanly manner; I had to see a doctor about this pregnancy. *My pregnancy*. I wasn't sure what to do next, because I was rarely sick enough to need medical help. I had an ongoing relationship with the local vet, because one sneeze from a cat or the dog and they were immediately whisked to the professional for help. I couldn't justify spending that sort of money on myself, and decided that a doctor would be cheaper in any case.

Going to the ancient retainer who'd seen to the Street family ailments for most of the thirty years of my life was out, not just because he was useless and still used Merlin's spell book, but also because I would meet every ailing friend and enemy of my parents and the bush telegraph would take over from there. Instead, I chose a trendy surgery off Grafton Street in town, which had the added advantage of a tropical travel clinic, where I could get shot full of typhoid and cholera vaccine should I decide to vacate the country for milder climes. It's always nice to have a back-door option for that quick escape. A doctor would see me on Tuesday at ten. Till then, I was to take care. I rubbed my abdomen with relief now that help was at hand.

I dialled Garvel Place Garda station and was put straight through to Hugo Nelson. When he heard my name, he anticipated my question.

'It's not her,' he said. 'The girl in the Central Morgue is not Nina Clancy. No birthmark, amongst other things. As you know from the file, Nina has a brown mark in the shape of Australia by her belly button. This girl doesn't. Didn't,' he corrected himself.

I thanked him, genuinely, for the information and reminded

him of our meeting later. Relief flooded through me, edged with hope: if Nina was not on a slab in a mortuary, there was a chance she was still alive out there somewhere. It was my job to find her.

There was a lot to be said for my new, clean-living regime. I had bounce in my step and verve to get up and go, as the ads might tell me to. I showered energetically and took delight in the feel of crisp clothes on my freshly scrubbed skin. I was aware of the world in a very tactile way, and it was pleasurable. I felt sharper, more alert. Time to put it to good use.

Rush-hour traffic had shifted to earlier than normal because of the good weather, so the roads were practically empty as I made my way to the city centre. No. 4 stuck his head out of the passenger window and barked greetings at sundry lamp posts, dogs and, for some reason, municipal rubbish bins. I pulled into the lot behind the Porsche, which had arrived simultaneously, and parked beside it. I began a bland greeting to the emerging form of the other driver as we disembarked, but stopped short when I found my eyes looking into the slate greys of the reformed alcoholic from the club. He looked as pleased to see me as I was to see him, which was not a lot. At the same time, the sound of hatred rose from an area beside my knee. No. 4's hackles were at full height for the first time since we'd hooked up. The reason was a white bull terrier with tiny black ears, newly released from the Porsche. The upstart arriviste was *built*, and lumbered with stated menace. To be honest, he was solid as a constipated stool, and just as pretty. His small, dark eyes were closely perched on either side of his long snout, and glittering as he drooled warning at No. 4. The two circled and bared teeth. I didn't want to interfere, in case my boy's macho image was dented or the other dog felt he had the upper paw. But I didn't want a fight either, because the other growler was a mean-looking S.O.B. Slate Eyes threw a disdainful sneer over the gathering and said, 'Come on, Rocky, before you catch something.'

Molly and I looked wide-eyed at one another, but couldn't manage a retort between us. No. 4 did a good 'hold me back, hold me back' routine. We watched our disappearing nemeses with resentful, stunned astonishment.

'I see what you mean about that fellow,' I said to Molly, and drew a quick veil over the incident. After some idle chit-chat to detract from our shame, I promised to return the dog after he'd run up and down the stairs a few times for exercise. He was going to need to get into shape if we were going to keep meeting the enemy like this.

'Oh, keep him fit, do,' Molly urged. 'There's nothing worse than a fat animal.'

Or a devious cleaning lady, I could have added.

I was following the dog's dust on the approach to Mrs Mack's hidey hole when I spotted her giving No. 4 a biscuit. She even rubbed his head for him. When she saw me, she announced that he was thieving her hard-earned snacks and might have to be reported to the landlord. I let it go with an angelic beam. She was top bitch of the Indigent Sweeps pack and asserting her position with me, that was all. I could live with this, not being as Alpha a female as The Mighty M. Or as prepared to do petty battle. I saved my energies for other tasks, like getting up those damned stairs. I was hoping this pacifist choice would prove lucrative for the company as a whole.

I was not the first to hit the office, which was a startler. The employee charter would be way off kilter if this sort of folly continued. Ronan Gillespie, the good twin, sat at the computer, tapping vigorously.

'Where's the evil half?' I asked him.

'Getting some bacon butties,' he told me, shyly.

I was suddenly ravenously hungry.

'Your name is in the pot, or . . . em . . . you know,' he added, blushing (a very charming sight).

'Good thing,' I assured him. 'Or I'd have to take a bite out of you instead.'

He looked positively terrified at the prospect until I explained that I was joking.

'I guess I'm too used to Ciara,' he said. 'She means stuff like that.'

I was subsumed by a mountain of spam mail when his sister returned.

'Breakfast's up,' she called, then pointedly looked at her watch. 'Such a time to stroll in at,' she chided. 'It's setting a very bad example for us younger members of staff.'

'I could always fire you,' I suggested. 'That would save you from my influence.'

'As if,' she mumbled, through a mouthful of crusty roll and pig. Or was it 'bullshit' all muffled?

Ciara sat munching and flipping through a set of snapshots. Her black hair was gelled into hedgehog spikes, setting off complementary black combats and a sleeveless tee-shirt. The caption across her chest was in letters so small your nose was in her cleavage before you read the warning, 'Don't even *think* about it'. I had made the mistake once before and didn't go there again.

'The wedding on Friday,' she told me, looking up from her task. 'I'm choosing the juiciest.'

'Or the ones in focus?' I wondered.

'Same difference,' she grinned, flecks of bread and meat dotting her perfectly even teeth.

I looked over her shoulder at a picture of a smiling couple

113

with the token, embarrassed-looking registrar.

'You'd have to wonder why he does it,' Ciara murmured.

'Perhaps he just loves women?' I suggested.

'Too much love, too many women,' she pointed out.

I had a vision of Andy Raynor, another man who loved the gals. My gut began to churn. Time for work.

'Did my package of Nina Clancy photos not arrive with those?' I asked. 'I was promised they'd be on my desk first thing.'

We conducted a search of the office between bites of our takeaways, but came up empty-handed.

'That's strange,' I said. 'They're normally so reliable.'

'Maybe the company uses a tracking system,' Ronan piped up. 'It's the latest gimmick for keeping customers occupied. You can look up the progress of your order on the Net. Worth a try?'

'Why not?' I said. 'It's time I joined the revolution.'

Ronan entered the name of the photographic company and came up with their courier service. As he inputted my order number, I noticed he was dressed in similar clothes to his twin sister, barring a tee-shirt caption, which disappointed me, strangely. What? Now I wanted to stick my face into the chests of teenage boys? I needed help. I dragged my concentration back as the screen told us the package had been despatched at 8 a.m. that morning and was marked delivered by 8.30. I was enthralled by the process, certainly, and relieved to have it as a focus for my scattered desires and sick imaginings, but the result brought us right back to the Middle Ages and its most enduring piece of technology, resident in our very own building: Mrs Mack.

'I don't need to go looking for aggravation,' I told the Gillespies. 'I've got her.'

'Her' sense of timing was as keen as ever, thus I met Kevin on his way up to deliver the parcel, with apologies for any delay caused and the slight mishap with the brown paper covering the photographs which had mysteriously burst a seam, despite a layer of gaffer tape. Unbelievable. And yet, so like Mrs Mack to get the week off to a flying start. Ciara was hanging over the banister singing 'Some day my prints will come' as I returned. I gently cuffed her about the ear.

Nina's face accused all who viewed her 6″ × 4″ isolation from the original of the Clancy siblings. I briefed Ciara on the situation, which didn't take long as not a lot had happened since Mary Clancy had chosen our plucky little firm to investigate the disappearance.

'I'm off to meet the cop who was in charge of the case, lunchtime,' I said. 'I'll start charging from then. In the meantime we have the delight of padding out a report for Declan Barrett, maestro of Moonlites.'

'Blame it on the boogie?' Ciara offered.

It's great to have help, you know?

I sighed loudly and knuckled down to the chore in hand, while Ciara looked after compiling the bigamy case report and bill. Ronan was banished from the computer for the duration, but continued his necromancy on a laptop he conjured from thin air. I could not resist asking him what he was up to. He glowed pale pink, now on ground less foreign than ordinary life. He swelled as he expounded on my chosen subject, and lost me early on. It amounted to his being a hacker not a cracker, which I took to be a lover not a fighter, or a good guy versus a bad one. Yeah, he was ethical, he said. He'd worked as a sniffer, tracking unencrypted traffic, and as a scanner, seeking out vulnerability in emails and programs which could be read easily. We were using words in our conversation that meant one thing to him and, more often than not, something else entirely to me; divided by the familiar in strange circumstances. Ciara looked on indulgently.

'The password is the weakest link, usually,' was a sentence I thought I understood completely.

Finally I tore myself away from the jargon and Ronan Gillespie's beautiful eyes. He was sitting on his delectably tight ass so I couldn't ogle that, thankfully. If it's true that pregnant women become either porridge or a whore, I seemed headed for the latter. The lovely boy was busy downloading a hacking tool from the Internet and didn't notice that we had finished our discourse, let alone my lechery.

My report seemed very mundane, but I did manage to beef up our efforts at the club, complete with security recommendations. Anyone with half a nous at all would have known these were mostly guff. The report looked professional, and it cost some pretty pennies by the time all of our woman hours were added into the equation, but ultimately it was hollow as an election promise.

I scanned Ciara's prose and totted up on the Mulholland wedding job: well done, but for one detail.

'The initial fee was for consultation, not consolation,' I pointed out.

Ronan spluttered lightly in the corner and even Mick Nolan seemed to smile in his portrait frame. Ciara was silent, perhaps the most deadly of her moods, her scowl dyspeptic enough to suggest flight to all lesser creatures. I took the hint.

'I'll leave No. 4 down to Molly on my way over to the Cop Shop,' I said. 'He's slept off the bacon roll now. I'll meet you here at 2.30 and we'll head to the club meeting together.' I was at the top of the stairs as I finished the last sentence. 'Have a look at the report and let me know what you think,' I shouted over my shoulder as my chubby legs picked up speed. Then I began to run.

I didn't feel safe from reprisal until I had crossed O'Connell Bridge and was officially the other side of town. At which time, I allowed myself a snigger.

The Garvel Place station was tucked between a youth hostel and a giant furniture showroom. The building was once an impressive Victorian structure, now a relic of old decency, but somehow a certain sturdiness endured. Late-century smog and pollution had stained and streaked the granite in an unhealthy tie dye of dirt. The angry and wounded of society busied through its ancient portals in neverending waves of misery and complaint. And, if you stood long enough, you'd even see criminals and some accused marched over the threshold.

Hugo Nelson shared an office, to the rear of the first floor, with what appeared to be everyone who worked in the building. The layout was more or less open-plan, with mountains of files and documents delineating various king- doms within this free world. I waited by a sickly potted plant until he was off his phone and ready for me. In the meantime I surveyed the man. He was of the middling dark and probably handsome variety, if you could see past the months of sleepless nights he'd had. I plonked a banana and raspberry smoothie on the battered desk.

'It's good for you,' I assured him.

'Too good for me, maybe. I'm supposed to survive on junk food alone. If I get into this healthy eating shit, I'm done for as a cop.'

'Tear up the manual and live a little. Just for today.'

He ripped the cap off the drink and slurped back half in one gulp.

'Needs vodka,' he said. 'No kick.'

Then he put his feet on the desk, tilted his chair back and blatantly gave me a once over. I think I passed muster. I got around to noticing his wedding band and a framed photo of a nice woman with two dirty-faced children.

'We haven't closed the Clancy case, obviously, because for one thing it's not solved. But it would be true to say that it's on the back burner for the time being. Nina is still mentioned in despatches and we keep an eye out, but honestly we just don't have the manpower to give it our full attention.'

'Well, that's what I'm hoping to be able to do.'

'And what her mother is paying you for,' he pointed out.

This was not a rebuke, just a laying down of responsibilities and boundaries. I was being told my place, sure, but I was clearly on the same side as the law on this, so we didn't have a conflict.

'Can you tell me any of the things that wouldn't have been in the file you released to Mrs Clancy?' I asked.

'Mmn. Right.' Hugo Nelson was weighing me up again. 'Okay, fuckit. We have reason to believe that Nina may have fallen in with bad company. It's the old, old story of a country girl coming to the big city and so on. From what we heard she was spending a lot of time around the Mayville area, which is not the best place for an impressionable teenager, but it's close to the bus station and the new arrivals know no better to begin with. However, when we tried to root her out she went to ground.'

He paused.

'Or plain disappeared,' I added.

'That's what we're afraid of. People vanish from round there

118

all the time, it's a bit of a Bermuda Triangle. We do know that she was very friendly with a local young wan called Cherry Phelan, who has a history of drugs and prostitution. But now Cherry seems to be gone too, along with her little brother, Damo, who lives with her.'

'Does Cherry have other family in the area?'

'Oh, yes. Most of them are up to their necks in trouble and well known to us. They all plead ignorance on the where-abouts of the girls and Damo, surprise, surprise. And I'm afraid that's about it.'

His shoulders sagged momentarily, an unconscious reaction to the world he had to face each day. He dealt with one rotten cog, another replaced it in the wheel: rollin', rollin', rollin'.

'The old brigade in here tell me you were trained by a good man. One of us, I believe. I hope you won't disappoint me.'

His voice had plenty of edge now, and I knew he had good cop and bad cop down pat, like all members of the Force should. Mick Nolan's disappointment haunted me every day. I felt I could handle Hugo Nelson's, if I had to. I stopped short of saying, 'When you've disappointed the best, why bother with the rest?' It didn't seem the right moment.

'So, any advice for me?' I asked instead.

'Be very, very wary of the people you meet out there,' he said, staring deep into my eyes as he did. 'And if you find Cherry, you'll find Nina. Good luck.'

'I'll need it,' I gushed, making light of the task.

'You will,' he confirmed, without humour. He scribbled on a scrap of paper and handed it to me. 'There's my mobile number, in case.'

I hate when 'ominous' turns up in a conversation. I swapped his number for mine to relieve the tension.

As I manoeuvred around a battered filing cabinet he said,

'Mary Clancy is a lovely woman, isn't she? Reminds me of my own mother.' His soft Cork accent was a caress as he praised her. Then he hardened it for, 'Keep in touch. You know where to find me.'

I left with a heavy step.

A glance at my watch reminded me, for the third day running, that it needed fixing. Time can be so repetitive. The Garda station clock told me I had a few moments to hang by Con's house with Nina's photograph, which was a lot more helpful, frankly. I sped along, weaving in and out of weary pedestrians with too many bags and hordes of kids hanging off them. I turned on to Mayville Street and spotted Billy.

'Someone rob yer car an' yer dog?' he wanted to know.

'I'm giving them the day off. I'm on my way to see Father Con.'

'The new lad?'

I nodded.

'Yeah, he's all righ', but.'

'He said you might know someone I'm trying to get hold of – Cherry Phelan. Do you know where she is?'

Billy looked puzzled.

'Or Damo, her brother?'

He darted his ginger head around quickly to check on the rest of the street. He paused and I held my breath. Then he turned on his heels and ran off.

'Leave me alone, yeh fuckin' pervert yeh!' he roared.

The little tyke.

I legged it up the road, not caring how guilty it made me look. I feared for my limbs. I should have brought No. 4, useless wretch that he was. I was sweating and exhausted by the time I rang Con's bell. He wasn't home. I put the photo through his letterbox and returned to the city centre via a different, slightly safer, route. I didn't fancy meeting whatever afternoon party Billy might have rustled up for me; lynch mobs rarely want to hear a 'pervert's' side of the story.

I was just not fit enough for the stairs of the office building, so I phoned from the doorstep, which I had to sit on for a rest. They weren't making me like they used to.

'Jaysus, you lazy good for nothing,' was Ciara's pleasant reprimand.

'Can it,' I warned. 'Bring the report and make with some niceties, or I'll kill you.'

'With you in two shakes,' she said sweetly. 'Isn't it awful the way old people get so cranky?'

She'd rung off before I could retaliate. Huh, what did she know? A whippersnapper who had her whole life and, more importantly, a good ride ahead of her. I felt very pregnant and neglected of a sudden. I shrugged it off. There was work to be done and a paying customer to schmooze.

ELEVEN

Declan Barrett was running late, and Simon Cadogan had called in sick, so the three o'clock meeting lacked a sense of urgency for the first half an hour, as Ciara and myself yawned and read magazines in the foyer of Pleasure Holdings Incorporated. A transparent receptionist in chiffon layers offered us tea, coffee or beer (rock 'n' roll, man). She tottered about the dense shag in impossible stilettos and made us nervous for her brittle pins. I had never seen a skeleton staff before and it was grotesquely fascinating. We declined refreshments, in case of an accident. I had just managed to get comfortable enough on the designer sofa to nod off, when our meal cheque arrived and spoiled my fun.

A small, round man in a loud shirt and shorts bellowed his way into the reception area. Our hero had returned, with a toy donkey in a sombrero under his arm and wearing socks under his sandals: not a happy sartorial mix. He slobbered over the X-ray on the desk, then swept into his office without taking his sunglasses off or glancing our way. Ciara caught my eye and gave me the little finger sign for 'small dick'. I returned a tiny 'tosser' gesture in agreement.

He kept us waiting a further fifteen minutes, but if he was trying to impress us with his display of power he was wasting his time; neither of us gave a hang. Not only that, we had built a charge into the bill for just such a contingency. We called it our Stupid Fuckwit Fine. It was true solace for our weary, irritated souls and had yet to be spotted by a paying customer.

When we were finally admitted to Declan's inner sanctum, he was showered, changed into a cream-coloured linen suit, and looking a whole lot less ridiculous. He then turned all charming and, most surprisingly, it seemed genuine.

'My apologies, ladies. I've just flown in from Ibiza. We've expanded our operation to include a club there. Nightmare! Plus delayed flights. Blah, blah, blah. But without showbiz, there's no biz. Now, Moonlites. Shoot.'

We did our best to inject a little excitement into our account of a week at the club. When we were done, and possibly overdone given the material we had to work with, he said, 'Computerised optics and a new electronic door system are being installed today, so that'll be a surprise for the staff when they clock on. Eventually, the tills, stock control, will be hooked up. Costly.' He clucked his tongue with annoyance. 'But it doesn't explain just how much is being creamed off now. Take me back to the tills again.'

Another body with me on the money trail.

'Ciara and myself took turns every night to be close to each of the cash registers as they were cleared out and the money counted into bags to go into the club safe. We saw nothing irregular.'

'Then Security signed out the bags with Cadogan and

brought them to the bank nightsafe,' Declan confirmed. 'Again, nothing unusual: all nine till bags plus the door bag present and looking correct each morning in the bank lodgement.'

'Eh, sorry,' I interrupted. '*Ten* till bags plus the door.'

'Pardon?'

'There are ten cash tills in the club.'

'No, there aren't. There are nine.'

We let that information sink in. Ciara gave a low whistle.

'Wow!' I said. 'The audacity of it. Someone or some people have put in an extra cash register.'

'And Security didn't notice because by the time they got the bags each night, there was the requisite number, nine, plus door take.' Declan Barrett shook his head. 'Simple but effective. And I'm sure the extra till bag was swelled with shavings from a few of the others.'

'It has to mean Simon Cadogan is in on it,' Ciara pointed out. I agreed.

'Is anyone else involved?' Declan wondered.

It killed me to let Val off the hook in any way, but I said, 'Not necessarily. He could have engineered this by himself, introducing a new system under the new regime and all that.' But I had to sow a seed at least. '*If* anyone else is involved, I'd be inclined to put Val Tobin top of the list.'

'I'll bear that in mind. Thank you, ladies.'

He scanned our bill and reached for a cheque book.

Then Skinny from reception buzzed through to tell Declan that his bank was on the blower again. We sat there for the call as he hadn't parted with our boodle. He grew whiter and whiter as the seconds passed, and finally banged the phone receiver into its cradle.

'Seems my General Manager banked not a lot at all over the

weekend. Suddenly, I feel he's not so much ill today as doing a very fast runner.'

Who would've thought Simon Cadogan had enough personality for such a sophisticated plan?

Without consultation, I knew that neither myself nor Ciara wanted to spend any more time on the Moonlites job, so I took the opportunity to assure Declan Barrett it was time to call The Law and send the uniforms after his errant staff. Happily, he agreed and moments later, after the final pleasantries of commerce had been observed, we found ourselves surrounded by the freedom of the open city. Ciara punched the air in victory outside the glass-walled building. 'Yess!' she cheered. 'We never have to go near that shithole nightclub ever again.'

I laughed along, equally delighted.

'And here's another wee treat,' she said, brandishing an envelope under my long nose. 'I took the liberty of delivering a very special wedding album today and got paid by the many wives of a man called Mulholland. He won't forget *this* honeymoon in a hurry.'

'You're a treasure,' I told her.

'I am.' She beamed.

Ciara disappeared to have fun. We would liaise at eleven the following a.m. when she'd wade in on the Clancy case.

'Have a good one,' I instructed.

'Oh, I will,' she assured me and left with a wicked grin decorating her visog. 'Why don't I have one for you too?' she shouted back to me.

'She's a wine taster,' I told a bemused passer-by.

My purse was overflowing with riches. I had the Moonlites fee, the Mulholland wedding money and the cash Barry had given me. I spent a blissful half hour in the supermarket buying human and cat food, and bread ingredients for the five loaves Breda Raynor had ordered for the next day (I assumed she'd organise the two fishes herself). I also bought a cooked chicken, which was far safer than trying to roast one myself; it's good to know your limitations and even better to respect them. I would team this up with lots of crispy salad items, creating a nutritious meal without the risk of burning pots, pans, or myself. And I had nuts to fiddle with for afters. The livin' was easy.

Marion Maloney's arse was swathed in a paisley skirt, cut on an unflattering bias, and sticking out of my front door when I arrived home. She straightened and turned, flustered to see me.

'I was just putting this through your door, it came to the wrong address.' I had caught her on the hop because the something was still in her hand and, wonder of wonders, it was unstamped fan mail for Barry.

Marion was always good at covering her tracks and I had no doubt that she'd make a fine poker player, so there was little to be gained from a major interrogation. I tried a minor 'Did you see who left it to your house in the first place?' but got nowhere. It seemed mighty suspicious to me that several letters had made it to the correct address, all delivered in the same manner, yet now the fan had undergone a memory blip and was visiting the wrong place. I decided on some fun.

'I'm a bit worried,' I told my neighbour. 'This isn't the first of these that Barry has received and I feel they may be from someone very disturbed.'

'Really?' Marion's eyes widened.

'Yes. They're innocent enough, so far. But I've made some enquiries into the subject, and it seems that inevitably the person sending such letters enters a complete fantasy world. Often, when they lose touch with reality, they become psychotic.'

A sheen of perspiration glowed on Marion's face.

'These people become a danger to themselves as well as others.'

I paused for effect.

'I'm thinking of going to the police actually.'

That did it. She fled, along with the letter. And I somehow thought Barry's fan mail would be missing a few instalments from now on. I was chuckling gently as I twisted the key in the lock.

It felt like playing hookey, not having to go to the pit that night. Or ever again, I hoped. I lounged through my tasks, taking obscene pleasure in languid movement. The cats and No. 4 were dashing around in a frenzy, driven scatty by the heady odours of roast chicken and cooking bread. They ignored their custom-made food, the strike signalling that they expected full portions of everything the humans were having. And so they did, minus the greenery. I mashed The Snub's meal up because she was toothless, aside from one fang at the front of her mouth. The purring and yelping was deafening, especially when I joined in. I wanted to curl up in bed for an early night and lashings of well-deserved sleep but my body clock was still operating on Moonlites' time, and I did need to check the Mayville area for Nina. As I bustled about before departure No. 4 stretched his left front leg to show me his canine watch; 'off duty' was the message.

'Overtime,' I announced. 'Just like the rest of us snoop dogs have to do.'

The cats were snickering as we saddled up: cheap but

effective mockery, from their point of view. We were hauling our tired asses out as Barry staggered up the path. For once it was not the result of drunkenness but hard work, would you believe?

'What a day,' he declared. 'I'm bushed.' He pecked my cheek and disappeared: ships in the night.

Monday night was as glamorous as the previous one on the Mayvilles. No. 4 refused to get excited about his guard-dog duties and became ever more determined to sleep off his ginormous meal. I dragged him along behind me, the effort hurting my shoulder muscles as they tried to stay attached to my arms. His claws scraped and scratched along the concrete. Then progress became halting because he found each and every pole or upright in the area needed christening with the message 'No. 4 woz here'. Where he got all the wee in his small body was beyond comprehension. Con's house was in darkness so I walked on by.

The streets were eerily quiet, although there were a few members of the world's oldest profession out. I tried to talk to some of the women, but they didn't want to waste their energies on idle chatter. I must have looked like an amateur to them, with my trainers, jeans and sensible cardigan. It was not an ensemble that would attract many customers in this game. And I looked way too healthy and new. Their faces were uniformly ravaged by the hard lives they led; days and nights of drug-taking, drinking, the harshness of time spent as street prostitutes available to any nutter with a car or money.

One girl, under twenty but going on a hundred, had a black eye and a red welt across her cheek.

'I was robbed two nights ago,' she said in a monotone. 'The prick took eighty quid and marked me for me trouble. I wouldn't normally do these slow nights but I have to get me gear, ya know?'

Another prostitute with a habit, another statistic.

I showed her Nina's photograph, but she didn't recognise her. I asked about Cherry and she turned away. I tried again. She twisted angrily and said, 'Take a bit of advice, luv, give up on her. Okay? For the good of yer health.' Then she walked off.

I was lolling dejectedly when an older woman came over to me. Her gaunt face was crudely painted with bright make-up and she wore a pink, cropped top over a blue Lycra miniskirt. Her belly dangled between the two, crossed with the stretch-marks of childbirth and too many hollow calories.

'Were you askin' abou' Cherry Phelan?' she wanted to know.

I nodded.

'She hasn't been round here for a week or two. Buh Ma Hogan migh' know where she's holed up. I heard she was wi' her a while back.' Then, almost to herself, ''Course, that's if she made it past Ma's.'

'Who is Ma Hogan?'

'If ya don't know that, luv, I can't tell ya,' the woman said, realising she was dealing with an idiot. 'I'll put the word ou' that yer lookin' to talk. She'll let ya know if that's interestin' to her.'

I thanked the woman, Sandy as she introduced herself, and gave her my card, one which neglected to say that I was a private detective. I showed her the photo of Nina, told her she was a relative and had run away and we just wanted to know that she was safe. She looked at it a while before saying, 'Maybe. I dunno. Maybe I seen her. Can't be sure. My brain isn't wha' it used be.' I didn't find that hard to believe. She was, almost certainly, not the woman she used to be either.

A car pulled up by the kerb and Sandy went to talk to the driver. After some bargaining she got in and they drove away. It was going to cost him fifteen quid for whatever they'd agreed on. I hoped she'd be safe.

I was feeling shivery and pulled my cardigan tightly around me. It wasn't from a drop in temperature, although there had been a slight one with the onset of evening, more that something creepy hung in the air. I couldn't shake the notion that I was being watched from the shadows and spaces between the murky slum buildings. I quickened pace, both to warm myself up and to give any watchers a sense that I knew where I was going and what I intended to do when I got there.

There was a lot of activity and light at a derelict site which edged the railway end of Mayville. As I approached I saw that it was a film crew setting up a base, with make-up and costume trucks and several caravans. A bleak, urban drama, I thought wryly, minus the grit of real life here in the ghetto: Hollywood as Hollowood, again. Hopefully, the natives got paid something for the exploitation, and subsequent abandonment at the end of their usefulness. Burly security guards manned the gate leading in to the waste ground. They looked at the human trade around them with contempt because that made them feel more comfortable.

I walked back to the car, which I had stationed outside Con's house in the hope that thieves would respect the house and property of a man of God. I was still having to haul the dog along, and it was doing my arms and his claws no good whatsoever. He didn't seem to care that he might choke to death on the leash if he resisted completely, as he was attempting to do. I passed a pointer strapped to a pole with the logo of the movie on it: a pair of scales. Then I remembered that Maeve was filming a piece called *Tough Justice*. Perhaps she'd be on set tomorrow, when I would have to return and continue my search. And maybe I wouldn't stick out so much if there were lots of new people swarming round the area.

A note gleamed under my windscreen wiper. At this hour, I didn't think it was a fine for a parking offence. Nor did I feel that meter maids would be tolerated long in the area. If the cops rarely bothered to intervene, it seemed safe to assume that other uniformed guardians of civilisation would follow suit. The message was handwritten in bold capitals and simple to understand: 'GIVE UP ON THE GIRL OR YOU'LL WIND UP LIKE TINY SHORTALL'. The world of Moonlites was not yet behind me, it seemed.

I sensed a movement to my left at the corner of the laneway. I tried not to jump too high with fright and wheeled around to face whoever, or whatever, had come to scare me. There was nothing. It was as though a cobweb had blown away leaving a vague stirring behind it.

I felt exposed and vulnerable, and my shivers returned on the march. Con's house was still in darkness so I had only one way out: the way I'd come in. No. 4 sensed my fear and began to bark and agitate. It took an age to get the key to work the car door because of the tremor in my hand and my rigid adherence to a semblance of calm. My back was in a seizure of 'casual' posture, like a smile held too long. At last the door opened and the dog nearly flattened me as he hurled himself past. I jumped in after him, and quickly activated the central locking system.

Get out of Dodge and quick, Street, I thought, the night is a

132

dangerous place. I fired up the motor and put my foot to the floor.

No. 4 began to act up, an accusation of cowardice tacit in his attitude. I wasn't having any of that.

'Scaredy cat,' I taunted.

That shut him up, sharpish.

TWELVE

Tuesday was the beginning of an adventure. I was finally going into the official recognition phase of my pregnancy, by involving a doctor. I would face this new challenge without fear and in a spirit of excitement I would be as exhilarated as Einstein when he discovered that space was curved.

As my belly soon would be.

Jesus!

I was flying solo.

Ah!

My stomach was suddenly very upset indeed, but I calmed it with some retching, a sweet mint tea, positive mental attitude and a lot of deep breathing.

Could I keep this up for another seven and a half months?

More deep breaths, Leo.

The spasms abated.

Driving through my childhood haunts, much less past my

parents' door, did nothing for my frayed sensibilities as I delivered Breda Raynor's bread order. I crouched as low as possible in the driver's seat without entirely losing feeling along my spine or sight of the top of the car bonnet. Anything lower was taking its own chances. Luckily, I caught the Raynors leaving for a round of golf and the handover was both pleasant and brief. I waved them off towards Howth while I turned for town a free woman, if a tad jittery and moist.

There was no shaking it: Andy Raynor's face was in mine for the journey. Every traffic light had a flash of his smile. The clicking of the indicators echoed his rhythmic laughter. I could smell him in the air, whether laced with the sea by the coast or the pungency of traffic fumes in town, all heady and drunken in their effect, yet lacking in the short-lived happiness of an alcoholic binge. The simple fact was that Andy was not the settling kind. My heart still ached for him, but he was unavailable, unattainable. Forget him, Leo, do not self-destruct.

The functional waiting room of the clinic was filled with business people in suits reading *Hello!* magazine, nipping in to see their physician before a hard day's number crunching and whatever else it is that business people crunch throughout a normal day. They all looked rudely healthy to me. Then again, so did I, so where was the mystery in that? I leafed through a glossy without reading any of the articles, if there were any. I remember some pictures, including one of Julia Roberts which, presumably, a waiting professional had pencilled a beard on to; looked quite fetching, as it happens, but then again Julia can wear *anything*.

Funnily enough, I was still pregnant when I did the formal medical test, and later when I left with my diet sheet and instructions to take folic acid. It hadn't all gone as fabulously as I'd expected, the doctor saying things like, 'I'm satisfied with your blood pressure *for a woman of your age,*' and writing the remark 'adequate' beside the space for 'description of physical appearance'. No matter, I felt excited and buoyant. I was bursting to share my news with someone I knew, but there was to be no telling yet. This gave a whole new meaning to the phrase 'keeping mum'. I would enjoy my secret in happy privacy, making it a special time for baby and me, before the news became common knowledge and a source for Valium-taking amongst my family. There is nothing like a crisis for bringing out bad behaviour in relations. I glanced at the beri-beri poster as I passed the tropical end of the surgery, but decided against buying any that day.

I was in the mood for a bagel and milky coffee by office time, so I treated Ciara to the same. She was shagged all right. And crowing about it. 'Best of all is I don't have to see him again for ages. Not unless I want to.'

'Do I get the impression that you like this boy, then?'

'Man,' she corrected, sternly. 'Ah, he's okay.'

From Ciara this was fulsome praise.

'He sounds hot,' I said, hoping I'd picked a vaguely cool term.

It seemed to do the trick because she was quiet for a whole two munches of bread and a further gulp of *latte.* Then, 'Enough of my wild and wonderful life. What's the story on this runaway?'

'Nina Clancy is not a runaway, exactly,' I qualified. 'She left home with the permission, or at least the foreknowledge, of her family. It's since then that the problem has arisen. She has disappeared off the grimy face of dear old Dublin town.'

I told Ciara as much as I knew, then she asked some questions, truncated by the last of her breakfast.

'Credit card?'

'No, just cash.'

'Very inconsiderate, no paper trail.'

'Agreed.'

'When was the last phone call home?'

'Four weeks ago.'

'Not good.'

'Agreed.'

'Last postcard?'

'Three weeks.'

'Bad.'

'Yes, but it did say "boo".'

'We need to chase the sister, Deborah.'

'Uh-huh.'

'Last sighting?'

'Unknown. People won't talk about her or her mate Cherry or Cherry's brother Damo.'

'We have a mysterious Ma Hogan too.'

I shivered as I agreed. I didn't know why at the time. I would be wiser and sorrier later.

'And Tiny Shortall mentioned in the note left on your car and possibly involved?'

'Yes. Weird.'

'And worrying.'

'Agreed.'

The queries were all logical, convincing me again that Ciara was a smart and clued-up woman, as well as a potentially great investigator. Some day I was going to have to press her to think about joining the Garda corps. On top of all her other irksome abilities, she had the height. Until the handing over came she was mine, and happy to dress in colours other than police navy and bright blue every day.

When she got to be plain-clothes again as a detective with the cops, she would be back to where she started, in a way, but with some meaningful opportunity to make a lawful difference to society.

She always maintained that legit was not for her, but I wanted her to have the power to do good some day instead of being a shortarse wannabe like me, always on the grey fringes between right and wrong. She might even get to use words like 'perp', and forget the sneaky life of a PI, which is boring as a dry cream cracker 98% of the time.

The moment had arrived to get a plan of action together. We mulled separately then agreed that we would take turns about on Mayville, as the natives were mixed in their opinion of me. Also, I might go loony if I had to spend all my time there. Ciara assured me I was constantly on the edge and she couldn't risk letting me over it until she knew the company bank account number and was a signatory on the cheque book. She rightly pointed out that we should be staking out the needle exchange on Price Street, just across the river from the Mayville area, and where Cherry would go if she needed clean works for her habit or methadone for maintenance if she was trying to kick it.

'As Hugo Nelson said, if we find Cherry, we find Nina.'

'We need to check on the Tiny Shortall situation too,' I said, reaching for the phone and dialling Con.

'Agreed,' Ciara said, smiling into my face, the cheeky chick.

Con explained that Tiny had been buried out of his mother's parish in the East Wall, next to Mayville, although he had lived on the periphery of both estates in life. Con had never met him, but had heard of his small-time crookery, mainly protection rackets and running hookers. There was probably drug money involved too, though the Shortalls would have been mere lieutenants in any organisation of that kind and certainly not big bosses.

'Con, I don't know why or how, but there seems to be a connection between Nina and Tiny. Could you dig around for information?'

He promised to try.

'Have you got a part in the movie yet?' I asked.

'Strange you should mention that, but no. I must ring my agent,' he chuckled.

Before he rang off, I remembered the other name I had been given. There was a silence from his end when I mentioned it.

'Con?'

'Sorry, Leo. Ma Hogan is an ex-nurse and so-called pillar of the local community. And she's bad. If the girls have had anything to do with her, I really would worry. She is a very bad person, Leo, I can't stress that enough.'

A chill spread through my bones and I found my hand on my stomach, pressing tight.

Price Street housed an eclectic mix of shop outfitters, stationers, pubs, offices, derelict sites and out-reach departments of Trinity College. It was also home to the inner-city needle exchange. Daytime visitors usually got fresh syringes and needles, condoms, methadone. I had never been inside but I knew that trade was brisk outside, as addicts sold their physeptome in soft-drink bottles, often for cash to buy more heroin. The 'phye' helped stem a craving. Clean urine samples for the methadone program could be got for a fiver: only those with clear pee got the stuff dispensed to them. Scanning the motley crowd outside, I was sure no one was over forty years of age. Disease and abuse killed everyone from there on up.

'My mother would die if she saw this,' Ciara said. 'And me in it,' she added.

'Mine too. Still, I'm happy for her to stay in her ivory tower. I don't think experiencing this would change her life for the better.'

'Mmn. People should know, though.'

'Well, now we do, so let's make that count.'

Ciara and I got out of the car and stood still a moment to acclimatise. The sun baked the road, the buildings, the people sitting on the clinic steps. I resisted the urge to leave my sunglasses on as information is always more forthcoming when the whites of the eyes are in full view. We were both armed with pictures of Nina, but no one professed to know her. I went to try the staff, leaving Ciara to pursue the search outside.

There was a lot of shouting going on in the tiny waiting room. It smelt of dirty clothes and bad breath. A bedraggled man at a hatch screamed abuse at a harried woman on the other side of the metal-lined glass.

'It couldn't be a dirty sample, 'cos I'm not on the shit.'

'It's dirty. It's showing heroin contamination. There's nothing I can do for you.'

He began to cry, then threw himself to the floor, flailing maniacally.

'Help me, dear Jesus. Will someone not help me?' he wailed.

None of the people queuing paid his imploring any heed. Some stepped over him to get to the hatch and collect their supplies. The man eventually crawled into a corner and sat hunched and whimpering between two plastic chairs. My heart was torn apart for him, but without a Class A drug or a wad of money, he wouldn't want to know I was alive. And sympathy was as much use to him as a cup of tea or a copy of the *Beano*.

This waiting room was a world away from the trendy version I'd visited earlier that morning. Here, the posters were all safe sex, tuberculosis and illegal drugs. The overlying despair was in sharp contrast to the confidence of the careful professionals looking after themselves a few streets further into the shopping malls of the city. I stood in the queue, guiltily taking the place of an addict who needed help, but determined at least to try to save one young girl from the Styx.

When I got to the hatch I held Nina's photograph against the reinforced glass. I was about to launch into an explanation when the woman buzzed me through to the back room.

'I'm busy, but Orla will deal with you.'

She indicated a tall, slim woman sitting at a desk amidst the shelves of needles and condoms and drugs. Orla pointed to a seat opposite as she finished filling out a form. I could hear the addict begin to shout again from his corner.

'My death'll be on yeer heads. All I'm askin' for is a chance. That's all!'

Orla looked at me. 'Gerry,' she explained. 'He'll be fine. Or at least he says he will, if the Corporation gives him a flat. If he had somewhere to live, he could get a job and get off smack and live happily ever after.' She rolled her eyes.

'But wouldn't he?' I asked. 'If he got that help?'

'Addicts never take responsibility for their actions. It's always someone else's fault. That's one of the first things you get to know in this job.'

She saw that I was confused.

'Put it this way: if they take responsibility for their own lives, they get off the shit. I know it sounds hard, but it's the truth.'

She finished her paperwork and gave me her full attention. Gerry started up again, but by now it was just a regular soundtrack to the business of the clinic and didn't warrant undue notice. It was awful to realise that we can get used to anything, even the howling misery of another human being.

'Yes, that girl does look familiar,' Orla said, fingering the picture. 'Should I know her?'

She had a piercing glance, which clearly didn't suffer time wasters or fools. Like Nina's in the photograph.

'You might have seen her with a Cherry Phelan?' I tried.

'Ah, Cherry,' Orla said. 'Now we're talking.'

I felt the excited stirrings of a case moving on, building up an identity of its own, departing from the beginning formula of any other job.

'Where has she got to anyhow?' Orla asked. 'She used to be regular, now no sign for weeks.'

My stirrings came to an abrupt halt.

'Oh,' I said, crestfallen. 'I hoped you'd be able to tell me where she was.'

'Sorry, no. Last I heard she was in a squat out the back of Farrelly Street. Madonna Mansions,' she remembered. 'Would you credit the fucking names they give these dives?'

A metal door at the back of the office rattled open and a huge, muscular hulk entered. He was introduced as Phil, and he was both beef and brains to the operation.

'Even in these enlightened days, a strong man is essential in a place like this,' Orla said. 'The medical experience is a plus.'

'I've got it all.' Phil grinned.

Orla showed him the photograph.

'Friend of Cherry Phelan's, isn't she?' he said. He thought for a moment. 'Cherry was in a state the last time I saw her. Said she was in bad trouble, and not just the drugs. She did

look frightened, which was odd 'cos she's normally all attitude. She didn't want to tell me what was up, said her friend
was helping, this girl here. What's her name?'

'Nina.'

'Nina, yeah.'

Phil hung his bicycle helmet on a hook by the metal door.

'How bad is Cherry's habit?' I asked.

'She's tried to kick it a few times,' Orla said. 'Once she
managed four months off the smack and I honestly thought
we'd have a success on our hands. I had hopes of getting her
into further rehab and all, but she relapsed.'

'Cherry was coming to us for clean gear,' Phil added. 'She
was back using so she tended to come at night, when we don't
ask for the urine sample. For all we know she's overdosed
somewhere, or left the country. We may never see her again.
It's constantly changing traffic through here from week to
week.'

'You could always ask Cherry's dad where she is, if you're
really desperate,' Orla suggested.

'I am,' I confirmed.

'Rather you than me,' she commented.

'He goes by the name of Doc Phelan,' Phil said. 'You'll find
him holding court in the Raven pub most days. It's by the
railway station.'

'I know it,' I said. 'I take it he's not a doctor?'

'Doc is short for Papa Doc,' Orla said. 'So you get the
picture.'

I did, and I wasn't happy with what I saw.

I thanked Orla and Phil for their help and give them my
card in case new information turned up or they remembered
something useful.

'Can we help you to anything else?' Orla asked.

I was puzzled. 'Like what?'

'Condoms?' Phil suggested. 'We've loads.' He gestured to the mounds of coloured boxes stacked on the shelves.

'They'd be wasted on me,' I assured them. 'Really.'

I left with a smile on my face all the same.

Ciara was sitting on the steps of the clinic eating chips with some of the Price Street clients. I accepted a few from her greasy offering, careful to avoid the ones with ketchup which is, frankly, the devil's own condiment. They were as ugly as they were delicious, roughly cut real potato and none of your reconstituted muck. The last thing I expected as I smacked my lips was an earthquake, but that's what started. The ground began to shake and the security chains on nearby gates and bicycles rattled. Ciara and I were the only people to look alarmed. I reached for solidity, but my shaking hand couldn't grasp anything that wasn't itself in a state of flux. The day grew darker and still no one paid much attention.

'That'll be the Japanese,' a scrawny young man said. 'They send the cars over in these huge ships, high as a house. That'll be one of them pulling up in the dock now.'

I went to the corner of the steps and saw that he was right. The tallest ship I had ever seen was passing slowly along the mouth of the river, home of Dublin's port.

'The cars'll be rusting already after the sea journey,' he continued.

'A bit like ourselves,' said another. 'Rusting from the inside, wha'?'

They all laughed.

We hung around for a while without saying or asking much, just hanging out really. It was an odd club to be a part of, with the camaraderie guaranteed to last only as long as the high or the methadone lasted. When we left, Ciara, who was on first-name terms with everyone now, shook hands all round and said she'd see them soon. Once in the car, she sank into a weary crouch. 'That is one depressing place,' she said.

'I suppose dinner cost you a fortune,' I prodded.

'They were hungry and so was I.'

She was more like me than she wanted to imagine.

'Find out anything indispensable about our girls or Damo?'

'No one's seen them in a while. Word is that Cherry's fallen off the wagon again, and some of the guys are worried that she'll end up working something they call "the fair", but I couldn't get them to tell me where that is or when. They wouldn't say more than its name.'

'We'll ask Con about it and maybe Hugo Nelson knows something. It would be good to check in with him one way or another.'

'We're gonna have to come back here later,' Ciara said.

I nodded, waiting.

'They call it the Night Train.'

THIRTEEN

Madonna Mansions was as grim a prospect as facing an Irish Catholic parent with a pregnancy but without a husband, not even someone else's. The grey-and-red-brick buildings wore tattoos of graffiti and looked derelict to the casual eye. In fact they were home to hundreds of working-class city folk, many of them without the work bit of the title. Cousins of the Mayville pigeons lived here too, and their trademark contribution stained the concrete of paths and housing.

I parked the car in a prominent position well away from alleys or blind spots. A pair of urchins offered to mind it for a fee of five pounds an hour, which was steep for the facilities, but they were the driving market force here, so I told them they'd get paid if the car was untouched when we got back.

'Fingers crossed,' I instructed Ciara after striking the deal.

'You'll be lucky,' she muttered.

The stairwells of the inaccurately named Mansions were littered with soiled nappies, Durex and spent needles. And for some strange reason there were a lot of odd shoes on each landing. Badly daubed paintwork said 'Pushers out' at intervals along the walls. It stank of despair and neglect and waste.

'Careful where you step,' I warned Ciara, as we made our way slowly and with an ounce or two of ginger. 'I'm glad we didn't bring the dog, he might have hurt his paws.'

'Or worse.'

Number 68A was situated on the fourth floor, past a boarded-up flat which had previously been burnt out. We hammered on the door for several minutes but got no answer. A wizened head peeked out from further along the corridor. 'Gone,' said a foreign voice.

'How long ago?' I asked.

A non-committal shrug was followed by, 'After the men came. After the shouting and the blood.'

'This does not sound hopeful,' Ciara said, for something to do as much as anything. She was trying to figure out how we could find ourselves in this filth, wondering if we'd get out intact. We were of a mind on this, though I neglected to mention it. If I had we would have run out of that awful place and only taken a nice, clean, middle-class cheating case load from then on.

I picked my way down the hall and showed Nina's photograph to the old woman through the crack she had opened in her door. She extended a claw-like hand and grabbed it.

'Yes,' she nodded. 'This girl comes back to get things. And then, whoof, she is gone too.'

'When was this?' I asked, sounding as desperate as I felt.

'Saturday.'

So, Nina was alive at the weekend, that was good. I turned to Ciara, smiling. She didn't see, because she was busy kicking down the peeling door of 68A Madonna Mansions with her steel-toed Doc Martens. Not seasonal footwear for late-June, but invaluable for knocking in poorly constructed walls, bad persons' shins and the like.

'Not a great piece of workmanship,' she said of the portal, as I followed her through the smashed planks.

The place was such a tip it was hard to know if it had been done over or if it was always this squalid. Drug addicts are not famous for their sense of tidiness, but as far as we knew Nina was not using and should have had some home-making skills in her repertoire.

'I thought I was messy,' Ciara remarked, walking through the devastation. 'Even my mum would baulk at this, and she's obsessed with cleaning since her menopause hit.'

'Not very feng shui, I'll give you that,' I added.

I had joined Ciara in talking out what we were experiencing. We were justifying this action and ourselves and making sense of the situation. We were cool professionals, in control; we could handle this.

Flies buzzed around the table, with its sour milk cartons and forgotten cereals. More dive-bombed plastic bin liners overflowing with rubbish higher than a soprano's top C or a newly shot up junkie. The used gear of a habit was strewn throughout the filthy rooms. The air was damp and the wallpaper curled away from the walls in protest at the moisture levels. Ciara shifted various piles with her steel-encased toes, then bent to pick up some pieces of paper. She placed them together on the bare arm of the sofa. They made up a photo of Nina, another girl and a Shortall.

'I wonder if that's Tiny or his brother?'

'My money's on Tiny,' Ciara said. 'The live guy at Moonlites has longer hair.'

'Hardly scientific,' I pointed out. 'People do get haircuts, you know.'

'It's a twin thing.' She shrugged.

I left it, not having a retort for that one, especially as she was the aficionado in the field.

'Let's go show this to the neighbour, see if she recognises anyone,' I suggested.

We took ourselves down the hall and sure enough the little lady said, 'Cherry,' pointing to the girl by Nina's side.

'Is this one of the men who was shouting?' I asked, pointing at the man in the picture.

'No, not him.' The woman shook her head. 'Tiny gone,' she added softly. 'Dead.'

I gave her a moment.

'He was kind to me. He carry things and fix my door when robbers broke it. Then he scare them away and they do not come back. They say a bad man kill him, because of the girl.'

'What girl?'

'In the photograph. The bad man does not like anyone who is nice to the girl. She is *his* girl. Only his.' Then she had closed the door and locked it in our faces. We hadn't even seen it budge.

'Which girl in the photograph?' I shouted through the barrier.

I didn't get an answer.

'That old dear sure can move,' Ciara remarked.

'I'd say it pays to be nimble around these parts.'

I don't know why but we propped Cherry's door back in its jamb when we were leaving. A new take on old-fashioned manners?

I wondered about the neighbour and her East-European accent. Where had she come from that was so bad Madonna

150

Mansions was an improvement? The thought was a profoundly depressing one.

We went back outside and decided to question a few brash kids who were smashing up crates for sport, then setting them on fire and daring one another to jump through the flames.

'I don't want to catch you doing that at home or anywhere else,' I told Ciara as we approached them.

'How much will ya give us, missus?' the ringleader wanted to know.

'I don't have any money,' I said. 'I just want to find my friend Nina.'

'Ya can fuck off if ya haven't got any dosh,' he told me. 'Yer worse than the fuckin' cops, wantin' somethin' for nuthin', so y'are.'

'Yeah,' his companion joined in. 'An' we're no' informers neither. Scum!'

They would have had an even poorer opinion of us if they'd known that we snitched on people for a living.

We had slightly more luck with the car minders, simply because they were getting money and didn't seem to mind throwing in some info for good measure.

'Papa Doc dragged them off the other day,' a whippet-thin one said. 'An' Cherry was screamin' for someone ta save her. An' her friend an' Damo tried ta, buh they goh a slap in the face for their trouble. An' I heard she was brough' over ta Ma Hogan's.'

The tone he took left me in no doubt that a visit to Ma Hogan was a nasty punishment indeed.

'Where does Ma live?' I asked them.

They burst out laughing. 'As if we'd tell ya tha',' they said as they scarpered, jingling my money in their pockets.

Both windscreen wipers were missing.

'Just as well it's June,' Ciara said.

On cue, pigeon shit splattered on to the driver's side of the window.

'Nice shot,' she judged.

'I'm ravenous,' I said as I started the car.

'I hope that wasn't provoked by the mess on the windscreen,' Ciara said.

I ignored the gross implications there. 'Let's let Con feed us,' was my suggestion.

'At least we know he can cook,' Ciara said, referring to the course we'd all met on, initially.

Con had been a good pupil, and I salivated to imagine what goodies he would rustle up. I phoned ahead to warn him.

'You're in luck,' he told me. 'I have a tin of tuna somewhere.'

'Relax, we'll bring the rest.' I rang off. 'He's lapsed,' I told Ciara.

She sucked air back through her teeth. 'It was only a matter of time.'

Con was repentant.

'I didn't realise I had let myself go so far,' he said, slathering butter on a multi-grain baguette then heaping on his tinned tuna, which Ciara had doctored with mayonnaise and red onion. He alternated bites with a side salad I had prepared. As Ciara reasoned it, there was no heat involved in its preparation, just rudimentary use of a knife and I seemed trustworthy with one of those. She changed her mind when I threatened her with it.

'You've lost weight from the neglect,' Ciara told him. 'It suits you.'

'Thanks,' he returned. 'And, eh, Leo, try not to break any Commandments in front of me. It puts me in a very awkward position.'

Ciara stood behind him and taunted me silently. I raised the weapon just high enough for her to see that we had scores to settle later. In point of fact it was quite a blunt implement, good for squashing tomatoes as opposed to slicing them, splattering their juice and pips in a wide and indiscriminate arc.

'This new parish is so different from anything I've ever experienced before,' Con was saying. 'It's a whole other set of problems and standards, a whole other world it feels like sometimes. And it's rough, you know? There's barbed wire fencing around the church and I have to keep it locked a lot of the time, which is killing me. I can only open it if someone is there to look after it with me. The money is just running out of the Holy Souls' box, and I have yet to see candle money even though I know the parishioners are paying it. Ah, I don't know what I'm moaning for, the problems here are much bigger than that. The money doesn't matter, it's just light relief for me, something to distract me from the daily misery. No one stays longer than a year and a half in this post, did you know that? They get burned out.'

Ciara grinned at him. 'Bet your bosses have to give you a seriously good holiday then.'

'Or an extra-strong strait-jacket in a place with very soft walls,' he suggested.

'You'd need it, looking at that all day,' she said, pointing at the picture of the fox.

'It's there to test my character.'

Con had not heard of 'the fair' mentioned by the Price Street addicts, but he had met Papa Doc Phelan, several times. 'He supports the boxing club, sponsorship and so on. He's been involved for years and no one wants to believe that he's using the kids to do his dirty work selling drugs, but he is. It's amazing the depth of denial people indulge in when they just don't want to hear the truth.'

'I'm going to see him this afternoon,' I said. 'Pay a little visit to the Raven.'

Con shook his head. 'I think that's a really bad idea, Leo. The Raven is as rough as . . . well, we'll not go into that. It's no place for a woman on her own.'

'I won't be on my own,' I said.

'Ciara is hardly old enough to be served in a pub,' he protested.

The teenager spluttered her status as a legal purchaser of alcohol in public houses. I cut her off.

'Ciara won't be with me,' I told him. 'You will. Only no one will know that, because you'll look like you're collecting a raffle prize or something from the bartender. Surely priests do that sort of thing?'

'Well, yes,' he conceded.

'Right. Then you can keep an eye on me while I talk to Mr Phelan.'

I was not for turning and my lunch mates knew it. Even so, they left a decent pause to allow me to chicken out of my latest spluckidoo plan. When it didn't work, Con hefted himself out of his seat with a cross expression.

'I'll go and phone the Raven and tell them the good news of their largesse,' he said, unhappily resigned to his task.

Ciara, on the other hand, was apoplectic with rage.

'Don't blame me,' I said. 'Con is the one who insulted you.'

'You've kept me close all day too. You won't let me off on my own, don't think I haven't noticed. What is it? Think I can't handle this case?' She kicked the table a few times and swore, in words so strong they sounded like a foreign language. Then she slumped in a sulk into an armchair.

'If you really want to know, it's me, you divet. I'm the one who doesn't want to be on my own. I really don't like the territory we're in at all. I'm running scared.'

This was a mush of truth and half-truth. I didn't want Ciara coming to any harm, and I had a feeling we were only at the tip of an iceberg of eroded values and atrocity. At that moment, I would gladly have gone home and stayed there for months, giving proper meaning to confinement. Instead, I dialled Hugo Nelson's mobile and asked him what he knew about Tiny Shortall and his untimely demise.

'He drowned,' the Garda confirmed. 'His lungs were full of water, which is par for a death in the Liffey. But, interestingly, the pathologist did not find river water in the body.'

He paused for effect, knowing that I was wriggling on the hook.

'It appears Tiny took a bubble bath, of all things, and died in that. The pathologist says it smelled of magnolia blossom, which may have been a nice change for him. The pathologist, that is.'

'Dangerous thing, washing,' I said.

'Positively murderous,' he returned.

Ciara's hump was put to one side when I shared the news. In fact her eyes had taken on the glitter of a detective immersed in a case, determined to see it through, figure it out. Did I still get that thrill, or had I become cynical from too many years in the game? Was I still as excited by the possibility of unravelling a mystery and putting all the pieces back together in the right sequence, or was it just a job to me now? And how could I continue with it when the baby came? This was not the most opportune time for the Big Picture questions, I decided, and pushed them to the bottom of the pile for later consideration. They joined a lot of other neglected issues there.

'Wow,' Ciara was saying. 'Extreme water sports.'

When Con returned, I mentioned Ma Hogan. He was reluctant to talk about her, offered to make tea instead. Said he was unsure where she lived. Did everyone have enough to eat? He hedged each query until I finally exploded and asked what the big deal was with this witch, and why was it that no one would talk about her?

'She's like the bloody bogeyman,' I shouted.

'It's not such an odd thing that the shutters come down when she's asked about,' he said, quietly. 'Ma Hogan is the local backstreet abortionist.'

None of us finished lunch after that. The fox on the wall continued to smile.

FOURTEEN

I enjoy a pint as much as the next gal. Or I do when I'm not pregnant. But the Raven was ugly enough to make me go on the wagon, even if I hadn't already been on it because of my condition. It was a square room, with tiny windows set high enough up the walls to be a waste of glass. The pervading atmosphere was brown, as was the decor. It was possible that another colour had been applied to the walls early in the century, but time and cigarette smoke had dealt with such frippery. Wooden tables bore the scars of fag burns and black stout and, now, the final indignity of beer mats too old for proper service. The cardboard squares bubbled and buckled on the surfaces but were not recycled as stabilisers; the metal bolts securing all fixtures and fittings to a solid surface saw to that. Stools sat sentinel throughout, seats shiny from years of wear. There was not one soft surface that I could see. A television in the farthest corner was showing a golf tournament, ignored by the patrons.

In the silence which greeted my entrance, I saw a motor-cycle courier delivering a package to the barman. At a nearby table a fat man checked his watch and nodded to himself. Con walked past me, without a glance, and went to collect his raffle bottle and put the chat on the staff.

'I've been expecting you,' a voice said.

It was the fat man. I made my way over to the table where he was holding court over a half-dozen hardchaws, ranging in age from late-teens to late-fifties. They were a curious assortment of grotesques, all facial blemishes and broken noses. One had an angry red slash from forehead to ear, and I didn't think he'd got it shaving. The man who'd allegedly been expecting me didn't introduce himself. Call me instinctive, but I had fallen under the impression that this was Papa Doc Phelan.

'There's no need to sit down, you won't be staying long,' he shared with me.

One look at his face gave the lie to the popular belief that a man of his size would be jolly. He also had the sort of halitosis that brought vultures out looking for carrion. I winced at the exhalation of breath that rose to meet my nostrils.

Normally a person physically below another might feel inferior or less authoritative. Not this man. Rather, he used his position to assert himself. He was trying to make me stoop to his level. I did not.

'You're a very curious young wan altogether,' he said. 'You know what that did to the cat, don't you?'

He oozed danger and my spine began to freeze. I focused on his gleaming tonsure, the natural outcome of going bald rather than monk-like shaving. The rest of his head was smooth too, but badly disguised by a comb-over of the seven hairs still growing long to the right side of his spiteful face.

I felt the edge of a table push against the back of my knees, but ignored it. The crowd seemed to be moving closer too.

'I want to find Nina Clancy,' I said, keeping my voice even.

A youngster with bad acne and poor hygiene flicked cigarette butts at me. I pretended not to notice.

'Listen carefully now,' Phelan cautioned, 'because I'll only say this once. You give up on Nina Clancy, and leave my daughter and son alone too while you're at it.' His voice dropped to a whisper. 'Tiny Shortall is a small example of what can happen to someone who sticks their nose in where it's not wanted.'

'Would you like to share a little information with me about his murder?' I asked, calmly. 'My friends in the Police Force would be very interested to hear whatever it is you know about that.'

The table edge slammed quite hard against my legs and I buckled slightly.

'Tiny didn't float, from what I hear,' Phelan said.

His entourage laughed heartily. A man got up behind me and pushed me aside as he passed, knocking me off balance. I righted myself quickly but was shaken. Doc Phelan smiled.

'Get out now and don't let me see or hear of you again,' he said, ever so softly. 'Or you will be sorry, and that's a promise.'

'Sounds more like a threat to me,' I remarked, as an ashtray tipped off the table and on to my shoes.

I kept my hands firmly welded to my sides because I could feel them quiver. My back hurt with tension. I was petrified. Below me, Phelan's nose hooked out from high up on his forehead; first time I'd ever seen a fat-faced eagle. I tried to let that image cheer me.

'Arrive alive, wherever you go in your blue car,' his voice advised.

Funny, how it didn't sound helpful at the time.

'I've told you you can go, so what are you waiting for?'

He reached for his pint and his liggers laughed again. Idly, I noticed that Cherry shared looks with her mother, who-ever that unfortunate might have been. As it was, being shagged by Doc Phelan would have been akin to a century's torture in the fiery rings of hell, no need for the visual reminder every waking moment of your day. I counted to three, turned steadily and slowly began to walk towards the door. A helpful thug put a foot out to trip me and I went flying into some stools, bashing my shins painfully. Con intervened with, 'Ah, now, lads, leave the lady alone, can't ye?'

'The culchie speaks,' Phelan announced. He turned on Con. 'Listen to me carefully, priesteen. Remember that you'll only last around here as long as I tolerate you. And I can get very fed up with meddlers. Do you hear me? Now take yourself and your girlfriend out of here and don't annoy me anymore.'

Con made to link me out. 'Thank you, Father, but I'm fine now,' I said, not wanting to advertise out friendship in case it jeopardised him. He exited, though I could feel his reluctance hang in the pub's smoky air.

As I made for the threshold to freedom, a suave type in a dark suit and glasses entered. He removed his Ray Bans. I stood to stare, surprised by those pale grey eyes, unsure of my next move. What's a nasty boy like you doing in a place like this? I wanted to ask. And where did you park your Porsche?

'Razor Cullen,' I heard Papa Doc call. 'You're late.'

Now I had a name.

A muscular lump barged past me. Rocky the bull terrier was on board, and looking as bad-tempered as his master. Phelan scanned the picture and I could see him mentally set up the hoops for us to jump through.

'Deal with this little bitch,' Papa Doc ordered.

Great, now the hoops were on fire. Time for a proof of loyalty from Cullen. Someone could lose an eye during these ceremonies of male bonding and all bets were on me to be the blinded that day. The malevolence on Cullen's face became a sneering grin. If there's one thing I hate, it's being threatened by a designer thug.

'I think we can leave this one to Rocky,' he said.

My legs were jelly, and all other muscles useless as I looked down at the dog. The brown surroundings of the Raven began to swirl as Rocky advanced, growling. He flashed sharp, saliva-dripping teeth. I forced myself to avoid his eyes, not wanting to challenge him further. Silence roared through the pub as the drinkers tuned in to the entertainment. I stepped backwards very, very slowly. Rocky matched my pace. I could feel the sun on the back of my neck and arms, which meant I was close to the door. I continued the terrifying journey, feeling the step of the threshold too late to save myself from falling out of the door backwards on to the scalding pavement. My elbows burned and my lower back screeched in agony as pathway hit bone. The dog chased me on to the street barking his hatred, slobbering on to the concrete and swaying with malice. He made a last dart at me, ripping away some trophy cotton to present to his master, then returned inside to applause. Terror and relief flooded through me, and I allowed myself to lie on the ground a moment and convince my bowels to stay put.

Con ran to my side and soon I was leaning against the sticky pub wall, gulping air into my seized-up lungs. I finally caught my breath and straightened.

'They are definitely off my Christmas card list,' I wheezed.

'Now you know what he's like,' said Con, cradling a bottle of blended Scotch. 'And I'm going to have to run a draw because of it.'

'Draw?' I scoffed. 'You're nothing but a big old bumpkin, Con Considine.'

We were putting space between us and the pub when Billy the underage dealer passed, headed in the direction of the Raven.

'Watch ou' for her, Father,' he called. 'She's a bi' of a perv.'

Con halted the boy. 'Are you going in to Doc Phelan?' he asked.

Billy nodded. 'Have ta. Me ma does business with him.'

'He's her supplier?'

The boy's silence answered the question.

'We're going to have to have a talk, your mother and me. I don't want you involved in this racket,' Con said.

Billy gave a little laugh. 'It's your funeral,' he said, and walked on.

'I'll have to take up a sport,' Con said. 'Get the anger out some way.'

I could see the knuckles pressing through his skin, white-hot with rage at the inequity of life around him.

'You could always join the boxing club,' I said.

He feigned an uppercut.

I didn't feel like Ireland's number one overachiever as a result of my encounter with Doc Phelan, and to be honest I was at a loss as to what to do next. Con shoved me under his shower to remove the ash and dust of my run in with the Raven. I slapped plasters over my grazes and Ciara patched my jeans with safety pins, giving a punkish element to my frumpy image, or so she assured me. The Night Train on Price Street was still many hours off, so I suggested to my regular staff that we check out the film set at the end of Mayville Street. It might inject some much-needed glamour into the case.

'*How* naïve,' was Maeve's pronouncement on that. 'It's dull as an empty suitcase. Now *your* job, *that's* glamour.'

Ciara and I exchanged glances, then left my actress friend to her misconception.

Maeve was wearing a long, red, curled wig, with green contact lenses and a pale, fake-freckled make-up for that 'Oirish' look so beloved of anyone who's never lived in the place.

'I'd better get out of the sun,' she said. 'They like me wan and interesting for this part.'

She led us to a small caravan with the name 'Maeve Marion' on the door.

'The American cameraman can't get the hang of my name, *keeps* calling me Marion. Our waggish assistant directors are responsible for the Robin Hood-like tribute. Pathetic, I *know*, but it keeps us sane. *Welcome* to my humble box.'

We were ushered in.

'I'm impressed that you've got your own one of these and don't have to share. Barry will be green when I tell him,' I said.

'Leo, *all* this makes me is white trailer trash,' Maeve hooted.

She ordered coffees and snacks for us from a showbiz Sherpa, a hot water with lemon for herself. 'One of the hazards of filming is the amount of *grazing* we do: I see, therefore I eat. I've put on *six pounds* since we started, and with the weight added by the camera, which *never* lies if you believe movie lore and I do, I'll look like a *house* when this thing is released. *Hideous*.' She laughed out loud. '*If* it ever sees the dark of day in a cinema, that is.'

'So it's shite,' Ciara guessed.

'Oh, *yes*. But they're paying me a *massive* amount, so I'm taking my chances.'

'What's it about?' I asked. 'Not that it matters.'

'*Correct*,' Maeve agreed. 'I'm an Irish colleen,' she gestured to her ringleted wig, 'reduced to *parlous* circumstances and a life of selling myself to the highest bidder. *But* a visitor to our Emerald Isle falls for me and *saves* me from drudgery and a dose of the pox. He helps me get my kids back, is *filthy* rich, and we live happily ever after in LA.'

'As you do,' I said.

'Someone should be making a documentary about filming this,' Ciara said. 'And showing the reality around these parts.'

'Not very *feel*-good,' Maeve pointed out. 'No laughs, no happy ending, and too many people with American names. These Yanks like their Irish to be called Shannon or Kerry or Begorra. Now, a few minor characters *do* end up dead in violent ways and *one* of the bad guys gets it between the eyes. With a high heel, as it happens.'

'Thank goodness for artistic integrity,' I laughed.

'Oh, holding the mirror up to nature,' Maeve assured us.

A hiss of walkie-talkie interference was followed by a head appearing around the open door. 'Maeve, we'll be ready for you in five if you want to go for checks. Tanty time is over.'

'Our leading lady from the US has a tantrum *every* afternoon at this time,' Maeve illuminated. 'Don't know if it's habit or hormones. Herself and our leading man are a hoot. He is *divine* on the eye, but thick as two short ones, I'm sorry to say. Has as much *air* between the ears as a Zeppelin. As for her, she's had so many bits reshaped and replaced I'm surprised she *recognises* herself in the mirror.' She sighed happily. 'There is *nothing* like a bitch to cheer a girl up. I'll see you both later, perhaps. And you should talk to Karl, he's the location manager and the one who deals with locals when we're out of the studio. You'll find him at the end of the next row beside the honey wagon.' She saw blank faces. 'The mobile toilet?'

Ah.

We were en route to Karl's gaff when we encountered a recent acquaintance of mine, Daisy, Andy Raynor's squeeze at the barbecue.

'Hi, Lee,' she greeted me.

'Hello, Dotty,' I returned. 'What are you doing here?'

'I was going to ask you the same. Great minds think alike.'

Yeah, yeah, get on with it, small talk, cliché girl. I ran my hands through my hair self-consciously, a little too late to wonder if it was looking manky. It felt full of texture, which was probably not good.

'I'm working on this movie,' Daisy said. 'Just a small part, but very important.'

'There are no small parts, isn't that what they say?'

'That is so true.'

It was clear from her get up that she was playing a whore, but a much better dressed, better cared for and more beautiful one than Mayville normally set eyes on. Nice touch of realism, just what was expected from this work of fart.

A bit rich, I know, but I was furious with her for being here. I felt like an intruder or, worse, a groupie. Andy's girl pal *belonged*. I felt vengeful as a dying wasp as I regarded her good looks and trim figure, while I faced into months of elasticated clothing and piles.

'I really must rush back, they'll think I've fallen down a hole,' she said, before realising that it was obvious she'd just come from the loo.

I met her look and was not the first to break the link.

When she had disappeared from sight Ciara said, 'Sheesh, Leo. I don't know what that girl did to you, but it must have been bad.'

'Huh,' I growled dismissively. 'You should see me when I'm really pissed at someone.'

'God forbid.'

Karl was receiving in a hut on wheels not unlike a horse box. He was a vibrant man, late-twenties with a head of hair that seemed to have been stolen from a floor mop. A tanned complexion showed he spent plenty of time out of doors and his hand was firm to shake. I could swear I heard a 'pop' when Ciara and he locked eyes. Then I found it hard to attract his attention again. His fetching body had language only for my assistant, and her own was busy communicating too. Most of his answers were directed at her, so I stood close in a bid to feel included. It worked medium well, at least enough to make me feel less like a mongrel at Crufts.

Karl had been told that the unit would be safe for its two days and nights on the Mayville estate if a suitable tribute was paid to a certain Doc Phelan. He had trekked to the Raven and handed over a brown envelope full of cash, and so far all was going to their mutual satisfaction.

'I've met Mr Phelan,' I said. 'Not a nice individual.'

'And did you get a load of that breath problem?' Karl gasped. 'He could be dead, it smells that bad. I get the feeling he's in that pub all day, uses it as his office. While I was there two couriers came to deliver stuff to him. The barman is like a part-time secretary, signing for stuff.'

'Were the couriers from the same company?' I asked, a notion stirring.

'No,' Karl replied. 'One was Wingers. I know 'cos we use them too. The other was from an outfit with one of those dum-de-dum names . . . eh, Door to Door, I think it was.'

I gave Karl my card, though I had no idea what more he could tell me. He pocketed it without a glance.

'I should take yours too,' he said to Ciara.

'I don't have one,' she explained. 'But why don't I take your number?'

This was Ciara lashing on some serious charm, though you might not have thought so. Karl nearly broke his nib in the rush to give it to her, if you get my drift.

'An interesting afternoon,' I commented, as we passed through the chain fence keeping the film unit in and the ordinary world out.

Ciara smiled blithely. 'I hope you're taking notes,' she said.

We strolled by a derelict playground ringed with chains to deter vandals. They had failed miserably. A mangled slide listed sideways, metal struts distorted as if pictured through a trick photo lens. The swings were without seats and a single roundabout was never going to fulfil its remit of turning again. Notably missing were the children who should have been tumbling through it all in loud play, whooping it up in a summer that would always seem longer in their memory than it had been, and with better weather than nature would ever provide again in any distant future. This play area was forlorn, like a heart broken by failed romance. It stood ignored by a group of kids kicking a ball over and back across the road, dodging traffic for thrills and trying to look cool in the 'hood'. I wondered how many of them would make it past their teens with such odds stacked against them.

Billy was doing business on his corner. He was selling a score to a slim young man wearing a tee-shirt, jeans and baseball hat. A very familiar ensemble of these items. For instance, I knew before he turned that the shirt said 'hot', the left leg of the jeans had a deliberate rip just above the knee and their faded blue colour matched the man's eyes: Barry Agnew's eyes. His brilliant disguise had not fooled me. It wouldn't have fooled anyone who watched television either. Anger rose in me from my toes up.

'There's that actor,' Ciara said. '*Now* I remember where I know him from. He offered me a spliff one night in a bar in town, then propositioned me.'

In a landslide of sudden understanding I looked at a restructured emotional landscape. What became crystal clear to me then was something I could not believe I hadn't noticed before: Barry liked his women young. I was way too old for him at thirty. He preferred girls. I was a handy mother substitute, and it made my skin crawl to think what that made of our love-making. Move over, Mr Freud, I'll be needing a patch of couch. Suddenly, everything made sense. Take his obsession with my fifteen-year-old niece and obvious delight in her crush on him. His constant complaints about the actresses he was paired with being 'too old'. His casual neglect of me, and my own ridiculous compliance with that. My laziness had finally come home to roost.

I was fair rooted to the spot on Mayville Street as I surveyed my life. I was about to be very single again, but with a beezer new twist: pregnancy. Barry, perhaps about to be a dad but oblivious of this and many other important aspects of life, turned in surprise. You ain't seen nothing yet, boy.

'Stupid prick,' I muttered.

I grabbed Ciara and propelled us forward, unwilling to give my flight mechanism a chance to activate. Truth to tell, I was feeling a trifle pugnacious.

'Allow me to reintroduce you,' I growled.

FIFTEEN

Life was not content with the amount of crap I already had to cope with, so it dealt out some more. I suppose crime statistics had to be maintained, or the Mayville estate might have fallen out of the top five black spots in the country. I was one of the very mean Streets of Dublin as I surveyed the four slashed tyres on my car. Poor old thing. Like myself it was injured, winded but repairable. A note suggested I take a hike before someone brought me on one, which I was guaranteed not to enjoy. I smiled to think of the trouble my vandal had had deciding where to put the fan mail in the absence of the windscreen wipers, which were now in the possession of two small guys at Madonna Mansions, or perhaps sold on in a lucrative piece of recycling. I grew tired of this correspondence, though, as it was rude of the writer not to have left a return address.

I rang Mull at Mullaney Motors to organise the car rescue. I could picture him in his orange jumpsuit, gently scratching his balls in contemplation of my problem, unsurprised at hearing my voice as I am one of his most loyal and regular customers. This last boast is a hollow one; I'd rather be seen once a year for a vehicle service, just as I'd prefer to see a doctor only as often, and for purposes of prevention rather than crisis. It had certainly been one of 'those weeks'.

Ciara was sent to get wheels for later. This involved bullying her mum so she was delighted with the task. In the meantime, I gave Barry his marching orders.

'Leo, you are over-reacting,' he said, in an astonished voice.

'Barry, read my lips: I don't care. Go. I am sick and tired of you compromising me on all fronts. And if you can't see that you're doing that to yourself now, by buying drugs on a street corner, then you're beyond help.'

'This was a once off. My regular guy has gone missing.'

'Gone to prison, more like. Which is what you can look forward to, with plenty of publicity, if you keep this up.'

I looked at my watch. Still 2.15. Damn, I really did need to get that fixed.

'I'm going back to the office, which gives you time to pack and leave. I'll understand if you can't do it all in one go. We'll organise other times for that, if need be.'

Why did I have this maddening habit of throwing in a nicety or kindness at the very time I was entitled to kick ass? It was an issue to be addressed and corrected, i.e. stamped out. I made a mental note.

'Leave your keys on the mantelpiece and feed the cats on your way out.'

I turned and walked away, relieved, years lighter.

Panic set in on O'Connell Street and by the time I had crossed the bridge I was hyperventilating with worry about the future. I stalled to let normal oxygen intake resume. Then my chest grew tighter than my profit margin. I staggered through Temple Bar like a drunk searching for a taxi. Work would see me through. Keep those brain cells occupied. I threw myself into a plan which had been forming in my head since my visit to the Raven and subsequent chat with the film location manager, Karl. I rang Ronan and asked him to hang by as soon as. The sight of him would cheer me up at least.

Molly was looking peaky and I told him so.

'Ah, when you're my age, you can expect that,' he said. 'I'm tired a lot. Maybe I'm not getting enough sleep.'

'Or maybe you should go see a doctor,' I suggested.

'You could be right. A bit of an aul' tonic might do the trick, what?'

He handed No. 4 over and I walked the dog to the former refuge for poverty-stricken chimney sweeps and up all of the many stairs to the offices of Leo Street and Co. By then I had explained the Barry situation and the dog had digested our change of circumstance. He took it well, all things considered, but needed a nap to help him through. He was wheezing stertorously in a box under my desk when Ciara's twin arrived.

I explained my plan to Ronan and he agreed that it was foolhardy, probably in the extreme, but without taking the risk we gained nothing. Not the most solid case for doing the dodgy, but we were clearly not going to bother arguing that amongst ourselves. He set to work on the computer, trawling through the maze of technological flim-flam that is the Internet. I turned Mick Nolan's framed photo to the wall, because I didn't like the way he was looking at me and if he started shouting I might lose my nerve. When Ronan had hacked through to the database of Day to Day couriers, he called me over. I watched in silent fascination as he called up Phelan's details using the company records. There were a few Phelans listed, but only one P.D. Phelan, c/o The Raven Public House. Cocky bastard was using his Papa Doc initials. He paid cash on delivery, and seemed a busy man.

'What do you think he's transporting?' Ronan asked.

'My guess is, and it really is only a guess, he's using the couriers to send drugs around the city without necessarily touching the stuff himself.'

'Even more dangerous to piss him off then,' Ronan pointed out.

'Yes. But I need to rattle him to get information about Cherry and Nina. If I can convince him that I have the power to take away or restore his precious parcels, maybe he'll give me something.'

'Mightn't be the something you want.'

'No. But I'm hoping it'll only be a short-term thing and that the risk will be small as a result.'

'If not, you'll be moving house.'

'Or countries.'

Papa Doc had two packages en route to the Raven the following morning. We sent them both astray. Ooh, he was not going to like that one little bit. I looked at my fag-ash-stained shoes and could not feel sorry for him.

'What will happen to those packages?'

'I've sent them into the maw of the company stores, so they'll be easy enough rooted out when the search happens. Should take the heat off all involved, and it'll look like a clerical error rather than outside interference,' Ronan assured me.

'Grand. We'll leave it at that for now,' I said. 'If we have to, we'll start messing with the other companies he uses.'

'We have the technology.' Ronan grinned.

A mean streak in me had been sated, momentarily. The fall out from Barry's mess up would be felt by the dregs of Dublin's inner city, I hoped, rather than innocent bystanders in my life. Seemed only fair. A good, handy tack to remember for the future.

Ronan had a mischievous glint about the eyes. 'Fancy a bit of fun?' he asked.

I was flattered – unseemly in a woman of my age, and misplaced. Still, I managed to croak, 'What did you have in mind?'

He cracked his knuckles. 'Well, I happen to notice that your credit limit is freakishly low, so we could start by correcting that?'

I nodded gratefully. He swished his hands over the keys and it was so.

'It's that simple?' I boggled.

'Uh-huh,' the youngster confirmed. 'Next, anyone been annoying you? Perhaps a company that's been unreliable?'

'As you mention it,' I said, 'there is an insurance firm overdue with a payment, and it's cost me a fortune chasing them.'

I gave the relevant details and, not seven minutes later, he assured me I could expect a cheque in the next run from the company, which included a little interest on the sum owing.

'Jeez, lovely touch, Ronan,' I gushed.

I was hanging over the back of his chair now, blatantly invading his personal space but beyond shame on that front.

As I didn't want to be too forward or greedy, on my first visit to such teccy matters at any rate, I finished by sending Maeve some flowers and giving Barry an extremely early pick-up call for his next filming day, whenever that would be. Ronan made sure the address could be changed to reflect my ex's new circumstance but the pick-up would always default to our early command. I thanked him and asked him to bill me for the time he'd spent on my behalf. He beetrooted up and said he wished all his jobs were this much fun. Yeah, it would be a right laugh altogether when Papa Doc Phelan copped on to what was happening. Instead of lingering on that, I indulged myself in a lingering gaze at my newest assistant. He was so easy on the eye . . .

I waited till Ronan had left before ringing Hugo Nelson's mobile. I needed to know just who I was in the process of pissing off so mightily. Of course, I neglected to mention that aspect of my activities to the cop.

'Doc Phelan is not the head man in that particular drugs pyramid,' the legit detective said. 'But he's high up and important. Runs a very tight operation, and keeps his lieutenants separate from one another. None of them would know everyone in the organisation, and not even the Doc has that information. It means that if anyone goes down, the operation is still viable even in the event of some squealing. It's clever, difficult to crack. He has a few other sidelines, his own interests, porn-related and most unsavoury. Altogether, a bad piece of flesh.'

'I'm assuming he's violent?'

Nelson laughed at my simplicity.

'They all are. Papa Doc rarely gets his own hands dirty. There are stories, though, of punishments he's taken it upon himself to mete out. He likes to wear a butcher's apron on those occasions, apparently.'

Fuck, my brain said, you've done it now. First chance I got I would remove Leo Street and Co. from the sequence I had put in train. I had gone a meddle too far and was fighting well out of my weight. I left Mick facing the wall when I locked up for the evening, unable to face a barrage of abuse about my reckless actions. My innards were feeling less than solid as I descended the stairs.

'You look terrible,' Mrs Mack told me, delighted.

'Thanks,' I replied. 'It's nice to know you care.'

That woman was like the Candyman; if you said her name enough times, she appeared. As the years went on, even thinking of her would do the trick.

I rang the house from my mobile before heading for the bus. The answering machine kicked in each time, so I assumed Barry had cleared out. We were safe for going home. I was usually easy pickings for his sob stories and warped reasoning but this was one time I would not give his sophistry a chance. We sat upstairs admiring the sea when it appeared to the right of the route. I wanted to turn the clock back, years if I had to, to a time when I was happy and Nina Clancy lived at home. No. 4 licked my face from time to time, to take away the tears.

Number 11 The Villas didn't seem all that changed when I stepped in. It still had three cats and they had been fed, so Barry had managed to remember that instruction. He also seemed to have moved out, at least in the short term. It was imperative that I stuck to the letter of the law on his expulsion and did not let him wheedle his way back in. The past has an imperfect grammar and memory is a trickster; they could not be allowed to gang up and remind me of good times at the expense of the bad. Otherwise Barry Agnew would be back the following day as if nothing had happened.

Already I could hear my traitorous mind saying that I was only angry with him because he'd been public in his stupidity. If he had bought the drugs at a comfy club, under cover of darkness and the leeway afforded his minor celebrity, would I have been so unhappy? And what was a bit of dope between friends? It was not exactly an inheritance of good pasture going back generations and now squandered by a blow in. It was just grass, just blow, the acceptable face of dabbling.

It was a focus, though, of all that was hollow and wrong between us. I had given myself an out here and I was not going to flitter it away with sentimentality. I rubbed my belly.

'It's you and me now, kid,' I said. 'Fancy a rasher sandwich?'

I added lettuce and tomato to keep us healthy and regular.

The answering machine flashed three messages. My mother was worried about me. No great revelation, she was an Irish Mammy, it was her job to worry. Con wanted me to meet someone the following day who might help with the Ma Hogan mystery. I jotted his instructions on the pad by the phone. The last message was of no consequence: my ex-boyfriend wanted to apologise, said we must talk. I wiped the tape.

The nail biting started small, then took over. I found a finger in my mouth and began to run the nail between two teeth. It snagged a little, so I bit off the jutting piece. Then I had another chew at the nail to even off the job. I ran it through my teeth again and found a rough edge, which I tugged. This ripped some more off and ended low down at the side of the nail in an ever-widening triangular shape. Which hurt, because it was attached more to flesh here than nail. I pulled at it, using my other hand this time, and it came away leaving a small dot of blood. The nail had split horizontally during its journey and I had only a thin layer on the upper part of the finger. This was sore, but I figured I'd have one last evening out bite. Then I was left with tender, exposed skin, normally protected by a tough outer shell. It throbbed, miserable and red, flanked by jags on both sides now, so I headed for the nail clippers in the bathroom. Precision steel left a short stumpy nail on my middle finger. It was tender to the touch and I was reluctant to press anything solid, knowing the discomfort this would cause. I immediately regretted the harvest, but told myself it would grow back soon. It was just one nail, I had nine more pretty enough to shift the focus from the injured one.

It's funny the things that annoy or provoke tears. Barry had taken his toothbrush, but left his shaving paraphernalia. Was he a presumptuous git who thought he'd be back before his beard got out of hand, or was it as disposable as our life in this house? Some dirty socks and skids were still in the wash basket, but his shoes were all absent. I spotted the pinafore dress I'd worn to the barbecue and remembered Andy's note. I fished it out with trembling hands, admonishing myself for my jitters. After all, it couldn't be any worse than the rest of the day I'd had.

'Dearest Leo,' it read (a promising start).

I'm not sure where things have gone wrong for us over the last six weeks, and you won't ring me to say. I think you may have got the wrong end of the stick with regard to Heather, who you met one morning at my house way back when. She always liked to call early and make herself at home. She's history now. I hope we are not.

Please call me,
Andy.

There was a single X after his name.

I had to sit down. That man's ability to leave me reeling was the stuff of romantic novels. I was on the bed I would no longer share with Barry, thinking of Andy, wanting to die with

177

trepidation for the future and regret for the past. Instead, I lay back on the pillows, closed my weary eyes and let sleep take me away. And when the dream came it smelled of Barry, tasted of Andy, and had Ronan Gillespie's face with Razor Cullen's eyes.

I could have kissed the telephone when it rescued me from my sweat-drenched stupor. The room was dark and brooding. I fumbled for the receiver and muttered my number.

'Get washed and ready,' Ciara ordered. 'We're back on duty. I'll collect you in half an hour.'

The house was quiet, just the soft burr of sleeping cats and dog audible. Soon it was joined by the hum of my shower. I stood in the pouring water, switching from hot to cold to revive my weary senses. I felt myself adrift, as detached as Nina Clancy had made herself from Clunesboro when she got on the bus headed east. My surroundings were familiar, but everything was changed. I was like an actor on a stage, not knowing what the play was or what lines I had to say.

On the outside looking in, I could see no other option than to continue. I moved my feet in rotation, got to the bedroom, dressed and was standing shining, numb and ready when Ciara pulled up in her mother's car. I was holding sandwiches and a thermos of coffee, but couldn't remember the action of making them. I wafted out and tried to look like I meant business. The effect was spoiled by my bashing my head against the car door jamb. Ciara chose not to comment. I fell heavily on to the passenger seat and busied myself with the seat belt.

'Drive,' I said in my best hard-boiled voice.

And keep going, I willed her.

Life goes on. And on. And on.

SIXTEEN

The Night Train was for the hopeless cases. There was no pretence here, no urine sample asked for or given. Clearly, these clients were never getting off their habit and most of them were dying, in the various late-stage ravages of AIDs-related diseases. They came for clean needles, condoms, methadone, anything that would get them through another few hours on this Godforsaken planet. These addicts were still using and the methadone was for maintenance, helping them dull the edge of their craving for heroin. The daytime clients were expected to use it as part of their detox.

We parked the car on the road opposite the clinic and watched for a while. Figures shuffled from the shadows of Price Street and, just as quietly, blended back into the darkness, ghosts in the works. Two big, red-necked cops sat in their car further along, also watching the comings and goings, dispassionately.

Ciara stared at me in the reflected light of a street lamp.

These moments were intended for some quiet psyching up and the mood wasn't helped when she asked me if I'd been crying.

'No. I've got hay fever and it's making my eyes water.'

'That and a dicky tummy. Jayz, you're not much of an asset.'

'Thanks for that. Don't forget that I still have the power to hire and fire round here. *And* I've got the sangers and the flask.'

'Absolute power doesn't suit you,' Ciara remarked. 'It brings out a nasty streak.'

'Thank your lucky stars I'm not pre-menstrual,' I said. Though you won't see any of that for months, I thought to myself.

A few stragglers sat on the clinic steps sharing cigarettes and doing deals with passers-by. Ciara and I joined them, not that they seemed interested in us. We were the haves, they were the have nots. I was surprised they didn't run us. Eventually, a woman called Alice introduced herself. She was a skeleton after twenty-four hard years of living. Every one of her features seemed to have receded, her skin and gums drawn tight over the structure of her bones. The back of her left arm throbbed with an infected boil. What body I could see was dotted with angry track marks, her immune system clearly unable to cope with the constant assaults of the needle. Her feet were swollen under dirty socks and shoes. I guessed she was using all areas of her body to find veins. A welt on her neck looked like someone had tried to throttle her. Perhaps someone had, she didn't say. One extraordinary feature remained intact: her eyes were vivid green emeralds shining huge and bright in the devastation of her face.

When she'd established that we were not journalists looking

for a good story, Alice opened up a little. She'd seen Cherry around and about, with a girl matching Nina's description. She recognised the dress from the photograph.

'Cute,' she said of it. 'Very Jackie Kennedy Onassis.'

An old man approached and amazed me by asking if anyone wanted to buy some pills. This guy was your archetypal granddad, with silver whiskers and a broad, healthy smile. He was doing a brisk trade in Valium. When he had offloaded his consignment he headed in the direction of Ringsend, well pleased with his night's sale.

'Did I just see what I think I saw?' I asked Alice. I was slack-jawed with amazement.

'Ah, yeah, that's Paddy. He's a regular.'

'And he's, like, a dealer?' I could not get my head round the concept.

'Well, not really,' Alice said. 'He gets all sorts of shit from his doctor for free, 'cos he's on a medical card. Tells him he has trouble sleeping and so on. Then he comes down here and sells it all for beer money. The Valium is great for calming you if you're late with a score, and it helps with the pain. Or you might use it to get a good night's sleep.'

'Is this a regular thing?' Ciara asked.

'Yeah,' Alice said. 'If it's not Paddy, it'll be one of the other pensioners from the area. They love their jar.' She shook her head affectionately at the old age scamps and their doings.

The cops in the car appeared to be laughing. They were also stuffing their faces with a takeaway from the greasy spoon so handily located beside their car. I couldn't tell if it was us or the food providing their good humour. Both, I suspected.

Alice didn't know much about Ma Hogan. 'I've never had need of her services,' she explained. 'Thank God. She's a bit of an animal, might as well be using a knitting needle is what I heard.'

I shook to my core at this description.

A young man with a cultured accent sat beside us on the steps and said his name was Ted. He looked like he was taking care of himself, washing and shaving, but his clothes were threadbare and he wore a coat although the night was warm. He placed a newspaper on the concrete before taking his place on it.

'I have to be careful of the cold,' he said. 'Kidneys are bad.'

Ted had been a student before falling into a life of drink and drug taking. He'd spent grant after grant on his habits, failed his exams and got turfed out of college. He assured me that all he needed was another chance. If he had a nice place to live, a job, he could start again. I remembered Orla's words earlier in the day about an addict never taking responsibility. They'd seemed harsh at the time, but in fact she was just telling it like it is.

Ted had studied History and Economics. He told me he'd been HIV-positive for years. I looked from him to Alice and back again trying to imagine them in health, flesh on their bones and colour in their complexions. No matter what they had looked like, no matter how different their backgrounds, they were both ruined now. Heroin was an equal opportunities destroyer.

I wanted to know about 'the fair'. Alice said it was held two or three times a year. Lost souls sold themselves for more money than they'd earn on the street, but they were also expected to perform out-of-the-ordinary tasks. She didn't want to elaborate on that. There were rumours that sometimes people made better lives for themselves out of it.

'That's hard to believe,' I said.

'Tell me about it,' Alice agreed. 'I've never met anyone who did well. They never came back to tell the story. They're probably dead. I don't believe the happy-ever-after shit.'

All anyone knew for sure was the date. This summer's version was to take place on Friday night. An hour before, word of a venue would hit the street. Everyone interested would be ready to roll at that point. I asked Alice if she was going this year.

'I'm not that desperate, love,' she said. 'Yet.'

I could tell they were both anxious to be rid of us, so we canvassed the others on the steps for news of the missing girls. I saw Alice and Ted exchange words, then disappear, Ted helping Alice with her painful walk. Ten minutes later they were back, all smiles and dilated pupils. Alice apologised for her rudeness earlier. I told her there was none. Her voice had taken on a curious, low growl. I found out later it's one of the signs that someone's just shot up.

I needed to know where this fair was going to take place on Friday, so I suggested we meet up again on the night. Alice laughed.

'I'll try,' she said. 'But who knows where any of us lot will be Friday? That's a long way off. I could be dead by then.'

I looked at the motley collection of humanity on the Price Street clinic steps. There was no guarantee any of them would make it to the weekend.

'Do you need anything?' I asked her. 'Money?'

'No. I robbed some earlier.'

She said this without expression or emphasis. It was a fact of her life, that's all, something that had to be done every day to support her habit: functional, effective theft.

Leo Street and Co. were headed back to the car when one of the cops decided to talk to us.

'Enjoy the entertainment?' he wanted to know. A smell of vinegar and grease wafted out through the rolled down window.

'Gas altogether,' Ciara said, without stopping to talk.

When we were out of earshot she called them BIFFOs. I arched a badly plucked eyebrow. 'Big Ignorant Fuckers From Offaly,' she explained. Ciara has always had her own distinctive respect for authority.

As we pulled away from the kerb, I saw Alice waving goodbye to us, Ted a frail shadow behind her. I waved back. She was six years younger than me, but looked older than my grandmother.

'I hate to bring this up,' I began, wondering how to word this.

'But you're going to anyway.'

'We need to talk to Tiny Shortall's twin, and the only place . . .'

'No, no, don't say it!' Ciara shouted, banging the steering wheel to underline her point. 'I can't bear to hear the name of that tip. I'll drive us there, just – don't – say – that – name.'

We pulled up at Moonlites five minutes later.

Security thought we'd been sacked along with Simon Cadogan. It paid to play along. Dublin is a small town and we might run into these people on another day's mission when the last remark you want shared is that you're a private detective. It tends to be a dead give-away.

'Nah,' Ciara said. 'Chance would be a fine thing. I just hated the work and couldn't face in this week.'

'Same goes for me,' I said, pitching my one and twopence worth. 'Bet I'll be back when I'm broke.'

'I wouldn't count on that,' Eamonn Davey said, grinning and shoving his belly forward. 'Val says you're a terrible bad barwoman.'

My professional pride was almost dented, but the truth was I had been almost totally shite at the job, so I learned to live with the criticism.

We explained that we were dropping in to find a friend and would not be long.

'And you want free admission, is that it?' Eamonn feigned amazement. Then, for just a second, I thought I saw the notion of making us pay flit across his brain. His short-term health prospects improved when he unhooked the thick red rope across the door. 'Ah, go on in, I'm in good form tonight, even if it is the first Tuesday of a month.

'I miss the boots,' he told Ciara as we passed by. She flashed him a mega-watt smile in return for his compliment.

'If he'd charged us, I'd've had his balls,' she assured me through gritted teeth.

'And the leching?'

'I've almost stopped noticing that, it's so fucking pathetic.'

We waved at Tanya who was looking tragic in her booth.

'Job satisfaction,' I whispered to Ciara.

'Oh, big time,' she giggled.

Inside the Mickey Money was being spent with pagan abandon. Women of all shapes, sizes and age were gyrating on the dance floor. They had their hands in the air because it was raining men, amen. Then, they swayed in unison, bawling out to Argentina not to cry for them, they hadn't left. Suddenly it was Gloria Gaynor's anthem and we were left in no doubt that these women would survive. The outnumbered men in the club held the bar up and looked very, very afraid.

'Girl Power,' Ciara shouted over the music.

Val Tobin greeted us like long-lost daughters. She was looking much more corporate with dark brown hair scraped into a French pleat. The hairstyle was somewhat more sober than she was.

'I'm the boss now,' she said. Her smile still had an unsettling quality. 'Is there any special way I can help?'

We told her we were looking for Tiny Shortall's brother.

'Shorty's not here,' was her information.

I was struck again by how original his nickname was, not. I didn't have one, or at least not anything that was ever mentioned to my face.

'Any idea where we might get hold of him?' I asked.

'Yes, actually. He'll be here tomorrow night.'

Duh, or course. He wouldn't be seen dead in Moonlites on Children's Allowance night. It was way too scary.

We were not delayed by a drink on the house.

'In a way, I'm not insulted by her lack of hospitality,' I said to Ciara as we left the nightclub.

'Yeah, but the pisser is that we have to go back there tomorrow,' she moaned.

'True,' I agreed. 'Unless you find Shorty in the meantime.'

'Good tactic there. You know I really, really do not want to darken the rancid carpet in that place again. Leave it with me.'

A mile into our short journey she asked about Barry.

'He's gone,' I explained. 'I threw him out.'

'If you want, I can stay over,' Ciara said, disarming me with the most unlikely offer of help I could have imagined at that time.

I looked quickly out of the passenger window, staunching tears.

'Thanks, but I'll be fine. It's nice of you to . . .'

'Yeah, yeah,' she cut me off. 'No need to mention it to anyone. I have a reputation to keep up.'

'You're a strange woman, Gillespie.'

186

'That's rich, coming from an expert.'

We pulled up outside my concrete, terraced two up-two down.

'Out you get. And be proud of what you did today,' she instructed. 'It was a blow for you. Well done.'

I could not look at her. My eyes were filled with gratitude and salt water.

One message bleeped on my machine. I pressed 'play' and quickly went to 'erase' when I heard Barry's voice. Noel miaowed by, complaining of his tough life and wanting a cuddle. I picked him up and stood looking out at the moonlit street, my mind trying its best to stay blank. The cat was strangely attracted to the pulled back curtain, watching it intently, not daring to purr.

'What is it, sweetykins?' I asked him, in a goofy voice.

His eyes were bright and wide, steadfast on the curtain. Then I saw a thin, black tail swish in the folds of the material. Noel dug his claws into my shoulder and neck, trying to get a steady hold before launching himself into an attack. His claws sank painfully into my flesh and I yeowled as I tried to prise him off. He was having none of it. The mouse began to run up the curtain and along the pole. I leaned over and extricated the cat from my flesh, ripping a shoulder in the process. When I looked back the mouse had disappeared. Shit!

I don't think I'm so different from anyone else in my fear of the unknown. It poses a threat because we can have no rational reaction until we understand it and therefore can figure how to combat it. Next, there's phobia, fear's first cousin. My own phobic fear is large spiders. Their silence and stealth gets me every time. And, boy, can they shift it on those eight legs. Aesthetically they're not my cup of tea either. All round nil points for the old arachnids. My brother Peter had the more impressive list of vampires and triffids when we were young. And Stephen was a monsters man. He would bang open the bedroom door, squashing the monster behind it, then jump from there on to his bed to avoid the monster underneath. So, fears and phobias are individual demons, and for me, along with spiders, I have to add surprises. I really hate those. In fact, I think *This Is Your Life* is the spookiest and cruellest show on television. And here I was with a surprise visit from a mouse, which had taken the precaution of disappearing. Action was needed, and fast.

I ran to the kitchen and pulled a pint glass from a cupboard. My plan was to capture the creature and release it. If I could find it. In reverse order, I would have loved support, help, someone else to do this. But I was on my own in a race to save one animal from the jaws of another, as well as to remove the unwelcome provider of surprises from my home. If he was willing to wear a bell, maybe we could come to an arrangement, though I didn't fancy his chances with the cats. Anyhow, my preference is for mice that live anywhere but my house though, to be fair, this lad had probably been reluctantly dragged in by one of my lads and couldn't be blamed for the entire controversy.

I returned to shake the curtain and the little guy reappeared. Noel stretched as far as he could from his new perch on the floor but was a good three feet short of his prey. The mouse was a nimble little fecker and led me the traditional merry dance. I settled for trapping him in the net curtain itself and then transferring his balled-up body to the glass. This was the only time I could boast of using the Net to full advantage. I threw the tiny fur bag into the front garden where he lived to mouse another day.

Noel was disgusted and railed loudly against my stupidity. I told him to shut up but he ignored me, as usual. I sank into the sofa, trembling but grateful that my rescue case was a mouse and not a rat. Or a big, hairy spider, with black eyes like feelers out on stalks. I shuddered and shivered and suddenly felt completely drained. And alone.

I looked across the room and saw Barry's keys abandoned on the mantelpiece. That did it. The dam broke and my face flooded with tears, hot drops falling unchecked to drench my shirt. I was miserable as I could be. I could see no light in any direction. All I could make out was tunnel.

SEVENTEEN

My body ached when I came to the following morning. Part of the reason was that I was still on the couch and had three cats and a dog nestled into my various nooks and crannies. In fact, they seemed to have created new ones, comfortable for them, painful relocations of flesh for me. I was stiff as a well-lacquered armoire and cranky as a traffic warden.

The furries did not take well to being moved. 'Tough,' I told them. 'I am bedding with attitude, you takes your chances.'

There was no point in consulting my watch for an accurate version of the time, so I dragged myself upstairs to look at the radio alarm. I slugged down a glass of water as I reviewed my options. I was dehydrated from crying, bent out of shape by the menagerie, pregnant. It was not a happy list. I decided, sensibly, on crawling under my duvet and allowing myself another hour's sleep. Being selfish can be a very rewarding experience and it did not disappoint on that occasion.

When I rejoined the household I found myself in a weird

animal Coventry. They were prepared to eat my grub, but left to do busy things elsewhere when they were done breakfasting. No. 4 frolicked with a striped ball in the back garden and seemed the least put out of all of them at my removal of my comfy self earlier. He really had no short-term memory and bore few grudges as a result. The cats had bitchery down to a fine art but even they would be back soon; they had standards of behaviour to maintain, that's all, nothing personal.

I was back in the bedroom when I realised that I could smell Barry in the air, hanging around like a fart in a jar. It got me revved up to rip off the bedclothes and replace them with fresh, clean covers, scented by a popular non-bio brand. I filled a wicker basket and hauled the lot down to the washing machine. I sorted items efficiently, by throwing Barry's stuff in the bin and dividing my own clothes into whites and coloureds. Then I stuffed the offending sheets and pillow cases into the steel drum on a hot cycle. Out, damn' Agnew! I celebrated with a cup of mint tea.

There was still something odd to the day, like that weird itch deep behind the soft palette of your mouth that you cannot locate, let alone scratch. What I needed was a good moan into someone else's ear. I phoned Maeve.

'The bitch bush telegraph is *alive* with your news,' she assured me.

'Is this my fifteen minutes?'

'Oh, I *hope* you'll manage even better, my dear, this is a mere practice run.'

'I'm feeling a bit of a heel over it now.'

'Don't be *ridiculous*, you should have done this long ago. It'll be character-building for him, not to mention handy for building a character on one of his future jobs. We actors are complete *tarts* and waste nothing, you know. *Now*, the very latest is that I've had your dear dejected cry into my face, and I can report that it was *not* pretty. He is very sorry for himself in*deed*.'

'How bad is he?'

'None of your worry nonsense now, he's *fine*. He got five out of ten from me, not bad but not enough: you've got to score an *eight* to get to stay on my couch.'

'How am I doing?' I asked, in a suitably miserable voice.

'You are always an eight, dear,' she said, gently ribbing me.

I related the mouse story with all my stupid self-spooking.

'Fear is a very personal thing,' Maeve said. 'I know a woman who is *terrified* of mohair, for instance.'

'Of course she is,' I exclaimed. 'That makes perfect sense.'

'Every man I've ever dated has been afraid of commitment,' she continued, ignoring my outburst.

'Until this April,' I felt obliged to point out. She was now shacked up with a high-flying legal type.

'I'm making a sweeping point here, don't interrupt.'

'Sorry.'

'There you go again. Oh, look, I can't be bothered finishing my brilliant observation now, you've beaten it out of me. All I can say is, *well done*. You'll be fine, even if it's hard at first. Stick with this, Leo, you'll be the better for it. Now I want *you* to do something for *me*.'

'What?' This was a surprise, I thought I was the one getting the sympathy and advice.

'Look up the word solipsistic, then behave accordingly.'

'Right,' I said, unconvinced. She'd gone batty.

'I take it the flowers were a thank you in advance for my *superb* advice and counselling, but you needn't have spent all that money, I would have offered it gratis.'

'You're welcome, and really they weren't at all as expensive as you might imagine. Bit of a steal, actually.' I had a pleasant flash of young Ronan Gillespie's elegant hands brushing the computer keyboard as he conjured up our villainy. I allowed myself a frisson of pleasure.

'Call if you need to let off steam. Stay strong. And do *not* let Barry wheedle his way back in. He may seem pathetic, and he is, but remember he's an *actor*, and a good one, and he can make you believe anything. That's his *job*. He has the power to manipulate, very convincingly, that's his profession. Consider him a method actor, bringing his work with him everywhere. *Okay*?'

'Okay.'

'I feel some retail therapy coming on. Let me get to grips with my schedule and we'll get those credit cards out. Now, have a lovely cup of tea, revel in your own space and *stay busy*.'

I did as I was told, starting with the dictionary. 'Solipsism (n), the theory that the self is all that exists or can be known'. I guessed Maeve meant for me to get selfish, but if she'd said just that I'd have ignored her. Now I'd made the effort to find the meaning of a parallel idea, and she knew it would lodge nicely in my brain. She'd said to keep busy, so it was time to pull my socks up and get to work. Those socks could look forward to becoming support tights as these fertile months passed. I groaned. Then I got on with life.

The first of the day's deliveries to Doc Phelan was due at the Raven at noon. This gave me time for cogitation and I made sure it was business-related. I had a pain in my butt from the personal aspects of my life and decided to put them to one side for now. I gnawed some toast as I thought of Nina Clancy and Cherry Phelan. Why had they been forcibly removed from their flat? Why was Cherry considering work at the fair? Was

Tiny Shortall involved at all, or just being used as an example of what can happen to meddlers by men who frightened for a living? Why didn't Nina call home to tell her mother she was alive, and perhaps well? And where did Ma Hogan fit in to the equation? What a great start to the day, a series of unanswered questions, most of them with danger attached to any possible solution. I did discover that mint tea and toast were an uneasy combination, however.

And then came a break, of sorts, the chink of light through rain clouds that you hope will lead to a rainbow. Mary Clancy phoned to say she had received a card from Nina in the morning post.

'It just says, "Sorry not to have been in touch, I have been very busy. Please don't worry about me, I'm fine. I'll call with all my news soon. Love, Nina." '

There was a pause during which I didn't dare breathe. I could hear muffled words in the background.

'Deborah says to tell you there's a "boo" on it.' She sounded confused by this and I was certain Deborah was in for an awkward Q and A session with her mother. She deserved it.

A plan knocking around the back of my mind wouldn't make her feel any better; I had a little surprise in store for the same Deborah.

'What does the postmark say?' I asked Mrs Clancy.

'Monday, 11.30 a.m., Dublin.'

I read this as a good sign. Nina Clancy had been physically seen on Saturday. This card had been posted on Monday. There was a chance she was still alive then. I wanted to believe this, so I did.

I thought a buzz to Hugo Nelson would follow on nicely. He answered on the third ring, his mouth obviously full of breakfast.

'Breakfast? You must be kidding,' he said, scathingly. 'I've been on duty for hours.'

His reaction to Nina's card was, 'So maybe she was alive Monday. Today's Wednesday. Let's not get too excited.'

'I'm wondering about the connections between Doc Phelan and Tiny Shortall? Are they drug-related?'

Hugo slurred his words as he drank and ate during the answer, but I made out the following.

'The Shortalls are supplied by a Turkish outfit based in London, whereas Phelan is attached to a Liverpool gang. So it's unlikely that they do business with one another.'

'I suppose it's not exactly like one pub borrowing a barrel of lager from another,' I ventured.

'No, not really.'

'So that brings us back to the girls and Damo.'

'It would seem to, unless we're on the brink of a turf dispute, and I really don't want to think that's a possibility. On top of everything else, if it is we can expect a terrorist element and those boys are a whole different territory. I'm not elite enough in the Force even to think about that area of trouble. Anti-terrorism is the prestigious end of the police baton.' This last remark was tinged with anger and regret. 'I'll ask the experts here and let you know.'

'Thanks.'

'I hope you're being careful.'

'Safe investigating all the way,' I assured him.

Pity I hadn't been as careful in my sex life.

I was packing my big handbag full of crap when I heard a powerful engine arrive in The Villas cul-de-sac. It seemed to stop outside number 11. Fact was, I didn't want to go near the curtains to check. I was done with adventures on that side of the room. When I thought of how long Marion Maloney spent at her window every day, I began to have new respect for her bravery. Sharp knocks rapped on the door. I thought this might be a courier and didn't want to open up. Doc Phelan used them a lot, for instance, and though I did too, the deliveries were generally to my office. A man called through the door. I started, nerves zinging.

'Leo, are you there? Leo?'

The voice had a familiar ring. Then again, anyone doing an impression of John Wayne would have sounded familiar too, if you see my point.

'Leo, it's Ronan. I've come to give you a lift into town.'

I threw my head back in silent frustration. What kind of shit-scared wimp was I? I'd have grabbed myself by the scruff and given myself a good shake if I could have. If I was going to quake at every unscheduled visit and worry about being alone I might as well shut up shop altogether and move back in with my Mammy and Daddy. The disgrace of it, and me a tough cookie gumshoe.

I opened the door.

'Ronan, brilliant. Sorry about the delay, I was in the loo.'

Mentally, I stuffed my hand in my mouth: too much information. Ronan Gillespie laughed in my face. I shrugged, knowing that I had brought that on myself. I looked beyond him in wonder.

'I didn't know you were a biker.'

A black, gleaming machine lolled by the kerb, nonchalant in its power and beauty. Its gleaming owner lolled nonchalantly by my front door.

'There's a lot about me you don't know,' he said, and I had the impression that he was teasing me. I didn't care. Whatever change had come over him had unleashed a handsome man in tight biker's gear, and it gave my hormones a welcome boost.

'No. 4 will be furious he didn't buy the motorbike helmet he had his eye on in Pampered Pooch last time we were in.'

'And my spare is on loan, shame.'

Ooh, those eyes.

I quickly gathered my belongings and flung out some tinned food. The dog was still chasing his toy in the garden, oblivious to my treacherous desertion. He could use the cat flap for the day in his forays to and fro, most of them trying to locate me, no doubt. I felt guilt, sure, but I was not passing up the opportunity to ride a hog. I was getting the hang of this selfish thing.

I climbed on board the monster at the kerb, held on to a man eleven years younger than me and enjoyed the purr between my legs for the next twenty minutes; part engine, part Leo Street. Mmn.

Molly was shocked, of course. He wasn't looking any better either and I began to insist that he see his doctor. He gestured with one hand to quieten me.

'I'm booked in for midday. All my customers will be here by then, and I've arranged cover till I get back.'

Mull had delivered my car to the lot and it looked quite smug in its new boots. The bill was stuck under one of two replaced wipers, and was as welcome as any other note I had recently received by this method.

I noticed the Porsche was in situ, too, and took down the registration for Ronan to hunt up with his magic computer skills; it might be nice to know a little about the owner. I scanned the vehicle and decided it was eight years old from the number and model. Classier than a spanking new one, according to my biker friend. Personally, I couldn't see any merit in Razor Cullen's showing off.

'Molly, any ideas as to where yer man in the swank car goes to after he parks here?'

The old man shielded his eyes from the sun, squinting as he located his target. 'He always goes into and appears out of that building there.'

I followed the spindly finger and took in a new set-up of shops and cafés, encased in the shell of an old red-brick warehouse. I sent Ronan to the office and took myself into the complex in search of Slate Eyes.

From the moment I entered the lobby I had a feeling I was on to a cold trail. A man dripping Armani and driving a sports car was hardly going to serve in a fast food joint or a newsagent's. I scanned the list of companies in the floors above and made a note to call them later if I hit a dull patch, but none of them leapt out as likely workplaces for my quarry. Mostly I was taken with the fact that the building had a way out into the city sprawl on the opposite side and my hunch was that Razor Cullen walked through and out the other side each day. I bought us some *lattes* and headed for work.

The sky had introduced grey and white wispy clouds into its blue. Temperatures were high and wind was low, giving a close, muggy quality. Air seemed short. I had to rest on each landing as I struggled up with the coffees and my bag balanced in my moist hands. It was an entirely precarious arrangement. I was in sight of the office door when Mrs Mack jumped out of nowhere and managed to frighten a spill of the boiling liquids. I aimed for the linoleum in the confusion and was told that she'd just cleaned that and I would have to mop up the mess because it was more than she was being paid for. A flying glance at the floor would have confirmed that it had last seen water and a promise in 1938. There was a lot to be learned from Mrs Mack's attitude, and none of it good, I decided.

My long and arduous climb was rewarded by a grim-faced Ciara. To put it mildly, she was not happy about my hookery with Doc Phelan. I felt Mick Nolan glow with approval for my apprentice. Amazing the way one situation replicates another.

'It's done,' I said, curtly. 'Let's try to make this work to our advantage. I don't think we have room for negative attitude right now.'

I could hear her mentally yell at me, she was that angry. She had every right to be. Scarier still, Mick Nolan's portrait was facing back into the office. How had he managed that? Now I had both of them to contend with.

I dialled the Raven and asked to speak to Mr P.D. Phelan. I lowered my voice to make myself sound like Alice and Ted from the Night Train, newly strung out. I pressed 'record' on a cassette player I had handy, feeling the conversation might be one to preserve for posterity. Something for the grandchildren to listen to on a wet Tuesday, or the police on a hot Friday, who knew?

'No one here by that name,' came the reply.

'Can you please tell him it's about his deliveries?' I asked politely.

When I next heard from the pub, it was Papa Doc himself speaking.

'Who the fuck is this?' he wanted to know.

'Someone who'll mess up your precious deliveries until you let Cherry go,' I growled. *If you find Cherry, you'll find Nina,* Hugo Nelson had said.

'Is that you, Shortall, you pile of shite? You better fuckin' get my gear back to me pronto or you'll end up whingein' and cryin' like your fuckin' brother.'

My, my, someone had upset his cider cart.

'Let the girl go.'

'You must fancy a swim or somethin', is it?'

'If she's not let go by tonight, I'll take more action. It's up to you.'

I put the phone back in its cradle in the middle of his stream of consciousness. If it's true that babies learn in the womb, I didn't want mine emerging with the complete Anglo-Saxon canon on board.

I switched off the recorder and turned to the Gillespies. 'I have no idea what'll happen now,' I said.

We sat in quiet contemplation of that, then decided eating would keep our strength up. We saw to that and planned our day. Ciara waved a makeshift paper fan before her face.

'This is murder weather,' she declared.

No one dared disagree.

I had an appointment with Con that afternoon to meet the contact who might help us with Ma Hogan's whereabouts, so I let a reluctant Ronan off to his own devices. But I had a special mission for Ciara. I sent her to Clunesboro to see what she could force out of Deborah Clancy.

'Nice,' she whistled approvingly. 'You're getting as mean as me. I like it.'

Ronan was stalling by the door with a hangdog expression on his lovely face. Ciara took pity on him.

'Oh all right, you can come with me. But this isn't a skive-off afternoon, you'll be working. You can put the chat on the locals while I grill the sister.'

She left with a jaunty skip and a hop. I didn't envy her interviewee.

I headed for the Bridewell, a sort of one-stop shop with Garda station and courts all rolled into one. It's one of Dublin's busiest spots, though rarely mentioned in the tourist brochures. Funny, that.

Con was standing on the steps outside court number 2

when I arrived, mopping his face with a handkerchief in the heat. His companion was shaking, visibly, yellow from a spent liver and green from nausea. Before we could be introduced the man doubled over and vomited on a spot behind him. He was totally mortified and apologetic.

'Don't worry about it, Dean,' Con said. 'You take a minute to gather yourself and we'll wait over there.'

He took my arm and steered me to a bench a few yards away. The waft of puke followed us. Con deliberately sat me down with my back to the sick man, which only ignited my interest. I looked back and saw why. Dean was on his hands and knees gathering up what had been inside him a moment ago. I quickly averted my eyes, somehow guessing what would come next.

'He can't lose any of it,' Con explained. 'He's had his methadone for the day and can't get any more. He needs that. Poor soul is so nervous about his case he can't keep anything down.'

My heart was strangled for a man reduced to these actions, trying to start over against such impossible odds. The drug robbed everyone of decency and pride when it got hold. In my mind, I wished Dean all the luck he would need to succeed but said nothing; the man's dignity was at stake. Some women began to row noisily on the steps, impervious to anyone's problems but their own. The chorus of shouts rose and fell, punctuating the ebb and flow of arrivals and departures from the station and the courts.

Dean sold papers on the corner of the railway station and Mayville Street, apparently. He saw the regulars of the area every day. He noticed the comings and goings from houses in the vicinity and knew who was driving what car. He also knew Ma Hogan and what she did for an illegal living.

'She moves premises every few weeks, 'cos the cops are on to her. Lately, I've noticed her coming from a place on the street that looks shut from the outside but must have been fixed up inside. She needs a table and . . . eh, stuff . . . eh, whatever.'

No one was meeting any other's eye at this point. We all had a mental picture of what Ma Hogan needed for her operations. My head became dizzy and my stomach heaved. I leaned forward until it passed.

'Are you all right?' Con asked.

'Yeah, fine. It's just not a very nice subject.'

NICE? a voice screamed inside of me. Why not add LOVELY while you're at it, and paint it all rosy and pink? Call it like it is or leave it alone.

'Dean, when is she usually at this house?' I asked.

'Day times,' he replied. 'Guess you could say ordinary working hours, really. She goes home then, regular as any other nine-to-fiver.'

If I wanted to scout out her lair without interruption, evenings were best. I made a note and thanked the lads.

'Good luck with your case,' I said to Dean as I left.

Con put his arm around the man's shoulders and said, 'He'll be just fine.'

I crossed my fingers as I walked away. The group of women started to scream and shout again and the symphony of the Bridewell resumed. Back in the car I rolled down the windows to get a bit of a breeze going.

I toyed with the idea of taunting Doc Phelan some more about his missing supplies but decided to give him more time to let the girls go or return to the open, whichever applied. I didn't necessarily want to accelerate a drugs dispute either, and felt that would go down like a lick of a pissy thistle with

Hugo Nelson. As it was, he'd be hopping mad if he knew what I'd already done. I nearly scared myself with the thought of it. I needed to pray hard that it would pay off long before it was discovered or beyond my control.

Ciara phoned to tell me that she and Ronan would stay on in Clunesboro to dig around some more.

'Anything interesting?' I asked.

'Nothing so far that can't wait till tomorrow,' she said.

I sighed with disappointment.

'Nina was seeing a lad called Jamesy Briarty, so me and Ronan are going to call on him.'

That would have to do for now. The women were still raging noisily against the system and I longed for a touchstone to soothe the ugliness away. There was one place I could go. It wasn't ideal but it would do till I came up with something better and more long term. I pushed down hard on the pedal and headed for my parents' place.

I spotted myself in a rear-view mirror pulling a ridiculous expression as I thought how nice it would have been to see Ronan again. Leo Street, dirty old woman.

EIGHTEEN

When we Streets got to our teenage years, my parents built a summer house at the end of our back garden. It was intended as a den for us youngsters, with a pool table installed to keep the lads out of the amusement arcade on the sea front, the arcade being, multiply, a potential occasion of sin for hormonal boys and girls, the road to the taking up of gambling, and the means of acquiring finesse with a cue – all activities, and in particular the last, leading to the wasting of youth in the time-honoured tradition.

The novelty of our own table lasted three weeks, by which time the lads discovered that they liked paying money for a game of pool, with a jukebox and women close by. The table was abandoned to dust and cobweb. Bit by bit, my mother squirrelled herself in and one day we discovered that an artist's studio had taken up residence in our den. From there on out it was known as the Streets' Pool Hall and Cultural Centre. This was where I found her, digging a palette knife out of a tear in a large canvas. Her face was dark with frustration.

'That thing is driving me cuckoo,' she snarled.

She wielded the knife, caked with oil paint, like a no-frills psychopath after a particularly gruesome murder. The red-stained smock she wore completed the image. I looked suitably afraid, I'm sure. I certainly felt it.

'A cup of tea might help?' I suggested.

'A large gin and tonic,' she stated, flinging the blade at the canvas again where it boinged and quivered like a circus knife by a lovely lady's head. Ah, the creative process.

We made ourselves comfortable at the kitchen table. My mother's agitation was considerably relieved by a large G and T, while I nursed an orange juice. I pleaded work later when she threw an accusatory eye my way after I refused any alcohol.

'Are you sure that's the reason?' she wanted to know.

A trickle of sweat ran down my clammy back.

How do parents do it? How can they sniff out a story? On this occasion, I believed my mother was fishing for information. On a practical level, there was a limited range of possibilities, so she was not working her evil genius too hard. If facts were pared to a minimum, I was not drinking for one of three reasons: a) I was taking antibiotics, b) I really did have work later, or c) I was pregnant. She was using the trusted means of suggesting the most explosive by innuendo. This did not stop my heart from jolting when her beady eye caught mine. I laughed it off, though not too hard: subtlety is everything when dealing with a suspicious parent.

'Yes, I am sure that's the reason,' I said. 'You have a terrible mind.'

'Hmm,' she hummed, sipping her drink. She let me go, like

a fisherman tiring his catch as he reels it in, slowly and gradually. 'Any news?'

'The usual: work, work, work.'

I made the mistake of relaxing a little. 'Is it very warm or am I having an early menopause?' I joked lightly, pulling my tee-shirt out a few times to circulate some air.

Then I sipped my drink, wondering how I could have mentioned the subject of hormones.

'I hear you have the house to yourself now.'

In shock at the unexpected words I actually sprayed the table with orange juice. Add horror to the shock, while we're about it.

'How do you know that?' I spluttered. 'I'm not sure I know it myself yet.'

Geraldine Street was serene as a dreamless sleep and secretive as an offshore bank account.

Lucy charged through the door, rumbling the mole system.

'I believe Barry's been in touch with you,' I said to my niece, still looking at my mother. It had not been one of my more arduous pieces of deduction.

'He's really upset,' Lucy said, in an accusatory tone.

'That's because he's homeless and has no one to look after him hand and foot,' I pointed out. 'Not because he misses me, I think you'll find.'

My mother registered the new playing field and said, 'Ah, now, Leo, you're very hard, he might miss you.'

This performed very nicely to the Lucy gallery. Geraldine Street was mistress of the good cop/bad cop routine and played both parts herself. It's an awe-inspiring Irish Mammy skill, honed by years of practice on her family, an archetypal mother trait as automatic to her now as suspicion or reading other people's post.

'You are shameless,' I told my mum.

She smiled broadly at the truth of it.

'The idea of Barry missing me is like that cat noticing that I'm alive,' I continued, gesturing to the whole, vast bulk of Smokey Joe Street as he sailed by. 'In other words, not likely.'

That cat liked nothing better than to make a complete eejit out of me as well as a liar, so he used this occasion to stop, put his front paws on my knees and miaow up into my face, lovingly. A conspiracy of cats, that's what their collective name should be.

Lucy was glaring at me, presumably on behalf of the slighted, nay, dumped Barry Agnew. I asked her if she'd like a drink. She left, slamming the door hard. I took this to be a 'no', with knobs on. The rambling house gave it a satisfying echo; 11 The Villas was so small you could hear a sentence before you'd uttered it.

The hubbub of returning men disturbed the sport in the kitchen, but if I thought it would be some sort of rescue I was sorely mistaken. My dad came through first, followed by my brother Peter and behind him Andy Raynor. My face fell, my mother's lifted skywards.

'Leo's single again,' Geraldine told him. Gleefully, wouldn't you know?

Andy raised an eyebrow and looked in my direction without further expression. If he had smiled I would have thumped him, he knew this. Same went for showing surprise or indeed any reaction whatsoever. I shrugged at him, a 'no big deal, happens every day' sort of signal. He nodded an 'I've been there' reply. I warmed to him, which matched the fire in my cheeks at my mother's announcement.

'We'd better have a jar so,' my dad said, fatalistically.

I lifted my glass to indicate I was sorted, my mother gave

hers over for a refill. The family got comfy and I promised myself I'd leave at the earliest convenient moment, i.e. very, very soon. I tried changing the subject. 'How was the golf?' I asked.

All eyes, including a pair of feline, turned on me as if I had lost my marbles thinking that ploy would work. There was nothing for it, I prepared to run.

I have never been the most graceful of creatures. I trip over loose match sticks, invisible bumps, cross words. I am especially prone to arse-over-heel activity when under family pressure. It was therefore inevitable that I would get up from the table, bang my thigh hard against it, recoil into the kitchen chair I had just vacated and keel over on to the floor. I was wearing a floral print skirt which reached to mid-shin when left to its job, but now shrouded my waist revealing plenty of knickered buttock. I was also on all fours, which was not an elegant pose. I let my forehead rest momentarily on the linoleum, trying a desperate spell to banish me to anywhere but here. A bronzed hand reached into view to help me to my feet. Andy's. As I was not exactly in a position to be choosy about where help came from, I grabbed his paw and he hauled me up. I made a deal of fixing myself while gathering breath and avoiding suffocation. My face was boiling with embarrassment.

'I'm fine, I'm fine,' I chanted.

I could hear the muffled gulps of the Streets as they suppressed their laughter. I looked at my watch and said, 'Oh, dear, this is broken,' as if my latest spill had done the damage. Anything to keep me motoring, really. 'Must go now.' I bolted for the door.

I looked back to see my mother clutching her chest. 'I needed that,' she said, smiling.

Andy wore the pained expression of someone who wanted to join in the fun, but didn't want to hurt my feelings. Nice, but a bit superfluous.

'Don't mind them,' I said to him. 'I'm the clown act round here.' I gave a self-deprecating shrug of the shoulders. Inside of me my chest had caved in and all pride was on leave. I felt resigned to it and almost didn't mind.

'I've got to go myself,' Andy told the gathering. He thanked the lads for the game of golf and they made the usual promises to hook up again soon for more of the same. He pecked my mother's cheek. Then he put his arm around my waist and said, 'I'll see you to your car.' It felt fine, actually.

And after that it didn't take much to bring him home with me. The pretext was a cup of coffee. We were barely in the front door when we started to claw at each other. My clothes stuck to me from apprehension and the cloying heat of the day. Andy's clung to him too which meant we both started from the same block, except that he knew what colour panties I was wearing, due to my earlier clumsiness. I couldn't have cared less. The cool cotton sheets calmed our ardour for all of twenty seconds, then we lost ourselves in pleasure. Well, I thought with handy reasoning, I can't get any more pregnant, might as well enjoy myself. I neglected to mention my happy news to the man I made love to.

After the first time, and before a number of others, Andy said, 'Guess I can date you now, seeing as how you're unattached.'

Another time that scenario would have been near future perfect in tense, but there was a baby now, and I could only be half-certain of its parentage.

'We'll see,' I said, after a moment.

We would have to.

I was dozing in Andy's arms many hours later when the phone rang. I murmured my number and a voice whispered, 'Cherry's home.' I started into a sitting position, jolting us both wide awake.

'Who is this?' I asked, fear caressing my spine and raising hairs all over my body.

The caller disconnected, leaving a mocking dial tone in my ear. I reached for the bedside light.

'Trouble?' Andy wanted to know.

'Probably,' I said. 'I've got to go somewhere.'

'Leo, it's midnight. There is no way I'm letting you out that door unless I'm with you.'

'Andy, I appreciate the offer, but this is not something that concerns you,' I explained. I was just covering my sorry ass. Of course he was bloody coming with me, I just had to get him to insist. He did. I capitulated. Result all round.

Madonna Mansions didn't look any more appealing at night than it did during the day. The block housing 68A was particularly dark. There was a reason: all the light bulbs had been kicked out. I couldn't quash the thought that this was no accident. I was glad of my male escort, but secretly; this was no time to go to pieces. Andy held a torch and I shone the penlight attached to my keyring. We made our way slowly through the clutter of stairwells and up on to the fourth-floor corridor with the broken door we sought. The complex was unnaturally quiet.

I moved ahead and reached for the door with my foot. The penlight faltered, it had seen too much pappy television. I shook it as I continued towards the entrance, but was pulled back by my companion in mid-stride. He pointed the flash lamp at a blood-filled syringe stuck in the empty key hole, its spike rusted brown with congealed human tissue. I screeched quietly and jumped back. It was a booby trap, but it had failed.

Andy kicked the door in and we followed his beam into the airless apartment. I tried the light switch but the darkness persisted, which didn't surprise me much. The stillness seemed unbearably loud. We inched forward, as quiet as the air around us. The main room was empty except for maggots feasting on the abandoned rubbish. My stomach wanted to heave in protest at the stench and the fluorescent wriggling of the grubs as they consumed their rotting meal. We turned into the bathroom. It had nothing to offer but my startled, pale face staring back from a speckled mirror. Then we entered the bedroom and a wail rose in my throat.

A young woman lay face down on the bed, her arms spread out towards the pink, velveteen headboard. The thin blue lines of her veins were scratched and pocked by the needle's damage. Their pulse was still now. She was dead. She wore a navy blue dress, and her body was twisted to reveal one large white button.

I was gagging gently into my handbag when Hugo Nelson arrived with his back-up team.

'It's all right,' I said, giving the cop a wan smile. 'I didn't contaminate the scene.' I indicated my ruined bag. 'Good thing I left my Gucci at home.'

They set to work, rigging lamps off a generator and shedding cruel light on the body in the bedroom. The flat teemed with busy personnel in white jumpsuits.

'I can't leave until they turn the body over,' I told Andy. 'If you want to go, I'll understand.'

'Don't be ridiculous, woman,' he said. 'It doesn't suit you. I'm staying.'

'Thanks.'

'You're welcome.' He paused. 'I'm loath to say "any time", in case you take me up on it.'

I repeated my wan grimace, it was all I could muster. Andy put his arm around me.

'I was impressed by how cool you were, calling the cops and all that.'

'Force of habit,' I assured him. 'It was drummed into me. I'll never get used to death, though.'

'The day you do is the day you should retire.'

He was probably right. I sneaked a lean into his shoulder and breathed his delicious, comforting scent. I wanted to tell him I loved him then. I wanted to tell him I was in love with him too. I believed those feelings right there and then at that moment. But the timing was off. We were within two yards of a dead body, and within orbit of a growing life he knew nothing about. It was not appropriate. I held my peace. And, oddly, it did feel like peace.

Hugo Nelson appeared in the bedroom doorway, tired wrinkles etched into his face. He looked half-beaten by time and the tide of wretchedness he had to wade through. I stepped forward, my frown matching his. He held my gaze.

'It's not Nina,' he said, eventually.

I let loose a cry I didn't know was inside of me, and felt Andy's supporting arm around me once again. My knees joined the rest of my body in the shakes of released tension and relief.

'No birthmark,' Hugo explained. 'It's Cherry, we think.'

'Any idea what killed her?' Andy asked.

Hugo gave him a suspicious look, he was an intruder after all, then decided to direct the answer at me.

'There's the remains of a deal and works on the bed, so she may have overdosed. You can't always tell immediately with a junkie. We'll have to do a post-mortem. I'm going to insist on priority, so we'll have a preliminary report tomorrow. Call me.

'Interesting detail in the bathroom,' he added conversationally. 'Bottle of magnolia blossom bubble bath.'

Tiny Shortall had been full of the stuff when he reached his watery grave. Yes, sirree, bob, very interesting indeed.

He walked away and we were dismissed. As we reached Andy's car, I realised that I had been using the term 'we' for the evening, instead of my usual 'I' for personal dealings. It was a habit I could not indulge myself in, but I was too tired and upset to start remedial action as yet.

Normality reigned at number 11 The Villas and I wanted to kiss every last hairy bit of it. There were exceptions, of course: Barry was gone, Andy was here, I was pregnant. Other than that, it was run o' the mill. Great. I filled Andy in on the main aspects of the case over tea, then tried to make him leave. He was as stubborn as me when he wanted. All the time, I suspected. I lost the battle, gladly, and chalked it down to knowing when to give in, a great and under-praised skill I hoped to become fond of. We went back to bed. I curled into his body and sailed into safety. I didn't care how long it lasted as long as it got me through these small hours. There are times when my own lack of ambition makes me want to cheer.

Later, when I woke, Cherry was still dead and Nina was still missing. But Andy was still in my bed. Be still, my beating heart.

NINETEEN

What's the first rule of a love affair? Don't know, couldn't tell you. And now was no time to be thinking about it because it didn't apply. I sat at the kitchen table in a cold sweat, realising that I was in a classic cycle of dependence. I had chucked one crutch out and the bin men had not collected his cast-offs by the time he'd been replaced in my bed. I was a textbook nightmare of jumbled emotions and needs. Andy would have to go.

The initial stages of organising this were easy, as he had to get home to change clothes. Not that the rumpled duds from yesterday didn't hang gracefully off his more than adequate frame. I pushed those thoughts to the back of my troubled mind and pushed him out of the door. He thrust his watch into my hand.

'You can have this until yours is fixed,' he said.

I looked at the chunky designer chrome and felt as uneasy as if it had been an engagement ring. I would deal with this later in the calm light of solitude. This afternoon *is* another time, I told myself in my best Scarlett O'Hara. My wrist dragged down to my side under the unexpected weight of the gift.

Ciara was walking up the path as I waved him away.

'You don't waste much time,' she commented, airily.

I dragged her through the door roughly. 'Booty call,' I said.

She rolled her eyes up. 'I tell you far too much.' She took in the watch. 'Cuffing costs extra,' she said. 'Amateur.'

She was drinking coffee and petting the cats by the time Ronan arrived. Bizarrely, I was glad he hadn't seen Andy, as if somehow that left me with more options. I administered yet another mental head smack as I reminded myself that Ronan was a child.

'I've heard of a two-horse town,' Ciara was saying about Clunesboro. 'But this is a two-*arse* one. Jeez, what a dump! One chipper, a SPAR, a bookies and seventeen pubs, right at the very back of beyond. No wonder Nina scarpered.'

'So that was the reason?' I couldn't hide my disappointment.

'Well, yes and no.'

I brightened.

'I didn't get an awful lot out of Deborah because she wouldn't stop crying. She's in bits that Nina hasn't sent for her.'

'Isn't Deborah the elder sister?' I asked.

Ciara nodded. 'Put it this way, Nina is a leader, Deborah is a sheep. Anyhow, the long and the short of it is that it was only a matter of time before Nina split. But it was hurried along by something.'

She gave Ronan the signal to continue.

'She'd been hanging out with the local hot stuff, Jamesy Briarty. He's first in line to inherit the biggest farm in the area and in the meantime he's driving a fast car and shagging women.'

'Nina?'

'Seems so.'

My heart sank to think she might be joining me as a statistic, in the unmarried mothers' section. What had been in the country's air for the last few months?

'Was she pregnant, then?'

'Deborah doesn't think so. If she were, she'd have written "boo-hoo" on a card.'

That was something, at least.

'So why leave town?' I asked.

Ciara started to laugh, then Ronan joined in. Soon I found myself grinning.

'What?' I asked. *'What?'*

Ronan eventually straightened his face. 'Jamesy told me he might've given Nina the clap.'

It wasn't exactly comforting to reflect that, in the last throes of the twentieth century, there were still towns in Ireland small enough to drive a person out, because news of a sexually transmitted disease could ruin a reputation or a whole family's name, especially if that person was a young woman. Was there no one she could have turned to?

'Presumably Jamesy is delighted with himself?' I enquired.

Ronan nodded. 'Very macho. And not the sharpest knife in the drawer.'

'Does Mrs Clancy know any of this?' I asked them.

'No,' Ciara said. 'And we didn't think it was up to us to tell her.' She looked at her watch. 'Don't you have an exam this afternoon?' she said to her brother.

'What?' I yelped. 'You're in the middle of your exams and we've been distracting you?'

Ronan blushed. 'Nothing I can't handle. It's kid's stuff.'

I shooed him out of the door, offering incoherent apologies and good luck wishes and generally making an eejit of myself. Ciara smiled knowingly at the scene, making me feel even more foolish. I busied myself with more coffee making to cover my tracks. She let me away with that.

'Oh, to round off my brilliant endeavours,' she told me, 'I got word to Tiny's brother and he's paying us a visit after lunch.'

'Nice work, Gillespie.'

I went through my own night's events, leaving out the more personal aspects. Without them, it didn't make for cheerful listening.

'Poor old Cherry,' Ciara said.

We took time to remember a girl we had never met; it made it all so much sadder.

'Right,' I said, shaking myself. 'You feed them.' I pointed at the fur brigade. 'I'll shower and then we'll pay Hugo Nelson a visit.

No. 4 might not suspect he was to be left behind if Ciara was doling out the goodies, I thought, the change might put him off the scent. We could still hear his barking and crying as we got to the corner of The Villas and turned for town.

'You are one cruel bitch,' Ciara said, twisting the knife.

The State Pathologist's suite reminded me of a hospital. Some rooms held worried relatives, others were theatres with many of the same surgical implements but none of the pressure to keep a patient alive. The job here was to unravel death. It didn't make the process any more wholesome to someone as squeamish as myself. We sat outside in a beige corridor surrounded by the smell of putrefaction and disinfectant, and watched trolleys of the dead being wheeled by at surprisingly regular intervals.

'There's a lot of it about,' Ciara said.

I settled into the annihilation of a range of nails. I shaved off slice after slice of hard enamel, leaving pink, throbbing flesh aching in air it should never have been exposed to. I well knew where my quick was by the time I got to the second victim, and it was a tender place, but I was on a roll and just couldn't stop.

'You'll regret that,' Ciara said.

'I'm an adult, I've made an informed choice and you're not suffering from toxins because of it, so bog off.' I was obviously racked with guilt at my vile habit.

'Ooh, defensive,' Ciara sang.

'Don't start,' I warned. 'You've got your piercings.'

'I've also got tattoos you've never seen, but I don't go round upsetting people by displaying them. Except for my parents,' she added. 'And that doesn't count because it's my duty as a rebel fiend. Your fingers are in a shocking state.'

'I know,' I confessed. 'But you have to admit it's a professional cull.'

'Observing you, it's not the first,' my companion judged.

I shook my head. 'You'd think I'd have learned from past mistakes.'

'I'm not so sure about that whole method of learning,' she mused. 'I mean, where's the fun in it? You've got to go out and learn the hard way sometimes, so that when you're reformed you can be a proper pain in the hole about it.'

'I like the way you think, Gillespie.'

'I've noticed.'

I returned to my munching. It was a habit as much as Cherry's or Alice's, with self-mutilation as part and parcel.

Only difference was this would probably not kill me.

If Hugo Nelson had slept, it had been in what he'd lain down in. Black circles ringed his red eyes. His hair seemed to stand on end. He reeked of cigarette smoke and bad news.

'She didn't die of an overdose,' was his opener. He had our attention and didn't need tricks to retain interest, but still he raised the game.

'Cause of death was an embolism, which is basically when a blood vessel becomes clogged. In this case, it was air: most likely the by-product of a botched abortion. Seems there's a big syringe used to pump soapy water into the womb and it can cause air to enter the system, enough for it to be fatal.'

He sank wearily into an uncomfortable plastic chair.

'Ma Hogan,' I ventured.

'Perhaps,' he acknowledged. 'If we could find her.'

I had my mouth open to tell him about Dean's theory as to where she was based when Hugo took a big breath and continued.

'We have another friend of yours in here,' he said. 'Alice. I believe you were talking to her last night on Price Street.'

The flimsy bottom of my world was rapidly falling away.

'What happened?' I croaked.

'Overdose in this case. But the interesting thing is she was using very high-grade heroin. Not your ordinary street brown. Quite a white powder. Very expensive. Would have been way too potent for her. The spike was still in her arm when she was found. I've ordered toxicology on the remains of the deal we found on her and she's here for the pathologist to have a look at. She'll still end up as an OD statistic 'cos she probably shot up herself, but whoever gave her the stuff would have known its effect.'

A long time later he met my eye.

'Looks like a lot of the people you're interested in are ending up dead.'

I was in that strange place ruled by anger and helplessness. I felt responsible for the two deaths. I had not lifted a finger physically against the dead and yet I might as well have pulled a trigger. Now I had to find out what had happened and bring these women some sort of justice, if possible.

'Follow me,' I said to the policeman. 'I think I can help you locate Ma Hogan.'

It was a start.

As we left the building I asked Hugo how he knew I'd spoken with Alice.

'There were two cops watching. They're not half as thick as you'd imagine.'

I could have sworn I saw the traces of a grin on his stubbled face.

I rang Con and brought him up to speed on events. He arranged to meet us at the building we thought was Ma Hogan's base.

'How did Dean get on?' I asked.

'Great. He got his kids back. It was one of the good days.'

This one did not feel like it was going to match that. On top of everything else, the chemical smell of the morgue was dogging me, and my stomach spasmed lightly each time I breathed in. As the car passed the railway station, I saw the newspaper seller at his post. He was smiling. It was heartening to see a little happiness in an ugly world.

The glorious weather only served to highlight the destitution of Mayville Street. My spirits rose a notch to see Father Con Considine striding purposefully in our direction. He passed young Billy, who promptly disappeared into the maw of a building. We formed a select group at the ad hoc entrance of a clapped out, three-storey house, still in sight of the main road with the disembodied sounds of its traffic faint on the air. Hugo's back-up wore protective clothing and latex gloves were distributed. Ciara, myself and Con were warned to stay well back and not to touch anything. We were being tolerated; that was a compliment. One wrong step, we were out; that was a fact. Hugo marshalled the troops, ordered some of his men around the back and prepared to go in the front with the rest. We seemed to take a deep communal breath, then moved forward with delicate purpose.

The dim interior was musty and lit by shafts of random light spilling in through cracks in the walls and slats in the loosely boarded windows. Dust danced and swirled gently in the patterned, second-hand sunshine. It lent a surreal, cinematic beauty to the scene. The smell of cat spray did not. I suspected the presence of spiders and their cousins. Perspiration began to gather high up my body, getting ready for a good run down my back. I was sure I smelt off, fear perfuming my aura.

Abandoned rooms opened in all directions. In one, a lone couch sat in the middle of the floor, begging company. Its arm was torn and stuffing escaped from the wound. It needed a cuddle and a good home. Suddenly there was a rustle at my side and something hurtled past in the air, brushing my face as it passed. I yelped. The company stopped to look. A pigeon had flown up out of the shadows past me and roosted, cooing, on an old picture rail.

'Sorry,' I apologised. 'Fucking vermin,' I whispered at the bird as we walked on.

'All God's creatures,' Con reproved.

We headed up some creaky wooden stairs. There was a

change in the atmosphere. The air smelt different. Perhaps the cold attack of bleach and disinfectant on the sinuses? Perhaps fanciful thinking on the part of a nervous private detective with an overactive imagination?

'Grand and dry,' Hugo commented. 'Forensics love that. They don't care for the spores in the damp, and they really hated Madonna Mansions for that.'

A matching set of empty rooms echoed the ground floor, with one notable exception, a large room to the rear of the building. I was reduced to shivers even before I stepped up to its portal; I really had to stop watching late-night horror movies on television. This was the place, I told myself. This was where Cherry had come on the visit which ultimately led to her death. It had to be.

A table sat in the middle of the floor, pine bleached white with scouring powder and elbow grease. Was this where the unfortunate 'patient' was operated on? A sofa bed lay in a corner, flanked by an armchair in a mockery of aftercare. The floor was swept clean and the surroundings were relatively dust-free, but not hygienic enough to deal with a human body at its most exposed. A roll of unused black plastic had fallen on to the floor and unravelled across the planks. Otherwise the room was empty, quiet witness to the secrets hidden in this building, many of them unimaginable memories now, invisible to the human eye.

'When is bin day round here?' Hugo asked, breaking a tortuous silence.

All attention turned on Con.

'Yesterday,' he replied.

A dull groan escaped from the group.

'Any waste from here went then,' Hugo surmised. 'Or got thrown into an incinerator somewhere.' He ordered a thorough search. 'Just in case we get viable scraps of DNA. Probably a fool's errand.'

Ma Hogan's mobile clinic had moved on.

Con stayed to pray, while Ciara and myself took our earliest chance to escape.

'I'm more of a coward than I thought,' I said, leaning against a wall outside. My armpits were moist and uncomfortable, my back saturated. I felt the grit of the stale air in my lungs, the contamination of dirt in the folds of my skin and the roots of my hair.

'I wouldn't be a bit surprised if that place was haunted with all it's been through,' Ciara muttered.

'Do I detect superstition in a Gillespie?' I teased.

'Parascientific observation,' she invented.

'Reason or rubbish, you decide,' I intoned.

She pushed me, but couldn't drum up any venom to accompany it.

An ashen Con emerged, looking as if he'd lived in the shade for years and was unused to strong light. He was battered by life at the thin end of the wedge and would need that holiday soon by the look of things.

'We have even more bad news,' I told him. 'Cherry was found late last night.'

'Dead,' he guessed. 'You know, I never met her but she was a parishioner, so I'll be burying her. Strange, isn't it?'

'I was the one who found her, yet I never saw her face,' I added, understanding his difficulty.

We were reluctant to leave a shaken Con by himself. He eventually convinced us this was part and parcel of his ministry, that he had a funeral to prepare, a flock to tend as well as the unexpected problems that came with everyday life in his parish. And, most pertinent of all, we would only get in his way. We headed back to the office to meet with the remaining Shortall twin. Anything was better than this awful place, I thought, scanning the landscape of hopelessness at Mayville. What awaited us at the Old Sweeps' place was more of a surprise.

I drove us back to The Villas first to collect Ciara's car and No. 4. The area seemed like a pretty Dingly Dell after the harshness of the inner city. I felt like a privileged popinjay in my cosy circumstances. I could have my baby, I didn't need to resort to the butchery of a back alley abortion. And even if I had opted for termination, I had my choice of clinics in England and the price of the operation and air fare; luxury compared with life on the margins.

No. 4 leapt into my arms and gave some heart-breaking whimpers.

'He's worse than a child,' I told Ciara, presuming this to be true.

'Or a big lump of a useless boyfriend.'

'Ah, no,' I assured her. 'Nowhere near as awful as that.'

I checked my messages. One was from Barry and sounded pathetic, so I skipped it. The second was a whole lot more trouble. It was from my grandmother, Mary Ellen Doyle.

'I've heard the news. Time you got rid of that gobshite. How's it going with young Raynor? I'll call over to you soon and we'll sort something out.'

Ciara saw my face. 'Bad?' she wanted to know.

'Worse than that. Looks like I'm going to have to move house.'

We were stalled at the traffic lights leading on to the Coast Road when Barry threw himself on the bonnet of the car. He wore a pained expression, which could have been the result of

225

the collision with the car or, hey, maybe he missed me. Either way, I was immune. I was also beyond platitudes and didn't listen too hard to the stream of pleasantries issuing from him. No. 4 was barking, too, which helped. Barry was big with the gestures and, when these moved on to the entreaty section of his performance, he even had the suggestion of a tear balanced elegantly on his lower lashes. It was one of his best, notwithstanding that I had vision but little sound. Mime's not a favourite of mine, so I was fine and dandy with this rendition of *Lassie Come Home*.

'He's good,' was Ciara's assessment.

'A bit over the top for my taste,' I said, as I revved the engine to warn him that we were moving off.

'Yellow card,' I muttered.

He didn't take the hint.

I revved once more, thus waving a motoring red card, took my foot off the brake and Barry Agnew ended up on his semi-famous backside in the middle of the road.

'Smooth action,' Ciara said, approvingly.

'Yeah,' I nodded. 'I have to confess I'm pleased with that myself.'

A worrying turn occurred when we got to the car park. Molly was missing and his deputy, Gerry, was on duty, hours before his shift usually started.

'He's not well,' we were told. 'And he mustn't be, 'cos the doctors told him to rest and he's actually doing it.'

This was not good news. No. 4 ran around the plot trying to find his friend. He looked confused and pale under his skewbald coat.

'Keep us posted,' I told Gerry. 'And keep an eye on Molly.'

'Will do. Don't be worrying now, he's been through a lot in his life, and he'll get through this.'

It had to be true. Too much of the old order was changing and I didn't want to have to do without Molly. I dragged the dog along as we left, and in turn we all dragged our feet, eight of them between us. It made a racket on the gravel.

'This is one piss-poor, shithole of a day,' Ciara summed up.

As ever, she'd put her finger right on the pulse of it.

TWENTY

'Do I know you?' I asked the man sitting on the top step of the stairs by the offices of Leo Street and Co. He seemed familiar, yet I was sure I'd never met him.

He was chunky without being fat, but still threatened to burst out of his suit. I suspected it had been bought when he was leaner, that bit of quality trotted out when the need arose. Sitting in it had only readjusted his dimensions and put further strain on the pressured seams. The shirt he wore should have been binned long ago as it almost certainly involved Bri-nylon, a sinister by-product of modern technology with the power to induce sweat and vacuum-trap it, all at once. His hands were vast spades, with the torn nails and calluses of work on the land. His face was ruddy from a life led outdoors. A farmer, I was willing to bet.

'I'm Aidan Clancy,' he said, in a mixture of accusation and vague embarrassment at being here unannounced.

'Nina's brother?'

'Right.'

He was drinking tea from a mug I recognised, but that did not compute as the mug was the property of Mrs Mack Ltd and strictly for her personal use. I said as much.

'She took pity on me,' he explained. 'I was a bit upset when I got here, what with the office being deserted and so on. And the worry about Nina and all.'

'Jesus,' Ciara swore. 'She has a heart. I need to sit down.'

'She was going to let me in, too, but I didn't think that'd be right.'

'It's never stopped her before,' I murmured.

We debunked to the interior of company headquarters.

'Strange thing,' Aidan commented. 'She told me I looked just like my sister. How could she know that?'

I remembered the missing package from Monday morning, which had so strangely fetched up in the hands of the Macks.

'She's seen Nina's photograph,' I said.

I introduced Ciara to him.

'I heard you were in Clunesboro yesterday', he said.

Ciara nodded. 'Didn't find Nina, though, so I didn't disturb you.'

Aidan smiled at her attempt to lighten the mood of the case. While we could still smile, maybe everything was fine.

We settled with various refreshments in the mismatched office seats. I planted myself in the most comfortable of them, because my ankle ached from its buggy rage run in, my elbows stung from my fall outside the Raven while my bottom and coccyx throbbed from the same. All other strenuous physical activity had involved pleasure, but it left its own brand of pain. I was bloody exhausted. And this was without adding the strain of the case. It took a while to convince myself that even the longest hour still had only sixty minutes and that I would eventually see the back of this interval in my life.

No. 4 chose the newest lap in town and his host did not object. I thought it might help him relax, and Aidan seemed calmer for it too. He got around to explaining his presence.

'I had a call from a cop. He said I should be here 'cos Nina would be turning up soon.'

'Was this Hugo Nelson?'

Aidan looked blank.

'Did he have a Cork accent?'

'No, now that you mention it. He didn't have much of an accent at all. I'd be hard put to tell you where he came from. He didn't say much either, just that really, that I should come to Dublin.'

I reached for the phone, intrigued. The short answer to my question for Hugo Nelson was 'no'. So who had called Aidan?

We sat around just looking at one another, which was bad for the image of a busy and vibrant detective agency. Especially when the client's son has arrived on the information of an unknown caller who is not charging for his services. I found a finger in my mouth, mid-chew. I removed the digit carefully, but then worried the nail with my thumb under cover of the desk.

'Are you staying over?' I asked our visitor, for diversion.

'Eh, yeah. I think I should.'

'Are you fixed up with somewhere?'

'Not yet, no.'

'Right. You may as well stay at my place. That way I can keep an eye on you.' I flashed him a beaming smile. 'All part of the service.'

He looked most apprehensive and I did my best to reassure him.

'I don't start biting people till after midnight,' I said. 'You'll be well tucked up by then.'

'That's not quite true,' Ciara corrected. 'There was that time when . . .'

I gestured with my hand to hush her. Aidan started to smile. We were going to get along fine.

He remembered something in his bag. 'My mother sent you these,' he told me, proudly handing over a mound of ham sandwiches, wrapped in foil. 'She says you don't look after yourself and you could do with some fattening up.' He caught my eye. 'She says. I think you look grand.'

As compliments went, it would have to do. In the meantime we chowed down on the unexpected feast. My nails breathed a sigh of relief.

Fifteen minutes later he was up to speed on the Dublin end of the week. I don't think the report left any of us feeling all that confident of a result soon, particularly a good one. I became even more concerned that my prank with the parcels had led somehow to Cherry's death, though she'd seemed doomed from the time she was reportedly dragged, screaming, from her apartment by unidentified men. I put another finger in my mouth and tackled a lengthy pinkie nail. Then, there was the Friday Fair to consider: would Nina go now that Cherry was dead?

We were all in separate, silent worlds when a knock rattled on the glass panel of the door. Three grown people jumped involuntarily out of their chairs and No. 4 barked up a storm. We calmed ourselves and were composed in a tableau as Dermot Shortall entered. Then we waited, frozen in our poses, for ten minutes until he stopped crying. The resultant stiffness cancelled out a lot of the sympathy we might otherwise have felt for him. Even No. 4 looked annoyed.

Shorty missed his twin and lost no time telling us that, once he'd finished dampening a whole pack of tissues. We were treated to childhood pranks, reminiscences, more tears. I had to get him on to Doc Phelan before his misery provoked the manic laughter of the recently driven insane, i.e. everyone else in the office.

The mention of the name produced an instant change in his demeanour. 'Bastard,' he exclaimed, which was neither surprising nor original under the circumstances.

'What's your connection with his daughter Cherry?' I asked.

'She and my brother were in love,' he replied, simply.

'And that's it?' Ciara let out. 'That's what this is all about?'

'Yes.'

Forget drugs, forget turf wars, think good old-fashioned Shakespearean stories of feuding families and star-crossed lovers. I almost smacked my head at the revelation.

'I'm presuming Doc Phelan did not approve,' I said, hardly needing to express the idea in words.

'No. The fucking hypocrite.' Shorty gathered himself. 'He was the one who got Cherry hooked on drugs in the first place. She used to sell for him, and eventually she got curious. She started small, 'course, and worked her way up to heroin. Phelan didn't care. She was totally under his control then, which is where he wanted her. It's where he wants everyone. But he couldn't have had that with Tiny or me, and not with Cherry anymore once she was with Tiny. He went bananas when she told him herself and Tiny were running off together. They planned to go to England first, then see from there. The only way to get away from that fucker is to leave altogether. And there was the baby to consider. Now it looks like I'll have to take her somewhere safe and into rehab and all. I don't mind, it's for Tiny. And

Cherry is all right when you get to know her, too. For a junkie.'

No one wanted to look him in the eye then. Eventually I said, 'I'm afraid there's some bad news about Cherry.'

He raised a lined face to mine. 'Ah, no,' he said, shaking his head sadly. 'No.'

'She was found dead in her flat at Madonna Mansions last night.'

He threw his head back, trying to recapture his tears, desperately fighting for control. I was oddly unmoved. Here was a man who sold potential death to the vulnerable, finally coming to know grief. He hadn't given much choice to the people whose lives he ruined daily, the ones he squeezed for protection, scammed out of their savings or supplied drugs to.

I let him wet another few paper hankies. Ciara had pushed a waste basket by his chair to catch the debris. Nice teamwork.

'This is Aidan Clancy,' I said to Dermot Shortall. 'Our priority now is to find his sister Nina.'

'How did Cherry die?' Shorty asked.

'I don't think the police have decided yet,' I hedged.

And then I let myself get angry and do a very impetuous thing. 'Ma Hogan seems implicated,' I said.

I knew immediately it was a death sentence, and that I'd had no right to give it. I won't blame my hormones, just a weird sense of craving justice for Cherry. But even that's an excuse. I had no right to cause another human being's death. I think of it every day now and if there is a hell, I guess I can look forward to it. I'll probably meet Ma Hogan there, and a few more I know, when my time comes.

Dermot Shortall got to his feet. 'Thank you for being so honest with me. I'll take it from here.'

'The police are dealing with it,' I protested, the words ringing hollow and late.

'There are lots of things the Gardai can't deal with. Relax. I've lived in that jungle all my life and I know a thing or two. Nothing bad will happen to anyone who doesn't deserve it.'

I was terrified, then, of the chain of events I had set in motion. I needed Shortall to leave so that I could tell Hugo Nelson about the carnage I had probably unleashed.

Dermot turned to Aidan. 'I've met Nina. She's a nice girl. I'll keep an eye out for her.'

I thanked providence he didn't want to shake our hands as he left. I didn't need a Judas kiss to compound my guilt.

'Will you quit whipping yourself?' Ciara said, crossly, a few minutes later. 'How long do you think it would be before he'd found out about Ma Hogan anyway? Let's concentrate on finding Nina, and forget situations we can do nothing about.'

I phoned Hugo all the same. Shit happens was the gist of what he felt, one less to worry about. I left a suitably appalled pause.

'If it makes you feel any better I'll try to have the witch picked up, but I don't hold out much hope of that if she's evaded us this long. Get back to the job you're paid to do,' he advised. 'And I'll go back to mine, if you'll stop wasting my time.'

I was stinging from his rebuke and my own to myself. For the first time in an age, I really fancied a drink.

'What better place than the Raven?' I said as I led our small posse forth. 'We can check out the Phelans in full grief.'

'If there is any,' Ciara pointed out.

I was talked out of this most foolish of my plans by the time we hit the Far Shore on Abbey Street. We took ourselves in, leaving No. 4 in the shade of the porch with a saucer of water for the heat.

'He can't be trusted to behave in a pub,' I explained. 'He has history there.'

I wanted Guinness, mentally adjusting from the notion that it was an indulgence to the idea that I needed iron for my pregnancy. It also felt good to be in a pub in the middle of the afternoon, my favourite time for a drink when I'm having one.

'This seems like an awful waste of time,' I said to Aidan. 'But the fact is the cops are watching Madonna Mansions as well as Mayville now, so we'd only be in the way. It's hard to stay hidden under those circumstances. And we're not charging for this either, so that should cover your next question.'

It did and he tried to relax. He took a mouthful of his pint, savoured it, then downed half in one mighty swallow.

'You know your way around that stuff,' I said.

'That I do.'

We settled into the vinyl seat of our alcove. I heroically resisted the urge to bite off a few more nails, just doing one in. It could hardly be billed as satisfaction.

Ciara stared at me, pointedly. I sniffed. She gave one of her snorts, the one which translates as 'you're full of shit'. I turned to Aidan.

'Why were you and your sisters so cranky-looking in the photograph your mother gave me? She said it was taken on Nina's birthday.'

'I know the one you mean,' he said. 'The neighbour who took it was a dirty aul' thing. Always looking in the girls' bedroom window and that. Nina swears he was stealing underwear off the washing line too. Still, he got his come-uppance in the end,'

I held my breath.

'Oh, not me,' he added quickly. 'I didn't do anything to him, though Mammy would've killed him if she'd known. No, he had his leg broken by one of his own heifers. After that we used to call her Mary secretly, in honour of our mother, for the laugh.'

'Nature's version of crime and retribution,' I ventured.

'You could call it that,' he agreed.

We were well comfortable, and trying to chat about anything but the case, when my mobile started flinging up calls in quick succession. First number to flash was Barry's and I ignored it. Then came Andy's, which I answered. He would join us soon. I must have been fidgeting with his watch because Ciara guessed who'd phoned, perceptive wench.

'It's not such a scoop,' I told her, loftily. 'He's on his way here now so you'll meet him yourself.'

Aidan looked frightened of the 'woman talk' he thought was going on.

'You grew up in a house of women, you couldn't be scared of us,' Ciara observed.

'It's because I did that I am,' he told us.

'A wise man,' I acknowledged.

The third set of rings displayed my grandmother's number on the screen but she was beaten to an answer by an extraordinary event. That was the moment Nina Clancy chose to walk through the door.

TWENTY-ONE

I have nothing against miracles, especially if they're helpful but, along with magic tricks, they annoy the legs off me if I can't figure out how they're done. Moreover, in the case of Nina Clancy's reappearance, I was blameless of great feats of deduction or classic gumshoe brilliance, which could have been an ego bruiser on another occasion. As it was, I was glad to see her, however she had effected this present manifestation.

It would have been a waste of breath to say we'd been looking everywhere for her, doubly so as she was buried under her brother's oxter and I was afraid she might disappear all over again. He released her, reluctantly, by which time Ciara had bought him another pint and I had moved on to fizzy water.

'What'll you have yourself, Nina?' I asked. 'To celebrate your return.'

'Something strong, with lots of vodka,' she suggested.

'Lemonade,' her brother said. 'She's only sixteen.'

She looked older: gaunt shadows under pale skin, the crimson-lidded eyes of sleepless nights and premature adult worry.

'Cripes, Aidan, how long have you been wearing that shirt?' she asked. 'It STINKS.'

'Good healthy sweat,' he protested. 'Nothin' wrong with it.'

He couldn't help the smile on his big, red, happy face.

'How did you know where to find us?' I had to ask, mistrustful of our good and welcome fortune.

'Razor Cullen told me. He made me come. Drove me in his poncey car, actually. Can I have a packet of crisps? I'm starving. Cheese'n'onion, not the vinegar ones.'

I pictured Razor's sullen, chiselled face, hair slick as the inside of an oil tanker. It was enough to induce a shiver, which it did.

'He said Aidan was in town too,' Nina continued.

She ripped open the crisps Ciara had thrown to her and stuffed them in her mouth, with table manners bad enough for a boarding-school pupil.

'My guess is that's who phoned Clunesboro and sent Aidan here,' I mused. 'But why?'

Nina knew the answer to that too.

'He said it'd call you off, that you were becoming a liability to his operation.'

I was gratified to hear I was a problem to the odious Cullen.

'We aim to please,' I said.

Ciara raised her glass in a satisfied toast to that.

'He's not the worst,' Nina insisted. 'He said he'd try to help Damo.'

'Cherry's little brother?'

'Yeah. Doc Phelan's got him back and God knows what'll

happen to him now. Razor's going to look out for him, in return for me getting you off his back. He's really pissed off with you for interfering. But he's okay, really.'

I hadn't the heart to get into an argument about a scumbag like Razor Cullen.

'We have to talk about Cherry,' I told Nina.

She turned two haunted eyes on me and promptly burst into tears, great heaves of misery rolling through her body. I was glad we were sheltered in the farthest snug from the landlord; crying, singing and snogging were all punishable by a barring from the Far Shore.

'You know she's dead, don't you?' I asked.

She gave a series of nods, then began to wail again. Aidan wedged her under his burly arm.

'Let it all out,' he told her. 'We love you, Nina.'

This time she didn't object to his body odour.

I ate two more fingernails, then changed hands. I was happy when Nina took a breather, on her behalf as well as that of my suffering paws. There were details that needed clearing up.

'I was the one who phoned you the night she died,' Nina gasped. 'Your number was on the photograph you gave our neighbour, Katarina.'

'Is that where you've been since Cherry was dragged off to Ma Hogan?'

'Yes,' she sniffled.

I looked at Ciara who was shaking her head at the revelation. We had only been inches away from Nina two days ago in Madonna Mansions.

Tears streamed unchecked down Nina's face, then dripped from her jaw on to a grimy pink sweatshirt. The wet stain spread by the minute.

'I was with Cherry when it happened. I didn't know what to

241

do. She just started to jerk like she was having a fit. We didn't have a phone so I couldn't call an ambulance. And anyway, she wouldn't let go of my hand. She was in so much pain and crying and there was nothing I could do for her. And then suddenly she stopped and I knew she was dead. I tried to give her the kiss of life but it was no good. So I ran out to find a telephone to call you.'

'Why didn't you call the police?' I asked.

'I wanted someone friendly to find her first. I wanted some-one else to know where she was and what had happened.'

This account of Cherry's death didn't tally with the scene as I had found it with Andy. I remembered the body strewn across the bed with a spent needle alongside it.

'So Cherry didn't try to shoot up before she died?'

The youngster shook her head. 'She didn't have any gear. I suppose the attack was the DTs, the withdrawal must have killed her.'

No, it didn't, I thought, the backstreet abortion did. But Doc Phelan got his people to plant a spike on his own daughter to make it look like her death was drug related. That man was one warped individual.

'Why didn't you call your mother more?' came a harsh question from an unlikely source. Ciara was angry, which was surprising as torturing her own parents was part of her life brief.

Nina looked sheepishly at her then back to Aidan. 'It's hard to explain,' she stuttered.

'Try,' Ciara ordered.

'I didn't want to be a failure, a disappointment. I wanted to have something to show for myself when I got back.'

Aidan shushed her. 'You have nothing to prove to us, Nina. That was plain foolishness on your part.'

242

'And selfish,' Ciara added.

I waved a hand to quieten her, feeling that Nina had learned a lot of cruel lessons on her prideful journey and didn't need that to be rubbed in even more right then.

'You'd better phone Mammy,' Aidan told her, hauling her to her feet.

'She'll kill me,' Nina cried.

'No, she won't,' her elder brother said. 'She's been worried sick and the least you can do is talk to her. And if she does give out to you, itself, remember you probably deserve it – and whatever you do don't give as good as you get, like you normally do. The poor woman's been out of her mind.'

Nina streeled off after him in a parody of a teenage strop. I had seen my own niece pull this manoeuvre and was rudely reminded that Lucy was only a year younger. There were kids out on the streets every day and night fending for themselves, most of the population not wanting to know of their exist-ence, much less their difficulties.

Aidan and Nina insisted on using the payphone to ring Mrs Clancy. I remembered my first day of the search for her, looking for a certain telephone, meeting Billy, hoping for an impossible break. Mayville was no longer a world away but right here, right now, ingrained on my psyche and etched on the day.

We offered both company mobiles but were rebuffed.

'She wouldn't want us frying our brains,' they told us.

It's amazing the way the mention of brain nuking can make my ears warm up and tingle. I can go for months not noticing the phenomenon, but one article in the newspaper and I've got a tumour. Therefore, I was a bit reluctant to answer my phone when it chirped, but the number was Hugo Nelson's and he was The Law.

243

'I don't suppose you know of any next-of-kin for Alice Murney?'

'No. I didn't know her surname till now,' I confessed.

'Mmn. We can't find any, and there's a body to get rid of.'

'I wish you wouldn't talk about her like that,' I said. 'What'll happen?'

'State'll cremate her, then who knows?'

'Such a lonely end,' I sighed. 'I can't let that happen.' Another part of me took over to finish the thought. 'If I can organise a service and a funeral and all, will you release her to me?'

'It's unusual, but let me check. The State loves a bargain and the chance to save a few pence.'

It was just Ciara and me at the table now, looking into the middle distance.

'It looks like the Clancy case is closed,' I said.

'Loose ends though,' she countered. 'You know I hate those.'

'And I've told you before, sometimes you just have to walk away.'

Before she could challenge me, I added, 'Good news is we've got a wake and a funeral to organise.'

Nina and Aidan were back to hear that last bit, but outside forces overtook us before I could explain.

Old age seems to afford its occupants the permission to be cranky, break wind at will in public and issue candid speech, often through a full mouth. With timing and tact borne of all of these, my grandmother, Mary Ellen Doyle, burst through the door, took one look at Nina and said, 'Cheer up, could be worse, you could be dead,' to the young woman. A fresh onslaught of weeping ensued and I was sure that now we'd be definitely asked to leave.

Gran could have taken the eye out of a hypnotist with her gear. Her dress was long and purple, with a design of stars and half-moons, reminding anyone who knew her that she had the power to cast spells and raise demons, including herself. It was also uncomfortably redolent of the decor in Moonlites, which in turn summoned unwelcome memories of The Dark Side for me. Sorcery, then, was her middle name in what my mother liked to refer to as 'this phase she's going through'. Her sandals were a red lattice with big silver buckles and her toenails were painted darkest purple to match her frock. A canary yellow knapsack adorned her back, no doubt full of frogs' legs and newts' gizzards for her alchemy demonstrations with her octogenarian gang later. She looked happy.

Ciara bought an emergency pint of lager to shut my gran up and that worked a treat. It even gave me time to gather some pathetic excuses for diversion when the conversation inevitably got to my single status.

'How did you know where I was?' I seemed to be asking this question a lot that afternoon.

'Friend of mine saw your dog outside, remembered him from something in Kilbride's a few nights ago.'

She waited for me to fill her in.

'I didn't see the . . . eh . . . incident,' I told her, truthfully.

'It was spectacular, if my friend's account is anything to go by,' she assured me. 'We have a network,' she continued. 'You never know when it'll come in handy to be able to lay hands on someone, so he passed on the info.'

Looked like I didn't get the detective gene from the wind after all.

'You're right on time for our wake,' I said. 'We've lost some friends today and we want to mark their passing.'

'Nice one.' She grinned. 'Andy can help when he arrives.

245

He's just leaving his car in the underground car park.'

And there was a conversation stopper if ever I heard one. Life is never simple. One of the reasons it's so wonderful, I guess.

'Stop biting your nails,' my gran said. 'You'll give yourself worms.'

We had no time to waste, as the heavy borrowed watch on my arm told me. I handed a wad of notes to Ciara and told her to stand any drink required. Barry's cash was coming into its own at last. Meanwhile, I went outside to phone Con in peace. I needed a priest, a funeral and a cremation. He was the man who knew which strings to pull. He was also the man to invite us to his house that evening to continue our sorry celebrations of lives lost and regained, and some still hanging in the balance.

I walked back through the door with Andy on my arm. It was a foxy entrance, I felt, and why waste an opportunity to be a little flash? I decided to postpone my rejection of dependency until the following week: no use in cutting off my cuddle to spite my love life. At least I appeared to have one now, however brief it might turn out to be. No. 4 howled at his abandonment from outside. I felt surrounded by family and a measure of safety. Hell, we had numbers, if nothing else.

The rest of the day soon became a disjoined series of events. First on offer, in our makeshift base camp, was the imposing figure of Father Con Considine, in the flesh. He had a coffee as he explained the plans.

'I've spoke with Hugo Nelson and the undertakers and Alice is coming to the church this evening. We'll have prayers at eight o'clock, and the funeral will be tomorrow after eleven o'clock Mass.'

'So soon?'

'No one likes to hang on to the AIDs sufferers for too long, especially the morgue. It's one of their more morbid traits. I've arranged a cremation in Glasnevin for afterwards, so she's getting all the trimmings.'

'Thank you, Con,' I said. 'I'll be footing the bill.'

'Grand. We'll raise a toast to her at my place. I'll see what I can do about a few sandwiches.'

These are just some of the reasons why Con can look forward to the kingdom of heaven for all eternity. Mary Ellen Doyle, on the other hand, was on a bad road. She refused to attend later, saying it was her cards night.

'Is it bridge?' Aidan wanted to know.

'My baldy butt is it,' she replied. 'Poker, man. Real cards.'

'That is not a nice old lady,' I said. But only after she'd left, blinding half the pub with a flash of her loudly coloured bag.

'I like her style,' said a red-eyed Nina.

'Very eclectic.' Ciara nodded, applauding the granny's individuality.

'You got off lightly,' Andy commented. 'Probably because I got the third degree on the street before she came in. Torquemada had nothing on her.'

'How did she manage if you were in your car?' I asked.

'She stopped the traffic at the lights, got in and ordered me to pull over. She'd have made a great cop.'

'Too short, like myself,' I pointed out. 'And if I'm not mistaken, she grew up when women were seen and not noticed except twice a week, going to Mass and the shop.'

'Great days,' he said, dreamily.

Ciara pinched him and I pulled his hair. There are times when I just love being a sophisticated feminist.

'When is Cherry's funeral?' I asked Con.

'Not till Monday. I've been told it's because there are relatives travelling from England. But if you ask me, the Phelans don't want to upset their weekend trade.'

He shook his head in disgust and I could see troubles in his soft, brown eyes. Then he gathered himself and was gone.

We needed to move on a few details. Ciara would spread the word at the Price Street clinic about the funeral and tell the staff.

'That'll be more needles and methadone freed up,' she said.

There you had it, the grim fact of life continuing, even for those under a death sentence from all their addiction had visited upon them. Alice would be forgotten by her comrades by tomorrow, tonight by Price Street if they shredded her file at the clinic. In reality she'd already disappeared; ignored by life, family, society. She was now thrust on the kindness and guilt of strangers.

'What a way to go,' I said aloud.

'Maybe, but let's do our best for her,' Nina said unexpectedly.

We were bonded in that effort now.

I loaded the jalopy and made for home with my new charges. When we got there, I realised I had been tailed by Andy. He pulled up behind me in his car and seemed very at home snagging an overnight bag from the back seat.

'That's a bit presumptuous,' I pointed out.

'I'm looking after you till this blows over,' he said, in a tone that precluded argument.

He thought.

I determined to tackle the problem later. Of course, even this postponement gave him leverage and sent off a signal that I had agreed to his attentions. I wanted to, but I knew that ultimately I could not. This was going to get ugly before it got sorted, but ugly and sorted it would be.

Then the ground rules shifted.

'I have to mind you,' he explained patiently. 'Geraldine rang and told me to.'

I stopped in my short-legged tracks. Ah, Jaysus, lads. What chance does a girl have against that sort of carry on? This was way beyond anything I would have given my mother credit for, even on the darkest day of interference. I had no answer or response to it; this was operating on a level that gave me a nosebleed it was so far beyond my capabilities. I sighed heavily and led my charges up to the house.

We had to step over Barry, who was slumped asleep on the doorstep. From the smell of him, I would have guessed he was drunk, very drunk.

'Isn't he the guy off the telly?' Aidan asked.

'Yeah,' I said, nonchalantly. 'National figures come here every day for some peace and quiet.'

I noticed a bruise on his cheek. 'He ran into a car earlier,' I told the others, softly, pointing to the mark. 'We'll let him sleep it off.'

I opened the door and we crept in, me carrying No. 4 over the threshold with my hand clamped on his snout to muzzle his happy barks at seeing his old mucker.

'I hope he's got some factor fifteen on, or he's gonna be one red actor when he wakes up,' I whispered. I pondered that a moment and didn't have the backbone to leave him to the elements. I grabbed a golf umbrella and placed it between Barry and the burning sun.

TWENTY-TWO

I was hunting out fresh clothes for Nina when Barry came to and knocked on the door. I left the youngster to root around the bedroom and went to face my ex-boyfriend and live-in pal. As predicted, in spite of my wimp-out intervention, he was pink as a boiled shrimp, his neck striped where his sleeping head had squeezed it down into an accordion, and two pale orbs where his shades had tried their best but failed to protect him. He had a wizened aspect that I suspected was an early stage of dehydration, so I let him in for a drink of water.

'You're supposed to ring ahead if you want to call,' I told him, brusquely.

'I've been trying but you never answer your phone.'

This was true, I decided, and let the point stand.

Through the kitchen window I saw that Aidan and Andy were having a beer in the garden, each with a cat posed artistically on his knee, the spare, Bridie, draped across the plastic table in front of them. No. 4 was marking his territory from some reserve tank hidden in his innards.

Barry sat on his ex-sofa and panted like a bad porn star. I brought him liquid, which soaked into him in one go, so we repeated the exercise. Then once more. Finally he seemed to have plumped his cells back up.

'What do you want?' I asked tersely.

I was getting the hang of succinct and it had its moments. I hoped this was one of them.

'What do I want?' he repeated, incredulous. 'I want to come home. I want an end to this nonsense.'

If he was trying a bullying tactic to cow me, he had misjudged his cow.

'Barry,' I said reasonably. 'This has been coming a long time. We haven't been doing so good for ages now. It's time to call a halt, and that way we can both leave with a bit of dignity.'

'Oh, right, so that's why I'm homeless and you're having a fucking party, is it?'

'This is a wake if you must know, not a party. We're all going to a funeral.'

The laughter from the garden was unfortunate, but one can't stage manage every detail, try as one might.

'Who the fuck are all these people anyhow?'

He was really stressed if he was swearing indiscriminately. Barry liked to ration his quotas of 'fuck' et cetera for maximum effect. This had a Tourette's feel to it and lacked his usual class.

'They're friends, old and new. And now you'll have to go. We have a church service soon. I don't want to be late.'

He grabbed my arms and tried to pull me close. I pulled back and toppled us both on to the couch where we were left with a skewed view of one another. It was not conducive to romance, reconciliation or good posture.

'Please, Leo,' Barry pleaded, from his slanted position. 'I'm begging you not to turn me out.'

He was a picture of regret, but hard to take seriously because of the sunburn patterns. He launched into a repeat performance of his roadside show. It didn't sound any better to me than it had looked earlier. The scarlet stripes and mottled blotches jerked comically and I was afraid I might laugh into his poor face, so I went to the bathroom for aloe vera.

'You should put plenty of this on,' I said on my return.

Then he knew he had trouble. His hands reached up to his hot face. 'Ah, God, no, not the face,' he exclaimed, rushing to the nearest mirror.

I could fall into a crater now and it wouldn't register. All that was important was Barry's looks and ultimately himself. He was already in the only home he really needed.

'I'm going upstairs,' I said. 'When I come down again, I expect you to be gone.'

A voice asked automatically if we could at least be friends, while all his concern centred on his reflection in the mirror. I didn't bother him with an answer. A short time later, I heard a taxi pull up and he let himself out of the house.

Nina insisted that Aidan change his shirt as the Bri-nylon would cause an electrical storm if he brushed against another false and treacherous surface. We found a suitably dull tee-shirt in a cool cotton mix and pushed him into it, once he'd sluiced off the trapped perspiration and odour of the synthetic fibre revolution. His new look was Country Casual Dismissive in its mixture of suit and tee, if still a touch tight.

Andy rustled up a casual navy linen shirt, which set off every attractive feature above his waist. A pair of matching linen trousers looked after the rest. If this baby was his, it could look forward to good bone structure and, hopefully, its father's metabolism as opposed to the Irish Slug to be provided by Mummy's side. I didn't once see him check a mirror. He was too at ease with himself for that.

Nina had unearthed the shortest and tightest of the skirts in my cupboard, just next to the skeletons. She teamed it up with a black lace blouse I had never had the courage to wear. This was the product of a day's shopping with Maeve; there is a whole shelf of my bedroom devoted to those outings, all with price labels still attached. I got into a sober long-sleeved dress and put my hair up. I did allow a pair of earrings.

'Classy,' Nina said. 'Shame about your nails.'

We made a respectable bevy of mourners when we were all primped and ready. Then the row over whose car to take lasted all of seventy-two seconds when I pointed to the likelihood of theft of a decent auto (Andy's) or the vandalising of any car (mine, Andy's) in the Mayville estate. We drove off in my blue number.

Whoever designed St Patrick's made sure it benefited from the evening sun. Stained glass captured the light and shimmered with a jewel-like quality. It was a kaleidoscopic crystal in a cold, grey concrete setting. Con greeted his meagre flock with genuine warmth at the tall wooden doors and ushered us to our pews. Alice's pine coffin stood pale and lonely at the top of the aisle, one white rose its only decoration. Ciara and Ronan were already seated, heads bent in thought. They were in matching black leather trousers and jackets, which Ciara had echoed in her make-up, though it was restrained, for her. We sat on the opposite side, to spread out the attendance. An organ played from the loft. After a few moments, a bell rang and we began to pray for the soul of Alice Murney, late of Dublin and a world she was probably better off out of. She had left it sooner than she'd anticipated, from a combination of trickery and her own human weakness. I hoped she was finally at peace.

The interior of the church was Gothic in influence, with a vaulted roof and carvings high up on the pillars. Everywhere there were stories to be read, from the Signs of the Cross, in paintings along the walls, to the stained glass windows with their saints and symbols and the marble carvings of the high altar.

Con spoke of the trials of life, and the rewards of heaven and the hereafter. He also reminded us that love and charity were as one. We prayed for the eternal rest of the soul of Alice Murney. I was surprised how many responses were still automatic to me, after years of lapsed Catholicism. 'May perpetual light shine upon her. May she rest in peace. Amen.' The organist let loose 'Abide With Me' as Con wafted incense from a jangling bronze contraption over the coffin. I cried freely in the comfort of the ritual and the beautiful sadness of the music. I heard sniffing to my right and left. We were invited to attend Alice's funeral Mass the following morning, and then Con walked away to his sacristy to change while we filed by the coffin to let Alice know we were there for her.

At the back of the church I saw a stooped and familiar back disappear through the open door and away. It was Ted, Alice's friend from the Night Train, as ghostly and shadowy a presence in this church as he was in society. There was another mourner in attendance. Doc Phelan had squeezed himself into the final row. He didn't exactly match the picture of sorrow, in spite of his daughter's death. As I passed he spoke, too loud for the occasion and the echo in St Patrick's.

'What was it they used to say in the war? "Careless talk costs lives", wasn't that it? Poor auld Alice, she never knew who to trust. She was never goin' to live long, was she?'

I'm sure a blood vessel burst from anger deep in my head then. Andy steered me clear through the door before my fist could land. It swung uselessly at the late-evening air.

'Think of Con,' said Andy, as he continued to point me away from the church and on towards the parish cottage.

I was furiously ignoring him when a smiling Ciara arrived with her twin brother.

'Don't fret,' she chided, when she saw my sour puss. 'Ronan had a little accident with some of the holy water. He filled a bottle up for our mum and it spilled on the slippery path, well outside church property, and poor Mr Phelan went for a bit of a slide.'

Her eyes were wide with the 'innocent' horror of it all. Ronan looked suitably downcast at his own clumsiness.

'He limped off, so nothing's broken,' he assured us. 'He did seem to be in pain, though.'

'Oops,' Ciara said, beatifically. 'How's it that song goes? "Accidents will happen", isn't that it?'

She turned a key in the lock.

'And did you get a load of that poor dental hygiene? Phew. He could curdle paint with it. Or maybe he's a walking, talking, flesh-rotted zombie – he's ignorant enough. A drink, I think, Ciara,' she said to herself. 'Thank you, Ciara, I don't mind if I do. And you, Ronan? You've had a heavy night.'

They fell on a bottle of wine, giggling, and I was uncomfortably aware of their similarity, which was made worse when I remembered my own lusty thoughts about the male half of the duo.

'What did Barry want earlier?' Andy asked me.

'Took you long enough to ask,' I pointed out.

'You know me, I'm a cool guy.' He smiled, meltingly.

'Nothing much, just the usual man bollocks that gets served up on such occasions.'

'Didn't work, from what I could see.'

'Nah. Heard it all before, have the stained tee-shirt.'

'I'll try not to add to the clichés.'

'Good line of attack,' I agreed.

Con arrived, accompanied by Aidan and Nina and an ancient I took to be the organist. She seemed to mutter a decade of the rosary in the corner, had a cup of tea and vanished.

'A treasure,' Con revealed. 'She plays like an angel, does a mean sandwich and, as if that was not recommendation enough, she is queen of the sausage roll also. Shall we?'

We fell on our feast and washed it down with fine wine and big talk. I like to think Alice would have enjoyed herself if she'd been with us. I said this.

'She is with us,' Con said. 'And so long as she is, even in memory, we have a duty to help all who suffer likewise. Here endeth the lesson.'

We raised a glass to our fallen, barely known comrade, then one to Cherry.

A short time later there was a knock at the door and when Con returned he was trailing Hugo Nelson. The cop got straight to the point.

'You can stop worrying about Ma Hogan and what'll happen to her. We have her now.'

I smiled.

'We weren't the first to get to her, though. She was found on a patch of waste ground behind some derelict buildings in Grangegorman further up the northside. Dead. Surprise, surprise.'

I had stopped smiling by then.

'Is anyone going to be left standing at all at the end of this week?' Ciara remarked.

'This is all my fault,' I said, burying my head in my hands.

'No, it's not,' Nina snapped. 'She got what was coming to her. You wouldn't have been top of the list to top that bitch, I can assure you. If you could have seen Cherry's face the night she was dragged out to go to that cow you wouldn't feel in the least bit sorry she's dead.'

'Two wrongs don't make a right,' I insisted.

'No, but they sure as hell help,' she spat. Her words echoed Dermot Shortall's speech at the nightclub on the night after Tiny's death, and the coincidence made me quake. 'Sorry, Father,' she said to Con. 'I can't help it right now.'

He didn't censure her nor did he condone her views, that was for the future. Nina was as much a soul to be saved as Alice was and he would see to it.

Hugo Nelson had questions for Nina, but only one set of them was urgent.

'Was Tiny Shortall at the flat the night Cherry was dragged away?'

'Yeah. They dragged her out of the bath and made off with her and Damo.'

'You went with Cherry?'

'As far as I could. They bundled her and Damo into a car and I could only follow it a few streets.' Nina paused. 'She was always able to get out of any scrape. I really thought she'd manage this time too.' She teared up, then added pathetically, 'I'd loaned her my lucky dress . . .' Her small voice trailed away.

'Did you go back?'

'Not that night. I was afraid, 'cos Doc Phelan and his thugs were still there.'

'Can you swear to that?'

'Of course I can. I'm not blind. I stayed with Katarina and only went back to collect some clothes. I didn't even have a key, but I didn't need one 'cos the door was broken down. Nothing had been taken as far as I could see. The place was in shit, though, much worse than we'd left it.'

Ciara and myself exchanged glances. We could help the police with their enquiries into the door matter, I'd wager.

'Don't go anywhere without telling me,' Hugo said to Nina. 'You can place Phelan at the flat, and hopefully forensics can prove it's where Tiny was killed.'

He looked around the small room.

'Not much of a wake,' he said. 'You need a bit of music, a few jokes.'

We gave a communal, dry grin to his retreating back.

'He's right,' Con said, putting a record on a prehistoric turntable.

The Beatles assured us all we needed was love, and none of us had reason to doubt them. We sang along with gusto.

Wakes are great parties where the guest of honour is missing. They're a chance for people to let their hair down and disgrace themselves without fear of reprimand. Thus, you can have singing, laughing, crying and fighting all in the one room, no bother whatsoever. So, it was inevitable that a guitar would appear from thin air. I think this comes under the 'fighting' bracket, but I'm not sure. Considine was responsible. He was a 'three chords and the truth' man.

'Do you now or have you ever done a Folk Mass?' I demanded, danger in my voice.

The Folk Mass was one of the more painful memories of my teenagehood. Jolly young Christians banging on tambourines and bawling out 'Kumbaya M'Lord's', swaying together in a vomitous love-in. Trite pop songs rehabilitated for Christ on cheap guitars and sentiments. Hand-shaking and hugs. Oh, no. No, thank you very much. Give me fire and brimstone any day. Hell and damnation, they're more my bailiwick: I'm an old-fashioned girl.

Con was laughing and admitting to long, shaggy hairdos and cheesecloth shirts. He strummed his few chords and launched into 'Yesterday'. Ronan followed on with 'Penny Lane', Aidan Clancy put an end to the Beatlefest with the ballad 'Arthur McBride', a song which takes seven or so minutes and no mean degree of skill to carry off. He eschewed the guitar, as he could not play, but as Nina pointed out, he couldn't sing either and that had never stopped him. This was all proved true over what felt like the next year. Finally the heroes of the song won out and we were released. It's at times like these that you appreciate how golden silence is. Softly, Andy began to sing 'Here, There and Everywhere'. Con took up the tune, then Ronan, and we were all hopeless mush by the time they were done.

'This is as good a time as any to announce our departure on "The Long and Winding Road",' I said, to well-deserved groans.

We cleared away what little mess we'd made. If only the same could be said of our lives, I thought. Then with a wave and a prayer we were away to our homes, to sleep off our excesses and plunge back in to the fray refreshed in the morning.

It was late on Thursday night now, and business was brisk on Mayville Street. A traffic jam would have been pleased with fewer cars. Women stepped in and out of the vehicles with lucrative regularity. Dealers lurked in the shadows. The drunks were back at their dilapidated bench, drinking and railing. The site at the end of the road was empty again. The film circus might have left these parts but the day-to-day carnival hurdy-gurdied on.

Later, I cuddled into the guardian angel my mother had chosen for me and it felt good. I thought of the baby. That felt good too. And even if the two good feelings could not hook up and were destined always to be individual and the sum of their own parts, this was better than a lot of other things, I decided. By a long shot.

TWENTY-THREE

A hose-pipe ban had been slapped on the city on Tuesday, due to the unseasonably brilliant weather. The town was now beginning to show the effects. Municipal parks, previously green and verdant, were now looking a shade more yellow. Some had cracks splitting the clay like chapped lips. The other residents of The Villas had been watering their plants from cans, it seemed, or in Marion's case probably ignoring the ban and spraying under cover of darkness, because we were still a leafy hollow. If you didn't count my little patch of desert.

We breakfasted at the table in the back garden, which was looking a bit crispy for lack of rain. What nature lacked in colour it made up in birdsong. We identified sparrows and tits, which led to plenty of smut. Bees buzzed, No. 4 cavorted and the cats begged scraps.

Showers were taken in relay, and I wondered how large families had managed to grow up in these houses without lashings of fratricide and the like. There was hardly space on the stairs for two people to pass one another, and if all the present residents chose to swing the three cats at the same time we were in trouble, humans and animals.

Andy had been Dad and gone to the shop for provisions.

'You'd be steeped to get anything more than a plate of cat food or some dry cereal here most days,' I told him.

'Is that meant to put me off?' he wondered aloud, his dark eyes teasing.

This put me off, my toast. Attention from a beautiful man so early in the day rattled me. When the butterflies and all other occupants of my tummy calmed down I finished my tea, but didn't dare reach for anything more in case my shaking hands betrayed me.

Alice had a few more people at St Patrick's today: the regular eleven o'clock Mass crowd were out in force, all eight of them.

'She has a lovely day for it,' Con said.

We shared readings among us, and some prayers from the altar. Aidan had a surprisingly moving style.

'He should stick to speaking from now on,' Nina whispered. 'He's pure *cat* at the singing.'

She didn't meet with any argument on that score. I looked at her troubled profile as she lapsed into the deep silence she'd been in all morning. It must have been hard for her to mourn a stranger while wanting to do the same for Cherry, her friend. There was a heavy weight of sorrow on those young shoulders,

Ted appeared from nowhere to bring the gifts of bread and wine to the altar at the Offertory, but was missing when we walked down the aisle with the coffin at the end. Outside, Con saw my confusion and handed me a note.

I have the priest's number. I'll phone him to say where to
go tonight if you're still interested. You did well by Alice.

Thank you.

Ted

I had forgotten about the Fair.

We followed the coffin on its halting journey through town
to Glasnevin Cemetery and Crematorium. Our select party sat
in two cars, desperately trying not to lose the hearse at the
various traffic lights and roadwork jams along the route.
When the high walls of the graveyard were in sight we had to
stall in a queue of other funerals waiting to enter and say final
goodbyes to their beloved. The sky was a cerulean canvas
above, calm as it gazed down upon us ant-like humans
rushing to stand still.

The previous group was still leaving the small crematorium
church as we filed in. Con said a short prayer, the curtains
opened and Alice's coffin trundled off on rollers through the
portal, transporting her earthly remains to a fiery end.

'Actually, there's a back up there too,' Andy said, bursting
my bubble. 'The Health Board have regulations when it comes
to cremation, and it might be a few days before they get to our
girl.'

'So I don't walk away now with an urn full of her ashes?'

'No.'

'Nothing is as it seems, eh?'

'No.'

Molly was still off and Gerry still on duty at the lot.

'The doctor is seeing him again this afternoon,' we were
told. 'Between ourselves I think he'll have to go into hospital
for a few tests. He won't like that, he hates the quacks. I'll

keep ye sussed with regular updates.'

I didn't see Razor Cullen's Porsche amongst the cars. He was probably too busy following us to have time to park it.

I was anxious to call into the office. 'God only knows what That Woman will be up to in our absence,' I explained. 'She's probably taken on a case, pocketed the deposit and sent Kevin to investigate it.'

'No way,' Ciara scoffed. 'She'd never let him out to do it. She'll have left him to do the cleaning and she'll be hot on the trail of a steamy affair.' She gave full relish to her theory.

I began to run towards our building, the image Mrs Mack out under the false pretences of my name burning a hole in my head. I collided with the diva of dust as she released herself into the community.

'No need to rush,' she told me. 'You've missed nothing. Your phone didn't ring once all morning.'

A smile spread across my silly face.

'And what's so funny about that?' she asked, indignant.

'Nothing, Mrs Mack. I'm just grateful to be in such good hands.'

Her eyes narrowed dangerously.

'Er, any post worth looking at? I don't feel like the trek upstairs, I've just been to a funeral.'

She cut me some slack. 'A few bills, nothing you can't ignore for a while, and that cheque you were after finally came from the insurance company you were chasing.'

Ronan's computer wizardry had succeeded. I wondered if Doc Phelan's missing package had been located and despatched from the courier depot yet. And, naturally, I also wondered, in startled worry, how Mrs Mack knew what was in one of the envelopes so accurately (and I did believe that she was right about the contents). She could see into the windmills of my mind and said, 'I felt the staple on the cheque and the remittance, so I knew what it was.' It was useless pursuing the matter to ascertain how she knew *by the feel* what company had despatched the cheque, so I thanked her and we went our separate ways. She'd saved me a climb and she was almost certainly correct in her estimation of the morning's postal crop. What an operator.

Barry's thousand pounds were still going strong and the money took the funeral goers to lunch at an Italian restaurant in Temple Bar. He was a lot more thoughtful and generous since he left. We made small talk, and drank wine at the cheery red-checked tables. It was the sort of place with candles in empty wine bottles at night. They were lined up behind the bar now, melted wax forming strange sculptures on their green sides. We ordered and nibbled on breadsticks until the rolls arrived and were attacked hungrily. The disadvantage of the stringent nail harvest was that my fingers hurt enough for me to think twice about ripping my roll in two and having to apply pressure in the process. I ate mine dry, which was healthier. I did not have the same difficulty with holding a drink, and indulged in a glass and a half of Chianti, which left me feeling a bit pissed. I began to gulp back water in an effort to counter the effect but I think it only made the alcohol travel faster through me.

'Do you have no job to go to these days?' I asked Andy. 'I know you're a journo type but this is a ridiculous amount of time to be getting off even for one of your lot. You'll never get a decent story out of us.'

'Not so,' he argued.

I stared in disbelief. Hurt and betrayal started a warm up in case they were mustered. If Andy was using us to get another of those top-of-the-Irish-heap journalistic prizes he was always collecting, he was in more trouble than he could ever have imagined. He had the morals of an un-neutered alley cat when it came to women and stories, but I never imagined, in my wildest dreams, that he'd sink this low. I found fury deep in my craw and let it begin an inexorable journey northwards.

'Leo, you're going purple, I wish you'd breathe,' Con said.

'So we're column inches for you, is that it?' I asked, my voice almost inaudible. The silence at the table, however, was not.

Andy didn't like that or the stern look he was getting from the commune, so he nipped in quick. 'I'm not on a story at the moment,' he backtracked.

'You'll have to do a little better than that,' I assured him.

'If you must know I'm on a bit of a holiday.' He had the good sense to look sheepish at that revelation.

'What?' I exclaimed. 'This is a holiday?' It beggared belief, really. 'You are such a sad individual if that's true.'

'It's only a few days off, a break then, not a holiday as such,' he said, defending himself.

I could not take the phrase 'as such' seriously. A golf club committee member and friend of my dad's used it constantly as punctuation, no matter what the meaning of his sentence or speech. He would say things like 'I used the five iron, as such, and it worked out fine', or 'I cut the grass, as such'. I tried not to laugh out loud but this gave me hiccoughs and tears ran down my cheeks as I choked on my own breath. Andy decided to ignore me and brazen out the scene.

'Besides, what's so wrong with wanting to spend it with you . . .' he took in the watchers at the table '. . . lot?' he finished.

Ciara made a slurping noise.

'She's right, you know,' I hiccoughed. 'That is way too

sloppy. You've gone to rack and ruin over the last while.'

'Good point. I'll return to form forthwith.'

He got a round of applause.

'Another one saved,' Ciara said, chalking an imaginary mark in the air. 'It was a close-run thing. We nearly lost a fine man there.'

'I thank you,' Andy acknowledged graciously.

Which was his style. He was a gracious, well-bred man. And a looker. So why was I uneasy having him around? I brushed the thought away, surprised that I had let it crop up at all. This situation wouldn't apply long. He might be easy on the retina but I was going to have to jettison all that as soon as my bump became apparent. I sipped more water. We had time yet before that pretty pass.

I was glad he was sitting opposite and not beside me. Initially, I thought this was because I could take him in without turning or making any effort, then almost to my surprise I realised it was because I wanted my own space too. As the meal wore on, my paranoia grew and I worried that I was a specimen in a jar for him to stare at, not that he was doing a lot of that, just more than I was used to. I began to fidget. Ciara kicked me under the table. I fidgeted some more.

'Do you need the loo?' she hissed.

'No, I'm fine.'

'Well, I'm not. Ladies', now.'

I frogmarched myself to where I was ordered.

'What is the matter with you?' she wanted to know. 'You've started this sniping at Andy and he doesn't deserve it. What's your problem?'

'I dunno,' I whined. 'It's just all got on top of me suddenly. I keep thinking he's staring at me, and it's creeping me out.'

'He's not, you know. He looks at you when you speak,

269

although all he's getting are snide quips so I don't know why he bothers. God, you're like a child. "Mammy, he's looking at me." ' She whinged the last bit, sounding very like I had earlier.

'I don't mean to be like this. I'm just not used to the attention. It's not natural for me, or comfortable. I'm used to a bit of neglect, and it suits me. That way I can get on with things without interference.'

'And I thought I had commitment issues. Babe, you need therapy.'

'No, I need an arrangement. Like you have. You know, a booty call type thing. And maybe a movie or two thrown in when I'm not on nights. And . . . so on.'

'In other words, the lot, and to your recipe?'

'Well, yeah. Is that so bad?'

'No. I just don't think you'll get it from that man. He might be looking for more.'

'Shit.'

'No shit, Sherlock.'

'I think I need the loo now. By the way, where did the Counsellor Ciara Doll come from?'

'She's always around, I just don't let her out much. I think she's a pain in the arse. I have no room for someone so reasonable.'

When I was washing my hands I saw I had red spaghetti sauce cat whiskers on both cheeks. No wonder Andy had been 'looking' at me. I needed to get a grip and start behaving like an adult, or a thirty-year-old, whichever was the more mature. When we sat back down, I leaned over to Andy.

'Sorry to be so narky,' I said. 'It's been a long week.' I turned to Ciara. 'Ain't that the truth, partner?'

She nodded. 'And how.'

We were on ice creams when Nina dropped her bombshell.

'I want to do the Fair tonight,' she said, in a quiet moment during hedonistic spoon sucking.

There was a fully fledged, one hundred and forty-decibel silence at that.

'Why?' I asked, finally.

'I owe it to Cherry, and all the others who'll be there,' she said. 'I want to bust it right open. And it might be a chance to find out where Damo is.'

I blinked a few times to clear my head. This girl was sixteen years old, she had no clue what she was proposing. None of us did, to be honest.

'She's right,' Ronan said, out of nowhere.

I'd forgotten he was with us, he'd been so quiet all day.

'I agree,' Ciara said, baling in with the other youngsters.

Great, kindergarten vigilantes, that was all we needed. Aidan Clancy was struck dumb and left with his mouth very wide open, still full of masticated tiramisu. Con toyed with his spoon and Andy was looking my way (again).

'You cannot be serious,' I said, in my best John McEnroe.

But they were.

We ordered strong coffees and prepared to reason them out of their craziness. I opened the argument by pointing out that we were a tiny band of liberal do-gooders against the might of some very evil people who thought nothing of murder or torture or both. We had no plan and we had no back up.

'Let's get some,' Nina said.

'Like what?' I asked. 'Ring the A Team?'

She didn't know what I was referring to. I sank into my mental Zimmer frame. 'Never mind the A Team then. Who or what can we get to help us here?'

'The cops,' she said, simply, almost innocent in her

271

assumption of what they were there for.

'She could be right,' Andy started, hesitantly.

If I'd had any nails left to bite I would have. I didn't, so I was left with the choice of joining their crazy plotting or leaving. I thought it best to stay as a voice of reason. I was suddenly very sober again.

'I don't think we should say any more about this until I've contacted Hugo Nelson and discussed the matter with him,' I announced, primly I'll admit.

When the expectant eyes at the table had burned through to my spleen, I fished out my mobile and dialled his number, willing it to be engaged. It was. I told the group as much and prayed for the miracle of forgetfulness to do us all a big favour. Two minutes on, Ciara pressed the redial button and handed me the phone. This time I was not so lucky, Hugo answered. He didn't seem surprised to hear from me, and offered to swing by the office in an hour's time, in spite of the fact that I didn't exactly talk up the attractions. My heart sank. Now the madness was moving on, taking shape, hoping for the stamp of respectability and approval from a law man. I really hoped he'd talk us out of it and send us home to where we belonged. Yep, I still have those hopelessly hopeful moments, and they almost always get shot to bits.

If I was narky before, I was a walking bitch now, and spoiling for a fight. Family are usually the handiest victims in these sitches because normal rules do not apply. You can, sometimes must, insult family and vice versa in the most casually, or calculatingly, cruel way, and forgiveness has to be dished out. Or generally that's true. Obviously if there's money involved, you're into feud territory and there's another book of etiquette for that. Closest thing to family I had at that gathering was Andy, and I couldn't really pick on him again if

Ciara's earlier prognosis of unfair carping was accurate. I think he knew it too, the grinny bollox, as he sauntered off to buy a newspaper. Everyone avoided me and dispersed for the free hour before our rendezvous. I think Con went to church to pray that I'd calm down.

I decided I was in a mood to tackle Mrs Mack on the lift issue now. I know, I know, but I was red-rag-to-a-bull angry. And foolhardy. And foolish. I had a lot of f-words in me then and was insistent on getting them out of my system.

There's no codding an old cod, or halibut in the case of Mrs M. She saw me coming a mile off and knew I was gunning for blood.

'The very woman,' she opened, and that stopped me in my murderous tracks. 'The lift is fixed.'

'I wasn't aware it was ever broken,' I retorted. I paid my rent, I knew my rights. And one of them was using the lift that *she* always commandeered.

'It's very temperamental, I'll give it that.'

'*It's* temperamental?' I was smokin' with the sarcasm.

She ignored me. 'I know you're not as young as you used to be, so I've made sure it's going smoothly for you now. I wouldn't want you missing business just because you haven't the juice anymore to make it up the stairs.'

You cannot deal with an opponent who's making the rules up as she goes along. Come to think of it, in that respect Mrs Mack is a lot like my mother and my mother's mother. You spend your life growing to an age of some reason and the time for leaving home, then walk right back in to the same set of strictures you thought you'd left. It's got to be a moth and a flame metaphor of massive proportions. My little forest fire led me, singed wings and all, to the elevator and watched me ascend, dumbfounded. She wore the broadest smile I'd seen

273

spread across her in a long time, but forgive me for suggesting it was due to her victory and not the pleasure of seeing me relieved of my normal climb.

I heard my own voice sounding very small and pathetic as it said, 'There are some people coming for a meeting later, can they use this too?'

The ancient machine cranked me up through the building and I didn't catch her answer. But I am sure I heard her laugh.

TWENTY-FOUR

I sat alone at my desk in my empty office and it felt like the old days. Mick Nolan's photo glared at me, of course, but its familiarity was almost comforting; never thought I'd find myself admitting that. It was the live members of the human race I was having problems with these days, and especially this day. What Nina proposed was dangerous. There was a very real risk of injury or death for anyone who messed with these criminals. I hugged my arms around myself and thought of the little one within. I did not want to put this new life at risk either. The future was something I could offer it, and I wanted to. All my hopes hinged on Hugo Nelson blowing the idea out of the water as he had to, surely?

I became more and more agitated as the hour wore slowly on. There was no ticking clock but the tension mounted still and all. Whoever came through the door first risked a sound verbal thrashing to ease my jangling nerves. It was Andy's bad luck to be the victim. I always knew it would be him, that's the way flak blows.

'Right,' he said. 'Let's get this row over with before anyone else arrives to get caught in the cross-fire.'

He knew me so well.

'I'm clearly in the major league bad books and I'd like to know why. Let's be having it.'

Faced head on with an opportunity to air the issues, I hesitated. I'm not great on confrontations when it comes to the personal, which is why Barry lasted so long. And I knew Andy didn't deserve to be dumped on because I wasn't used to normal romantic attention and was under the pressure of trying to save some kids from making a big and potentially fatal mistake. Even if there had only been one of these things to deal with, I would have found it difficult to put proper words to how I felt. But I gave it a lash, now that the opportunity was with us.

'I'm worried about the way things are turning out,' I began.

'Do you mean with the girls or us?'

Great, right into the deep waters, which were not at all as still as I'd heard tell. I couldn't find my reverse button, no option but to continue. 'Both, I suppose.'

'That's honest at least.'

'Andy, I'm on the rebound, for God's sake. It's the worst place to be when it comes to making long-term life decisions.'

'It's not just that. I'm annoying you too and I don't know why.'

'I'm a very independent woman. I've always had to be. I don't like being crowded and I am right now.'

'Jesus, Leo, you really know how to send out conflicting signals. It's okay to stay with you at night, in bed or trailing after you to make sure you're protected. But come the daylight I'm to disappear.'

'Love vampire?' I chanced.

'Don't trivialise this,' he snapped. 'I can't spend my life waiting around for you to make up your mind about whether I've put in the necessary time and effort to be included in your life, on your terms. *I* want things, too, you know. I want a home and a family. I want to live with a woman I love, even if it's not the woman I always thought it would be. I want to grow old with someone. And time is running out whether any of us likes it or not. I don't know how prepared I am to take the abuse I'll have to if I stick around to wait for you to come to terms with yourself.'

That was one almighty speech and I hadn't liked any of it. I felt despair. I was in no position to offer him what he wanted, not with doubt hanging over me like a guillotine. We had known each other a long time, and we could have sorted ourselves out with my rebound in the mix, and all the other peccadilloes we'd both picked up along the way. But I had a bigger secret and it could not be sorted. I had to let him go.

'I'll understand if you decide to leave,' I said. 'And I will be sorry, be sure of that. But I can't offer you what you want just now, and I don't want to waste any of your precious time.'

He misjudged the tone of my final words and looked at me stung by the opposite of what I'd meant. 'You really are a bitch to me,' he said. Then he walked out the door. It had only taken two minutes to ruin my life. A lifetime's aspirations condensed and destroyed in the blink of time's eye. I began to understand relativity. No wonder Einstein had a sense of humour, you'd have to, dealing with that sort of speedy annihilation.

I had ten minutes to cry and I did, massive racking sobs of anguish and regret. Then, a rush of heat throughout me sent me hurtling to the loo. I leaned over the bowl and threw up the breadsticks, dry bread roll, tagliatelle bolognese, some salad and a glass and a half of Chianti. I knelt at the bowl, cooling my brown against the porcelain rim. I had destroyed the best chance I would ever have at near-perfect love. I sank to rock bottom and stopped caring what happened to me or my stupid body. I would channel this negative energy against the repelling pole of the thugs who ran the Fair. There was no other way to use it. It didn't matter if Hugo Nelson helped or not, we were going and we would make a difference for all the unhappy wretches caught in this web of fear.

I had applied a new face by the time the stragglers returned. I'd used my pale, unseasonal winter make-up but it was infinitely better than the mask of heartbreak on the layer beneath. I explained it by citing the return of the dicky tummy. We arranged ourselves on sundry chairs and Ciara sat on top of the filing cabinet, her legs dangling in mid-air. Mick's picture was in the triangle between her arm and body and the metal surface, as if she had her arm slung around him. I was warmed by the look of it. With these people for me, who could triumph against?

'I've been having a think,' I said. 'I may have been wrong to reject out of hand the idea of going tonight. There may be something in it if we plan well and insure against injury. Though how we do that is beyond me,' I admitted.

'I suppose that's why you called me,' Hugo Nelson said, silhouetted in the doorway.

It was bizarre to think that we had summoned the police to a rooftop in the heart of a booming economic quarter to plot against an underground force of murderers, thieves and perverts, but it was Friday and it was Anything's Possible Day, all day, that day.

Hugo started with a general note.

'I'll only say this once: you are not going to the Fair this evening. If you do, you'll jeopardise a police operation that has taken nearly a year to put together, not to mention putting lives at risk, your own included.' He turned to me, and not in a nice way. 'You're know to the ringleaders of this scheme, and therefore a major risk to us. My first instinct is to slam you into a cell to ensure we know your whereabouts, but . . .' He shrugged. Obviously the law was a wuss for denying him this option. 'We've put together an expensive and dangerous plan, and I don't want to see my people or any of the innocent parties hurt or killed, both of which are real possibilities if any stupid interference occurs. *Don't* fuck this up for us.'

He turned and swished out the door, leaving the bitter tang of authority in the air.

It was a classic paradox: I had never been in so much trouble without being in trouble. The only way to deal with this black hole of logic was to ignore it. In time it would evolve into me actually being in trouble, I knew, so there was little point wasting mental energy on figuring out how I'd managed to wedge myself in the strange no-man's-land in between.

'Earth to Leo,' Ciara shouted.

'Sorry, lot on my mind,' I murmured, trying to return my attention to the office.

'We noticed,' she said.

I didn't look like I'd be much use organising a bark from a dog, so Ciara stepped up to the helm.

'Looks like we're about to disobey the powers that be and piss a lot of officialdom off?' We all nodded on cue. 'So we go then?' Another, communal bob of heads. With extraordinary sensory perception, we began to act as one, and swiftly. We agreed to go to our respective billets until Ted called Con and gave details of the venue for the Fair. Ciara suggested we all rest up till then.

'Mrs Mack seems to think you're in need of it more than most, and I'm inclined to agree with her, looking at the state of you.'

I must have rallied my misery puss slightly, because I got a stern warning never to tell the doyenne of dirt that Ciara had said such a thing. But, 'Go home, go to bed, then work out some sort of disguise or we'll have to leave you behind,' was a killer. I began to pull myself into an acceptable rag order. Sleep did sound a wonderful idea, it usually solved my aches and pains. It took a desultory while but I finally gathered myself and my things, Aidan and Nina, and we made for the car.

We met Karl, the location manager, and his amazing mop head on the stairs. Clearly, Mrs Mack had withdrawn lift privileges once the law had left.

'Scouting for a location?' I asked, chirpily.

'Eh, yeah. We're using a newly done up place round the corner to be a traditional and dingy pub, so I thought I'd call in to say hello.'

Don't know why I didn't think greeting me was going to satisfy him, I was that out of the loop.

'Ciara's upstairs in the office. See you round,' was all he got from me.

He had a spring in his step as he tackled the stairs in leaps. I gave him till the second floor before he slowed down and gasped through the rest. It was hardly likely to cool his ardour. Ciara might. Who knew? I left further pondering on the nature of human relations alone, as clearly I knew fuck all about it if my history was to stand testament to my expertise.

Romance was perfuming the inner-city air that afternoon. In fact, it was rancid with the stuff. As we turned on to a satellite lane for the car park, I took in the memorable sight of a pissed Barry Agnew weaving his way along the cobbled streets towards Leo Street and Co. He was following a single red rose clutched in his right hand, of which I'm sure he saw two, and thrust forward for the inamorata of his choice: me. I quickened my pace and escaped notice. Ciara would have her hands full with two suitors descending on the office. The thought lifted me, fleetingly.

Gerry's news was that Molly was in hospital for the same tests he'd predicted for him only hours earlier.

'And, sure, that's the best place for him to be,' he assured me.

Mortality rubbed its icy finger along my spine. It had nothing to offer but the unanswerable. Why did the world have to change? Why did some people have to move on, others die? Why were some of us left behind? What use was any of it? I preferred stupid questions, I decided.

Andy hadn't lost much time. A note under my new wind-shield wipers told me to leave his bag at his current paper's front desk whenever was convenient for me. I could hang on to the watch indefinitely, he had another. Disposable people. Disposable time. I was sick to my dicky stomach of it all. At home, I took to the bed and let three cats and a dog join me. We curled up and shut out our demons, and waited for the night to cloak us in a kinder light than the brash strident day and its cruel illumination.

Just as I dozed off, I wondered why Hugo Nelson hadn't told me about the Fair when I'd asked him about it. Perhaps it was true at the time. Or was he protecting the Garda plan to scupper it? Just a detail, but I would ask. I yawned and drifted away.

Nina woke me with a cup of tea, which is always acceptable.

Dusk was stripping the end of the day from the sky and the room was grey and shadowy. She sat on the edge of the bed as I sipped a brew strong enough to march an army of mice on, and petted The Snub who was toasty warm and not to be shifted.

'I have a cat called Bella,' she told me. 'I miss her,' she added, in the voice of a little girl longing for home.

She let me come to before throwing out ideas on what I might wear and what make-up job would best disguise me. I was convinced unhappiness had twisted me beyond recognition by then, but further alteration was needed according to my stylist.

'How did you hook up with Cherry?' I asked, curious about two girls from such different backgrounds becoming firm pals.

'She saw me crying outside a café and came to help. Street was full of people, she was the only one who bothered to ask me what was wrong.'

'What was?'

'I'd started my period, and it was really heavy, and it ruined my favourite jeans. I didn't have the money for somewhere to stay that night either, so Cherry took me in. Robbed me a lovely new pair of trousers too.'

'Did you know she was a junkie when you met her?'

'Yeah, she was very up front about all that, didn't think it was fair to tell lies to people. And she wasn't bad on it, you know, she was mild-mannered, maybe even happy. And she had a good thing going with Tiny. They were determined to get her off the gear, and have a healthy baby and a life together in England or maybe even America.' Nina gave a series of gulps, unable to speak, then whispered, 'Didn't work out for them.' She hung her head and cried some more.

'Jamesy Briarty is saying he gave you the clap.'

282

That rallied her.

'Jamesy Briarty is a fuckin' moron. Thrush, that's what I had, though I didn't know it at the time. I hope he still has an itchy mickey from it, so I do, the fuckin' loser.'

'I take it you're over him, then?'

'What do you think?' she scoffed.

Nina had learned a lot in her weeks away from Clunesboro.

'You had a fight with Andy, didn't you?' she said finally.

My heart hammered painfully against my ribs. 'Yes.'

'Is he gone now?'

Those tears were never far away. 'I think so.'

'That's a shame, I like him. He's nice. And he's really dishy.'

I almost laughed; I hadn't come across the word 'dishy' since I was a teenager myself, long, long ago before granulated sugar was invented. A laugh would have been welcome. I didn't get one. Nina wanted to talk about Cherry and Tiny. All they'd wanted was a regular life with the regular trappings. That wasn't too much to ask, you might have thought. It's what Andy wanted too, but I had judged it too much. How can so straightforward a desire become so difficult to attain for any or all of us, regardless of our standing in the cosmic scheme?

'I want to do this for them,' Nina said. 'I want to get at that bastard Doc Phelan. And if we can get just one kid away from him, that'll be a victory.'

'Did Cherry ever talk about him?'

'Oh, yeah, hard for her not to really. And he wasn't her dad either.'

'No?'

'No. She was given to him.'

'I'm gone all hard-of-thinking,' I admitted. 'I don't know what you mean.'

283

'Cherry's mum gave her to Doc Phelan in exchange for a deal. She swapped her for drugs. Same goes for Damo, though he had a different mother.'

I shook my head to clear out the wax. I must have misheard. There was no way she had just said the words I thought she had.

'He's had lots of kids that way, just doesn't always adopt them like he did with Cherry and Damo. Double psycho weirdness there.'

My blood chilled, and the dizziness preceding nausea began to spread through me. Phelan was *collecting children*.

'It gives him power. He likes that, gets off on it. Girls, boys, he doesn't care as long as he owns them. He's a very fucked up man. I think something bad must've happened to him when he was young, though that's no excuse.'

I agreed with her, it was no reason to perpetuate the misery on others.

'He owns that little guy that sells on the Mayville corner too, as far as I know.'

'Billy, is it?' Now my heart stopped completely and a flatlining buzz deafened me.

'Yeah, that's him. His mother is a complete flake, out of it all day, every day and has loads more kids, I think.'

This was getting personal. I roused some anger. There was no room for domestic hand wringing and hoping other people had the situation under control. Billy might regard me as a strange woman, but I felt like I knew him now and I couldn't let Phelan ruin him as he had so many more. We were going out there to help protect that little boy. 'You and whose army?' a voice in my head demanded to know, in what I can confidently describe as a mocking tone. I wanted to leave the details for discussion later, but one thing was sure: I would

284

have felt calmer if I'd had a gun, and I don't believe in weapons.

I have never been comfortable with violence. I don't enjoy watching it in a movie or on television. I would rather run than stand my ground, and I have only ever tried to hurt someone else physically if they've threatened a comrade, a relation, or one of my animal charges. When it comes to myself, I flee, because I have damn all pride to lose and possessions aren't worth protecting if it means someone has to get hurt. There have been occasions when I have cuffed another person for sexism, or finishing my pint, and occasionally I have attempted to give Smokey Joe Street a gentle root up his hairy, feline arse, but I have always (bar no time) come off worst in that scenario. I don't kill spiders or snails or slugs and I once spent a sunshine holiday fishing flies out of the hotel swimming pool before they drowned. Yet violence was only a breath away that night, and I prepared myself mentally for a kick-ass approach. I only wished that forewarned was forearmed, with some big fuck-off sticks and chains, and perhaps a Colt .45 like the cowboys used so successfully. If it was good enough for John Wayne, it was good enough for me.

'Time to get ready,' I announced to Nina, my body now full of the embalming fluid she had so cleverly disguised as refreshment. 'What look had you in mind for me?'

There was an argument that my own mother might not have recognised me when Nina was done. She'd probably have taken me for Ciara Gillespie's sister, an older one, sadly, but then I have lived that much longer and am so much wiser than my apprentice. I could just imagine Ciara's expressive snort at that last piece of whimsy.

'Is it fancy dress?' Aidan wanted to know.

'Haw-haw,' his sister said, inflicting damage to the back of his head.

We were what could be termed 'pathetic punk' with Goth make-up and tatty clothes, but the tat just too worn to scrape by at a Pistols gig. We also looked fairly strung out.

'Your nails are just perfect with this look,' Nina said. They did match our unkempt, bedraggled air. It was probably too much trouble to have gone to, but the devil was in the detail.

'I'm a perfectionist,' I told her.

Aidan, for his part, found an old overcoat of my granddad's that I wore for gardening in the rain. It had seen better days, and better nights than the one it was off to partake of now. He looked homeless in one broad stroke. 'Sorry, Nobby,' I whispered heavenward, hoping he'd understand, and that I'd got the direction of my glance right.

I had a fierce time convincing the Clancys that No. 4 should be allowed to come. Nina said he had no proper gear to wear so I put a ripped red kerchief around his neck and he looked quite the doe-eyed pup seen with all the best crusties. There was a more serious row about his unreliable behaviour, which the dog resented as much as I did, i.e. a lot. But the crux was that they were worried he'd get hurt.

'Let's let him decide,' I proposed.

I put the case for and against to him and he ran barking to the door.

'There you have the answer,' I said. 'The pooch travels.'

It was for me, of course. I wanted him with me as a focus and lucky charm, and hadn't Molly said he thought that was a name No. 4 recognised?

'I won't let him come to any harm,' I said. 'I love him.'

He also made me feel safer, although he had never furnished me with any scientific reason for thinking this. And so, it's fair to say that I might have been raving at the time. I bundled us out of the door before the protest started again. We drove to Con's house, because it was torture sitting in The Villas, waiting for the phone to ring.

Ciara and Ronan felt the same way, and were there ahead of us.

'The nails are a nice detail,' Ciara mocked. 'You saw this night coming a long way off.'

'Obviously.'

It was standing room only in the hut, or it would have been if there had not been an Andy Raynor-sized space in the middle of the floor. No one was crass enough to mention it, not even Ciara, surprisingly, but we all knew who was missing and why.

At 11 p.m. Ted rang and spoke to Con. There was a lot of uh-huhing before the latter hung up and revealed that the Fair would commence at midnight in an abandoned warehouse further along the docks. The site itself had formerly been a holding area for human cargo in the glory days of sailing; amongst the unfortunates were the lepers of Ireland waiting to be taken away and dumped on some remote island in the Indian Ocean to fester and die. This bleak spot was, and is still today, called Misery Hill. Ted would meet us there.

287

TWENTY-FIVE

Dublin stayed open twenty-four/seven, generally. But there were still areas devoted to dawn business which were deserted from early afternoon until daybreak the following day. Many of these were by the docks between Butt Bridge and Ringsend, accepting the bounty of the High Seas. For centuries boats had been arriving here to offload cargo, riches, and the odd invading marauder. Peppered through and around these centres of commerce were empty spaces inhabited only by weeds and rock, patiently waiting for a builder to develop yuppie apartments and charge a fortune for the result. Misery Hill was deep into this forsaken territory.

We needed to arrive in relay to avoid undue attention. In a reversal of sinking-ship protocol, the three men went first. They were supposed to case the joint and make it safer for us delicate flowers of Irish womanhood. They planned to light a fire and make like tramps around it. Each had a prop bottle in a brown paper bag and without a formal check I guessed that two of those contained whiskey. I warned Aidan he would suffer wrath and vengeance of biblical proportions if any harm came to Nobby's coat. This tactic circumnavigated accusations of sentimentality or terror nicely, but it all boiled down to one thing: if the coat left the scene unmarked so would the man. I wished I could threaten Con and Ronan in the same way, but I hadn't loaned them anything. We took a collective moment to stand still, but stopped short of a group hug, which I regretted as I watched the lads shuffle off.

A short time later, it felt uncannily like a century's worth, three women and a dog made tracks for the abandoned warehouse described by Ted to Con. We were entirely silent for the brief walk across the river from Con's house to Misery Hill. Dublin twinkled, innocent and familiar, lights shining in the night air and fluttering in the reflected water of the Liffey as it joined the sea in gentle kissing waves. The order and beauty of the night-time town was massively juxtaposed with the mood of our group: each of us was sick with nerves, even if No. 4 covered it better than his human company. The kerchief suited him and I was sure he knew he was under-cover.

In colour scheme, we were an old black and white movie, blending with the shadows of the bleak and rocky desert of the stretch. Occasionally, a street light picked out the tan spots of the dog's coat or his red collar. And from time to time we noticed other travellers making for the same place as ourselves. We were the unseen of the city, the ones no one wanted to know about, the disposable human waste of the burgeoning Irish nation. In the near-distance, the orange lights of Dublin 4 blinked in their safe, myopic prosperity. They could have been on Mars, and they might as well have been.

Our boys were standing around a flaming oil drum when

we arrived. The waste ground was quietly teeming with people, none over forty as far as I could see. In that regard we fitted in perfectly, in others not. The majority were sketched in chiaroscuro, and few were more than a vague set of hollows arranged in a general approximation of a face or form. These were wisps and wraiths, once full, fat and able, now the shadows of mankind. As we tried to relax and meld into the surroundings, I felt the gulf between the energies of panicked deprivation, exacerbated by poverty, and our own group's centred safety, calmly believing that something would always turn up to take care of us.

Rows of cars lined one side of the site, their darkened interiors holding the customers for tonight's perversions. The very shapes of the vehicles seemed to suggest a menace beyond conventional words – fanciful, really, when you realised these were the family four-doors that ferried the kids to school, wives to salons and whole families on picnics and breaks. The police would have their details on a computer database by now, and it would take some explaining if the vacation journey was halted, the car pulled over to one side of the road and awkward questions asked. I shivered to a stop beside Con and asked what we'd missed.

'Not a lot. Ted is here, but he hasn't gone in yet. Doc Phelan hasn't arrived and nothing will happen until he does. It's his roadshow and he won't allow anyone to handle the money but him.' He let his eyes wander. 'Can you tell which ones are cops?'

I couldn't. Good.

A flimsy chain fence surrounded the warehouse selected for this strange 'party'. With a change of clientele it would have made the perfect spot for a trendy disco, the sort used for the ultimate staff Christmas do or the launch of the latest Irish boy band's newest chart-topping album. Two hired beefs with Alsatians patrolled the outer perimeter of the property, but it was a meaningless show of strength; anyone who wanted to was going in and most of them were too frail to constitute a threat anyhow.

A roar of engines preceded the arrival of the convoy bringing Papa Doc Phelan and his circus. The earth rumbled, trembling vibrations from our toes and on upwards. By the time my cranium began to bob, fat, muscle and bone had enjoyed a thorough sonic workout. First into view was a battered van, driven by the thug with the scar from the Raven. He pulled up inside the compound and when he opened the back doors a dozen youngsters spilled out. They all looked frightened. He herded them into the warehouse. Next was a carful of sundry drinkers I recognised from the pub, and finally an open jeep with Doc sitting regally in the back. He was not alone. My blood froze and I felt Con stiffen; Billy was sitting on the seat beside Phelan, looking tiny, and on the other side was a youngster I just knew to be Damo. They both looked terrified.

With the main players now inside the gates were open to all.

'I'm going in,' Nina said.

'We promised Hugo Nelson we wouldn't get in the way,' I reminded her.

'So? He can arrest me and send me to jail, I don't give a shit, I'm going in there. Who's with me?'

We all were, of course. Again we staggered our actions. Aidan took off Nobby's coat and draped it over his arm.

'Looking around, I don't think I look like I'm selling, so I'd better pose as a buyer,' he said.

It hurt Con to join him, but he did.

'I'm jail bait,' Ronan grinned.

It was the last half-laugh of the evening.

I was stopped by the security men at the gate and had a mini heart attack on the spot. I'd never seen these goons before, which meant they didn't recognise me, so what was the problem?

'What's the deal with the dog?' one of the flat-featured Godzillas asked.

'He goes everywhere with me,' I explained. 'He's very tame.'

I was surprised that my voice sounded even and unworried. I was in tatters; it was unthinkable that I should continue without my mate. He was my talisman, and I felt so spiritually alone, it was impossible for me to face any immediate future that didn't feature him.

'He's not goin' in,' Flatface No. 2 said.

'If I tie him up just inside the door, would that do?' I pleaded. 'He goes mad if he can't see me. And he's afraid of your dogs, so I don't want to leave him out here. *Please?*'

Flatty No. 1 sized up what he thought was the situation. I was happy with two plus two being his five, even prepared to support his mathematics, if only it kept my dog within range. I gave him the look, which confirmed that it was his right to make this call, as he was clearly the only one with the brain and imagination to do that. Flattery will always get you somewhere.

'Inside the door then,' he said, not wanting to turn away product and, therefore, profit from the evening.

We passed on through. The goons' eyes were burning into me, so I draped the dog's leash through the nearest loop I could find. It looked like a dungeon manacle attached to the building's crumbling brickwork, and I could not banish visions of mediaeval tunnels and torture chambers from my troubled head.

It's hard to describe the sheer degradation of the human spirit in that place that night. Selling humans as a commodity was a centuries-old trade, but this had taken slave trading and prostitution to new depths. Phelan cynically exploited the cravings of the young addicts. He withheld their hit, sold them on, then gave them their deal (and a little extra for 'being a good sport'), subtracted an entrance fee, the money for the drugs and his commission. By the time the kid had pumped the drug into his vein he didn't care who he was with, how much he'd made or what he had to do to earn it.

I checked out The Team. Ciara slumped angrily against a wooden crate, Ronan mirroring her stance and attitude. Con and Aidan looked aghast and frustrated and Nina had disappeared. I thought I saw her wide on my field of vision, skulking near Phelan and Damo, but couldn't be sure; she was the elusive pimpernel of the season. Phelan was stationed by a wall at the back of the main reception area. From there, a number of doors offered options of other rooms to the customers, and trade was brisk. We were acutely aware of the proposed Garda bust and powerless to interfere until then. Helpless is not a look that I like on me, regular as it is, so I decided on a walk outside, around the walls of the warehouse. I untied No. 4 and made for the exit. The goons were intrigued.

'She mustn't be desperate for her hit yet,' one of them announced to the nodding other. 'She'll be back.'

I would, but not on their terms.

If life imitated art, dark clouds would have gathered, with thunder and lightning waiting on the celestial sideline for a call-up. Instead, the balmy night hung clammy over its creatures. I sagged under the weight of atmospheric pressures without and within. If this had been 'just' a job, I would have pointed me and mine towards home and headed on out of there. But this was a living nightmare that had to be addressed, and lives were at stake. I squared a shoulder or two against the negative charges and delicately picked my way along the perimeter of the building. No. 4 followed suit.

The rear of the property was bathed in an unexpected hush, given that events here were as interesting as they were surprising. I watched for ten to twelve minutes before figuring that undercover agents were waiting in all of the satellite rooms and quietly removing gagged and handcuffed customers and their prey to police wagons, hidden behind carefully positioned towers of industrial pallets. I marvelled at how calmly oiled the action was; the Force had planned well to prevent the alarm being raised. I could see two more security men patrolling with dogs, but presumed them to be under-cover officers when they didn't interfere with the work of the cops out back. No. 4 made a timid effort to growl and bristle at the bigger animals, and was relieved when I hushed him. He'd showed willing and that pleased us both: satisfaction is a subjective matter at any time.

I crept back around to the front entrance again. Outside, two middle-aged men were smoking and having a chat. It was casual and they could have been waiting to tee off at the golf club. In fact, they were exchanging notes on other fairs.

'They're a much better idea than the dog fights or the bare-knuckle boxing. This is far more enjoyable. And no one cares if the junkies come back or not.'

'Just as well,' his comrade laughed. 'Joe cut up a bit rough the last time, I doubt that young wan made it to the next day.'

'Who gives a fuck?' the other snorted. 'They're better off dead, most of them. We're probably doing a social service, getting them off the live register.'

They gave themselves big slaps on the back for that. The casual dismissal of another human being's right to a decent life was wiped away in hearty laughter. The bastards. I prayed they'd be next to be carted off in a Black Maria.

As I slipped back into the building they gave me the once over. They made no attempt at secrecy as one asked the other, 'Would you?'

'Bit old and raddled for me,' came the answer. 'I like them younger and with less meat on them.'

For once I was grateful for the insult.

Ted was just inside the door, dressed loosely in white. It gave him the look of a prophet, and there was certainly a quality of the apostolic about him. He beamed at me, and I would have laid a tenner on his being stoned.

'Glad you could make it,' he said, surveying the newest of Doc Phelan's kingdoms. 'Something else, isn't it?'

I nodded glumly.

'Don't worry, I have a feeling it's all about to go awry.' He winked and moved away, seeming to float in a shimmery aura.

No. 4 was edgy as an octagon. He sniffed the air and pawed the ground, anxious about some deeper problem only he was aware of yet. I really couldn't conceive of anything worse than what we were experiencing now and did my best to soothe him. He was enjoying this as much as a pig in a bacon factory, so I understood his reluctance to come with me on a tour of the room, getting stuck into the thick of the event. I left him by the exit again, his leash loosely draped through the unsettling metal hoop.

I edged closer to Phelan and Billy, who was pinned miserably by his side. He looked all of his scant eleven years and I wanted to bundle him up and spirit him away. Ciara and Nina were hanging back by a side door with Con and Aidan close by. Ronan was fielding an approach by a punter. The interior was oddly quiet for a place with fifty or so people in it and more arriving by the minute. So it was all the more startling when the shouting started.

Ted had got to Papa Doc Phelan's table and was making a racket.

'Someone take this fucker out and give him a good kickin',' Phelan ordered.

But Ted had more in him than anyone could have guessed. He wrestled the responding attacker to the ground and wriggled away from him. Then he lunged for Phelan but missed. He was only a delicate sliver of a man compared with the bulk of his prey. Phelan could have snapped his neck in two with little enough effort. I could take no more of the waiting game, especially as lives were being ruined all around me. I had to act, so I rushed forward to intervene, but the bigger man had kicked over his makeshift desk and pulled young Billy to one side. He had the youngster in a head lock which looked like it had cut off the boy's air supply. Ted took stock for a second. In that breath Phelan took a knife from his pocket and held it to Billy's neck.

'If you don't quit, I'll slit this little fuck's throat. Got it?'

Billy cried and strained against his gigantic captor, but he had no chance of escape. A stream of urine spread a dark stain over his combat pants. The gathering held its breath. Then, out of what we all like to call the blue, an unlikely champion jumped forward.

No. 4 hurled himself at Phelan and took his attention away from Billy just long enough for the crucial opportunity of freedom to present itself. Phelan swiped at the dog and Ted threw himself on to him. In the mêlée, Billy fled to the wings.

I ran to him followed by Con and the rest of our posse. As his bemused thugs hesitated and looked on, redundant, Doc lost balance and crashed to the floor. Ted was on him immediately, kneeling on his arms, pinning him there. He fished out a syringe from his jacket and held it high for everyone to see. It was full of a brown-red substance.

'Don't come any closer or he'll get this in the neck,' he shouted, his clear voice echoing through the startled air.

No one budged.

'Don't listen to the crazy fuck,' Doc ordered. 'Get him off me.'

Still no one advanced.

'Do you know what's in this?' Ted asked him, waving the syringe before the hook-nosed face.

His captive shook his head.

'It's a very lethal cocktail I made especially for you. Now, wasn't that thoughtful of me?'

Doc began to groan and whimper. No. 4 crouched close to him and growled very low and dangerous.

'My little friend thinks you should shut up,' Ted pointed out. 'And so do I. But before you do I want to remind you of someone. Do you remember a woman called Alice Murney?'

Phelan shook his head again.

'Oh, I think you do,' Ted insisted. 'In fact, I think you remember her very well because a few nights ago you gave her a very special present, didn't you? A reward for being such a good customer all these years. And do you know what?'

Again the head shake.

'Well, you don't know much, if that's the case because that deal killed Alice. And I hold you responsible. So, now I'm going to deal out a little justice for that, for Alice.'

Phelan let out an agonised howl of animal fear and pain as

Ted plunged the needle deep into his chest, as close to his heart as he could get within the many folds of flesh covering it. He emptied the contents into the screaming man beneath him.

'I'll tell you my recipe, shall I?' he shouted. 'That's as pure as I could afford, not your common brown muck, and it's mixed with citric acid and water, like usual, but the extra-special ingredient is my very own potent, HIV-ridden blood. So if the heroin doesn't kill you, and it should with the amount I've put in, the HIV will cook away nicely in there, and that'll see you off.'

He left the syringe in his victim's chest, stood up and kicked Phelan hard in the side.

'Should help you lose weight anyhow.' He grinned. 'You're the first to try the exclusive Ted Diet.' He laughed, stood tall and proud, arms outstretched, awaiting his bloody fate.

A dozen men leapt on him, dashing his slight frame to the floor. I ran forward to ward them off. The first blow to fell me was dealt by Scarface from the Raven. He got the side of my head, trapping air painfully in my ear, and I went down, crunching an elbow against the ground as I landed. My arm was disabled. Agony screamed through me and became the shape of my entire body. A mate joined and they rained a beating down on me. Pain darted through me, torturing now an arm, now a leg. A boot connected with my ribcage and a searing, poker-hot jab ripped into me.

I lifted my head and saw the prone Papa Doc Phelan, not two feet away on the ground. His whale-like bulk was heaving and jerking uncontrollably as heroin-induced seizures took their grip. His face was crimson and froth gathered at the edges of his lips. He wheezed impossible gasps of air into him, each more desperate than the last. I didn't think he'd last long enough for the HIV to have any effect. He probably died while I was looking at him. Beyond him, Ted's body lay still, a bloodied rag. Con leaned over him whispering the Last Rites. And still the boots kicked into me.

My face was pushed roughly into the planks of the floor, the blows rattling my teeth, splinters tearing at my flesh, dirt up my nose and grit in my mouth. I tasted metal. No. 4 attacked Scarface's leg and was thrown clear across the room. I heard his agonised wail as he hit a wall, then whimpering, then, worst of all, silence. I began to cry for the brave little fellow. I curled into a ball, shielding my stomach, but boot after boot met its mark and my body cramped into a spasm of pain.

Far away, it seemed, someone shouted, 'This is the police. Everybody up against the wall.' Another victim of too much television.

I heard the click of a flick-knife snapping out and knew that I had only moments to live. I raised my head to see Razor Cullen running at me, his face dark and twisted in rage. His dog Rocky snarled and foamed at the mouth as he launched himself at me. As I waited for the blows and kicks and bites to come, I could have sworn the dog actually licked my face. And then I felt warm blood begin to run down the inside of my leg. I was sobbing rhythmically as I passed into unconsciousness.

TWENTY-SIX

When I wake I am underground, damp seeping into my bones. I touch my face. It is swollen, right eye puffed and tender. Blood is caked at the edge of my lip. I don't think I can stand up, but I have to. The room is small, brown, dark but for a shaft of milky light from a boarded window high up above me. I pull myself up the wall, my hands sore and useless, no fingernails to dig into the surface for purchase. Finally I am upright, fighting waves of dizziness as blood returns in a rush to my legs. I stay still until they pass. I am fretful and short of breath. I do not know this place. I do not like it. I must leave it. There is only one choice of exit, one door. I choose it.

A corridor leads long and far away, a light beckoning. I know I have to go there, but I also know that I will die if I do. I cannot go back, I do not want to go forward. But what harm can there be in dying, now? What is there to live for anyway? Resigned, I begin to walk. The corridor is suddenly truncated and I am in a bedroom. I find my pregnancy test on the bed. I am staring at the blue lines when I see that they are the veins on Cherry's arms as she reaches out, to safety; Tiny Shortall holds her hands and she is smiling. On her dress big, white buttons gleam in the bright light. I walk on.

I burst a door back hard against the wall and walk up some stairs. The room at the top is darkened and dust swirls on a white wooden table. I can smell Dettol and cat. A woman is scrubbing the table, her back to me. I call to her but she walks away, leaving Doc Phelan's body lying there. I am beside him when he rears up and grips my throat. I smell decay and evil. I try to pull his hands away, they are choking the breath out of me. I cannot scream. I cannot scrape his face or gouge out his eyes because of my blunted fingers. Suddenly I am free and running, but I do not move, the air a foetid quicksand dragging me down. A hand reaches from under the table and trips me to the ground. I look to the side and see a grinning spidermouse, his tail swishing from side to side, whishswish, whishswish. I scramble to my feet and make for the door. My legs are heavy with acid pain. A weight presses on my chest, forcing away even the scratching dust. My lungs cannot take in the life they need. I am fainting. I have to get to the door. I reach out to the handle but it is a white rose and cannot help me. I feel myself in free fall, not caring about the outcome. I lie back and release myself to these final moments.

Then Mick Nolan roars, says I have to go back. He calls me Leo. He never calls me that name. I am Street. I am anyone but Leo. Alice says I have to listen to Mick. She tells me to go back too. She is sitting on the steps with her gallant Ted and her green eyes are huge and shining. Go back Leo. There will be other babies. Go back. And then I know the baby is gone, and I do not want to go back. Go back, Leo. There will be other babies. Other babies. And I am running again. I reach a place more familiar, but cannot find its name. Brightness bursts on to me. I can see Andy and he is lifting me up and I am safe now. I lean into him and smell comfort and love. I'm sorry, Andy. There will be other babies.

I am only safe until I see Razor Cullen and Andy cannot see him and he does not know there is danger now. I let the scream rise and it's out and it's loud and I scream and I scream.

TWENTY-SEVEN

My mother was holding me tight as I continued to holler. I pointed a finger at Razor Cullen but she didn't react. She had no idea what danger we were in. I tried to shake her off but she held me fast.

'It's all right, Leo,' she said. 'You're safe now. Everything is all right.'

The overbright room was slipping in and out of focus, an otherworld exacerbated by my inability to feel my own body in the time-established way of simply *being*. I was disaffected from abstract limbs, which existed but throbbed in an anaesthetised, dream-like state. That'll be the painkillers, I thought.

'She's mad on the drugs,' my mother stated.

I began to gasp and hyperventilate, struggling in the circle of her arms.

'Poor girl is out of her mind.'

I had to make her understand one thing. 'I can't . . . fucking . . . breathe,' I managed.

She laid my trembling body back on the bed and gave me a master class, super-deluxe, pained expression.

'No need for that kind of talk,' she admonished. 'I was just trying to help.'

I had no feist in me to challenge the martyrdom. Besides, there were other pressing matters to deal with.

Hugo Nelson walked through the door and stood behind Cullen's chair, leaning his hand on the back of it. Were these people blind? Could they not see him? I took the standard deep breaths to calm myself and made matters worse by pumping too much oxygen to my confused and agitated brain. Now it was twice as addled and unsure. I had to make them listen and know that we were all in great danger as long as that man was here with us.

'I'm so sorry to have frightened you, Leo,' Cullen said, heavy on the syrup.

How dare he call me by my name, be so familiar with me, after what he'd done? I blocked his voice out, the better to formulate a plan of escape. I looked around and saw that I was in a plain, off-white room with shiny walls. My bed was metal with cream curtains hanging on the rail above it. Everything was too bright, too hot and smelled of lilies, for crying out loud.

Hospital.

I sank into the forty pillows stuffed behind my head. I tuned back in to Cullen but must not have returned to sanity, even my own faulty version.

'I couldn't tell you before,' he droned. 'I'm a detective. I'm a Garda.'

'Yeah, right.' What? *What* did he just say?

Hugo Nelson was nodding vigorously, as if he believed this latest titbit. I knew, without looking, that my mother was in their camp too. This was all a farce. I was in hospital. And Razor Cullen was a cop. Next we'd be hearing that the world would not end at the millennium. I closed my eyes and willed them all to leave. I had nothing left to give.

Then they were open again with a start.

'No. 4,' I said urgently. 'Is he dead?' Huge tears rolled down my cheeks without check. I had not even felt them start.

'Relax now, pet,' my mother said. She got up and walked away, an odd thing to do when you're trying to reassure your only daughter. She opened the window and seemed to talk to the world in general and no one in particular. I couldn't make out her exact words, but heard a final, 'It'll be fine for two minutes.' When she turned back to me I saw the cheeky, canine face of No. 4 Street. He barked in her arms and was shushed by my mum.

'You'll get us all thrown out,' she said as she carried him to the bed and allowed him to slobber all over my face and neck. If dog's tongues did have healing powers, I was a new woman.

His chest was bandaged. 'Cracked ribs,' my mother explained. 'He's been playing up jigs and reels over them. Likes to be carried everywhere now, though the vet says he's not in much real discomfort at all. Your grandmother has him ruined, of course.'

'Is that who's outside?'

'Oh, sure now, who else would it be?'

She grabbed the mutt and handed him back out of the window. My gran's head poked through and said, 'I suppose you think this is a great excuse to skip Mass today, miss, but God is looking and He knows what you're up to.'

I laughed. 'He knows where you live too,' I told her.

So, it was Sunday and I had lost a day. I looked at my wrist but all I had on there was a plastic tag with my name and date of birth, in case I'd forgotten who I was. It did nothing to distract from the gap a certain timepiece and its absence left in my life.

'Your watch was in bits after . . . that business on Friday night.'

'No harm, wasn't mine anyway,' I said, an extra pain joining the general ache.

I paused. The whole shebang came crashing down. My body was battered, it hurt to breathe, and I wasn't pregnant any longer. I let the tears flow, not caring who saw me or them, or how disfigured they left me. Cullen and Nelson crept away, muttering embarrassed goodbyes. My mother let me get on with my sobbing.

I could conjugate the past over and over, it would not change the fact that I had lost the baby no one knew about, and a man I loved dearly. There might be other babies but they would never be that precious baby. And there could never be another Andy Raynor.

I shut my eyes tight, trying to block off the places I was in no fit state to go to, the situations I could not face. I heard my mother whisper, 'There will be other babies, Leo.' Startled, I looked at her, and saw that she needed no explanation, and didn't expect one. I was overwhelmed by her love and understanding. I looked down at our intertwined hands, identical but for the years between them. My mother was watching over me. I was safe.

I don't remember falling asleep but I must have because the next thing Ciara was bursting through the door.

'This place smells like a feckin' funeral parlour,' she declared. She took in the vast arrangement of lilies. 'Why did that eejit Barry pick them of all things? Like they're really gonna to win you back. Men!'

'Has he been here?' I croaked.

'Ah, yeah, crying into everyone's face and snotting up the room. Bloody pathetic.'

'He was shocking all right,' my mother agreed. 'We ran him yesterday, but you're probably due another visitation.'

Ciara barrelled on. 'The nurses say you're fine for getting up, so do and I'll give you a surprise.'

As I've mentioned before, a Ciara surprise was a daunting prospect. My mother protested but I knew better than to argue with La Gillespie when she was on a mission. I struggled into my robe, which someone had brought from home, my home, number 11 The Villas. There were cat hairs all over it.

I tried a step, but sagged weakly.

Ciara gave her Lauren Bacall impression. 'You know how to walk, don't you? You just put one foot in front of the other and go.'

Mum and Ciara each took an arm and we waddled down the industrial by ways of the hospital. We had not got far when I had to beg a pit stop. Ciara softened and let me use the loo. She chattered on merrily.

'You'll never guess who I met yesterday,' she told me, so I didn't try. 'Val Tobin from the club. Seems Simon Cadogan couldn't live without Tanya after all and he came back one night to get her. Security nabbed him and he's clapped up in Mountjoy awaiting trial. I know you're always telling me people do stupid things but that has to take top biscuit for a weekday. Nearly there.'

I was listing badly and willing a wheelchair to appear, even though the ignominy of being pushed around in one might kill me. We were in a ward called St Jarlath's when Ciara finally stopped us, at the door to a private patient's room. She knocked and a quavering voice asked us in.

Molly was propped up on a hundred pillows in his bed.

'I have private health insurance so I get more than you public patients,' he explained. 'They're awful uncomfortable, though. I think the nurses're trying to finish me off by breaking my back, that way there'll be less work for them. And they have the blood supply to me legs cut off with the tightness of the sheets. But I have news for them – there's plenty more where I came from.' He chuckled merrily.

Molly was recovering from a triple bypass. 'Not one, not two, but three,' he told me, proudly showing the number with his fingers. 'Another day, another few hours even, and I could've been a goner.'

We smiled at each other, battle-scarred but alive.

'Your grandmother smuggled wee Lucky in to see me. He's been in the wars, like yourself.'

'Yeah, but you should have seen the other guys,' I said. 'We won.'

I raised an eyebrow at Ciara, wondering.

'Yep, we did okay,' she said. 'And your house is packed with people now. You still have Aidan and Nina, and their mum and Deborah have arrived, and young Damo is on the couch. I think Nina is hoping he can go home with them, for a while anyway. She's taking over from Cherry as his big sister.'

A tea lady arrived and dispensed strong brew to us all. She had scarcely milked and sugared the stuff when the duchess of dirt arrived. Mrs Mack grabbed a cup of her own and waved a packet of Jaffa Cakes in the air.

'Now that's timing,' I said to Ciara.

Kevin Mack timidly insinuated himself by a beige wall. 'You two have had us all very worried,' he revealed. 'It's great to see you up and eating a bit.'

'I left Ronan in charge at the office,' Mrs Mack told me, confidentially. 'At the moment, there's nothing happening that he can't deal with.'

I choked on a swallow of tea. How many cuckoos would be in the nest by the time I had recovered? Ciara put a comforting hand on my arm. 'Nothing I can't handle,' she hissed. I was going to have to trust her on that one.

'That mop-headed film fella was in to see you again,' Mrs Mack aimed at my aide-de-camp, smiling knowledgeably at this juicy information. As Ciara reddened, I knew she'd have her hands full over the period of my convalescence. It made me smile to think of the political shenanigans about to be unleashed at the Indigent Sweeps' gaff. Then a pertinent fact struck home and froze me to my bowels.

'Why would Ronan need to man the office on a Sunday?'

'Some stuff has come in,' Mrs Mack said.

'Nothing for you to worry about,' Ciara added.

I was paralysed by a diaphanous dread, but unable to deal with it. I let it wash over me. It gave me a reason to get well *soon*; nothing like a bit of motivation.

'We nearly have the makings of a party,' Molly said. 'That nice Andy should be back soon.'

'Andy?' My heart doubled its beating.

'Yes. He's gone out to get something for you.'

'Me?' Clearly, I wasn't able for anything with more than one syllable.

'You have a lot to thank him for, I believe.' Molly looked to Ciara for affirmation.

'Andy was the one who hauled those brutes off you,' she said. Him and Raymond Cullen, with Rocky standing guard over you all.'

Andy, Raymond, *Rocky?* These were not names I'd expected

311

to be discussing out loud with people. And certainly not in these glowing terms.

'I thought he was gone,' I stammered, uselessly.

'You didn't really think Andy was going to let you off into that pit by yourself, did you?' my mother asked, scornful that she had raised such a dim child. 'Of course he followed you. And you can thank your stars that he did. I know I do. I don't know what we'd have done if we'd lost you.' Then she burst into tears.

'Ah, yer poor mother,' Molly said, as if I was to blame. I looked to see if a wheelchair was one of the pieces of furniture afforded the private patients too. No. Damn, no escape without the hired help.

My mother turned off the tap with remarkable efficiency. 'I don't want to be upsetting you anymore than you have been already,' she said in the particular tone she kept for extra-special occasions. I had a vision of a day a month into the future when I would get the full lecture about the worry I had put her through and the years I had knocked off her life with my latest escapade. Already I could anticipate the line, 'And I bet you weren't even paid for it.'

'You have a big evening ahead of you and you should get some sleep,' she said, preparing to haul me back to my ward.

'What do you mean "big evening"?' I asked apprehensively.

'Visiting time is from six till eight and the whole gang are coming.'

'I thought hospitals were for recuperating.'

My mother waved a hand dismissively. 'Yes, yes, that too.'

'Con is bringing Billy in,' Ciara chirruped. 'He says you're not bad, for a pervert. And Ronan will be along.'

Yikes, I was going to need some make-up as well as a snooze.

As we got to the door I asked Molly the question burning me up inside: 'What did Andy go to get me?'

'I shouldn't tell you, but it's a new watch. He says you never know the right time.'

I smiled. 'I might be able to learn it, though.'